More praise for *Pull Me Under*

'Both dark and illuminating. Reminds you just how many lives women can, or must, lead simultaneously in order to survive. Kelly Luce has amazing control over this fragmented experience with a narrator that draws you into the eye of the storm.'
– Olivia Sudjic

'*Pull Me Under* will bewitch you.'
– *O Magazine*

'A novel about secret lives and selfhood … an intimate portrayal of one woman's search for identity.'
– *Booklist*

'Beautifully written and utterly hypnotic, *Pull Me Under* is one you can't miss.'
– *Bustle*

'Luce's prose is sharp and powerful. The Japan of *Pull Me Under* does not read as a caricature of the country, but rather a genuine experience that is both atmospheric and nearly tangible. *Pull Me Under* does so much so well. The mystery surrounding the plot and the family drama can hook you as a reader, but it's the emotions and inner workings of the narrator's mind as you flip through the pages that will keep you fed.'
– *BookPeople*

'Luce deftly evokes Japan without exoticising it ... The final act is the novel's strongest and most confident, weaving the book's threads together and leaving a lasting reverberation.'

– *Publishers Weekly*

'Luce's debut novel is psychologically seductive, and the prose draws the reader into its loneliness. *Pull Me Under* shines brightest as an inquest into whether a split psyche can ever be made whole once the past becomes its own foreign country – and the tyranny of being taught that a dark past is not to be trespassed upon.'

– *Ploughshares* ('The Most Necessary Books for the End of 2016')

'I was sucked into the prose and character in Luce's latest accomplishment from the very start. Rio Silvestri and Chizuru Akitani bring both the familiar and the terrifying parts of our psyche to the surface and then pull you right back down into the depths of this stunning debut novel.'

– *Book Culture*

'Luce manoeuvres the reader through this story seamlessly; she is a virtuosic jack-o-lantern carver, slicing and hewing away at her characters until their pulpy interiors are exposed. And from inside that space, she shines a light.'

– *Electric Literature*

'By turns, *Pull Me Under* is a finely crafted mystery, a portrait of a fractured family, an evocative travelogue, an aching coming-of-age tale, and an insightful contemplation of our inescapable histories in an increasingly globalized and digitized culture.'

– Stefan Merrill Block

PULL ME UNDER

KELLY LUCE

DAUNT BOOKS

First published in Great Britain in 2017 by
Daunt Books
83 Marylebone High Street
London W1U 4QW

1

Copyright © 2017 Kelly Luce

A CIP catalogue record for this title is available
from the British Library.

ISBN 978-1-911547-05-1

Typeset by Marsha Swan

Printed and bound by T J International Ltd,
Padstow, Cornwall

www.dauntbookspublishing.co.uk

For my family, far and wide

PULL
ME
UNDER

Excerpt, Kyoto Wow!
English-language newsmagazine,
October 14,1988

On a cloudless afternoon in the peaceful Shikoku city of Tokushima, twelve-year-old Chizuru Akitani, Japanese-American daughter of acclaimed violinist and Living National Treasure Hiro Akitani, walked into the staff room at Motomachi Elementary, covered with blood and clutching a letter opener. Panic swept the room, as people assumed the sixth-grader, known for her introspective nature, had seriously hurt herself. The English teacher, Ms Daniela Townshend, was the first to approach Chizuru. As she neared, the girl raised her palm and stilled the room with five words:

'This is not my blood.'

BEFORE

KAWANO JUVENILE RECOVERY CENTRE occupied a compound originally built to house orphaned A-bomb survivors. It was turned into a detention centre for juvenile delinquents during the seventies. Some kids claimed the bomb survivors had brought radiation with them and infected the place, that no one could recover there, but for me it became home. I was twelve when I arrived, and I didn't leave until my twentieth birthday.

Those first days did feel like the aftermath of an explosion. I both did and did not know why I'd been sent there. The shock of what had happened – what I'd done – kept my mind cloudy, my memories watered-down. I met twice daily with Dr Kankan, a white-crested psychiatrist fond of naval metaphors. Dr K told me I had hurt someone but he would not elaborate. I wanted to know who – was it someone in my family? A stranger? I worried about my parents.

'We'll discuss that when you're anchored,' was his unchanging answer.

But other patients – inmates, we called ourselves – managed to learn what had happened. There were no secrets at Kawano. It didn't matter that we weren't allowed to read the juicy parts of the newspaper, or that, back then, the world was Internetless. Knowledge seeped in anyway. I killed a kid at my school, a boy whispered to me in the cafeteria. Stabbed him to death. Did I feel like a murderer? I didn't know how to answer. I knew what he said was true, but I also didn't know what feeling like a murderer meant. Still, if I'd killed someone, *shouldn't* I know?

I noticed at a young age – four years old, five – a dark presence in my chest, a blackness, clinging to the back of my heart. Mostly, the thing lay dormant and I could put it out of my mind. But occasionally it swelled like an infected gland. These were the times I felt hurt or angry, the sensations so closely linked that I never separated them until a therapist pointed out the difference. My anger was an organ.

I feared this black organ. It was responsible for the evil thoughts I had – the visions of hurting the person who hurt me, Tomoya Yu, his taunts of *Fatty Potato!* ringing in my ears. And those visions had come true. I was not in control of my body.

The kids didn't make fun of my weight at Kawano. Relatively little teasing happened there. Instead of insults we gave each other practical nicknames and my extra flab paled in comparison with other personal details. They called me *Sutabi-gyaru* – Stabbygirl – or *kireru*, the term the doctors threw around in their hushed conversations; it meant 'to split', or 'snap'. Like a wishbone, or a rubber band stretched too far. Before I left Kawano eight years later, seven more *kireru* kids would come. Three girls, four boys, each in their early teens. All killers, with

6

the exception of one girl who'd pushed a handicapped boy off a roof but 'only' (her word) succeeded in paralysing him.

Dr K carried a yellow notepad in his coat pocket and pulled it out often. He said it was good I had some time away. I was allowed no visitors for six months, not even family. 'Your subconscious needs to be bailed out,' he said.

He was worried for me. My mom had only been dead a month, a fact I kept forgetting. I talked about her as if she were alive and asked when she'd be able to visit. Dr K listened. Then he'd remind me that she was gone. He had me tell him how I'd felt when I'd heard the news, wanted to hear the story over and over. He believed her death and my 'outburst' were directly connected. Which, of course, they were. Her presence had soothed the black organ. Three weeks after she killed herself, it took control of me and Tomoya Yu was dead.

I'd been in history class, learning about the role of the shogunate, when I was called into the school nurse's office. Tachiyasan was there that day, the only male nurse on staff and my least favourite adult at school. A spaghetti sauce stain ran down the front of his white coat. He told me there'd been a car accident; my mom had swerved to avoid a child in the road.

'It was a quick and noble death,' he whispered, drumming his fingers on the table.

I stared at his fingers. Dark hair swirled above each knuckle. When I found my voice, it said, 'She doesn't drive in Japan.' I grabbed his hand – he leaned back but did not pull away – and added in English, 'Fuck you.'

I learnt the truth from my father, who was never one to spare details: she jumped off the new Ōnaruto Bridge while the tide was going out and the whirlpools were at their peak. She must have consulted a tide table, which meant she'd been determined; my mom was never one for schedules. She referred to herself as a 'quintessential Pisces'. When I was little, she explained that a Pisces was a fish and for a long time I thought she was part mermaid. Her looks backed this up: her amber hair was long and tangled and lightly waved, her eyes a bright grey, and the way she walked, as if gravity didn't affect her, was a little like swimming. I understood later why she never wore make-up, never styled her hair the way other moms did, the way, as a child, I wished she would. Any embellishment would have made her beauty garish.

We took her ashes to a temple near the house and had them blessed, but we did not take them to the Akitani family grave in Ehime Prefecture. There would be no funeral. My father told me, it was better that way. 'Remember her at her best,' he told me, handing me a stack of photo albums. I didn't know what that meant or what I should remember.

My mom's father had died by then – I never met my grandpa Bill – and her mom and two older sisters, who still lived in Texas, refused to have anything to do with the remains. They were the ashes of the worst sort of sinner. Hadn't she brought enough shame on the family already? The list of her sins was long. The first was leaving the Lone Star State – and for a filthy New York City commune, of all places. Fornication (with an Oriental!), wasting her gifts on those smeared canvases she called 'art', and finally, leaving the US of A altogether. Her own religion, people, country weren't good enough for her, and God would punish her for her pride. I learnt all of this from my mom's younger sister, my aunt Peggy, in the letter she mailed to me at Kawano. 'I believe Jesus would have said about Elena: live and let live. Though I don't condone her choices, she was my sister. We shared a bed until we were confirmed. I must afford her some grace.' I sent her half the ashes in the small porcelain urn I kept in my room. She wrote back with a card that said, 'Bless you, child.' I never heard from her again.

I didn't display the urn when I was still at home and I didn't display it at Kawano. I tried a few times, setting it on a shelf or near my pillow when I slept. But these attempts felt vulgar; I'd look at the urn and try to feel something and inevitably succeed only in feeling wretchedly sad at my failure. Finally, I put her away for good. My mom was not a decoration. What did I need a handful of dust for? Certainly not as a reminder of her. She was everywhere.

My father made me go to school, arguing that it was best to keep busy and not wallow at home, overeating. I don't remember those days well. The other kids stayed away from me even more than usual, as if death were contagious. Even Tomoya took a break from ridiculing me. But the grace period extended after my mother's death only lasted a couple of weeks. She hadn't killed herself in an honourable or a glamorous Japanese fashion – a lovers' double suicide; or a seppuku – so soon I just became the fat *hafu* girl with a dead mom. I made people more uncomfortable than ever.

I don't remember much about arriving at Kawano. Hiro must have brought some clothes and personal things for me, since I had the ashes along with some of my after-school clothes. But he forgot underwear and for weeks the only pair of shoes I had to wear during outdoor time were the red patent leather flats I'd worn to one of his performances in Tokyo.

I wished for the orange shoebox. Mom and I kept the box a secret from my father. Inside were three rows of cassette tapes arranged alphabetically. Aerosmith, the Beatles, Blue Öyster Cult, Depeche Mode, Dire Straits, Heart, the Moody Blues,

U2, the Who: bizarre, beautiful names I knew through her, my umbilical cord to the world of Western popular music. She bought a new one every month during her trips to Mitsuya, the high-rise department store downtown that carried her favourite brand of acrylic paints. The organisation of the shoebox was in sharp contrast to the bottom of the family stereo cabinet, where my parents' classical tapes lay in a foot-high heap. One of my earliest memories is of watching my mom pluck a tape from the shoebox and slip it in the player. The *click* of belonging as it fell into its place – a place it was expected, that had been made for it. The sounds that came from the speakers made more sense to me than classical music. They matched something in my body. I could tell my mom felt it, too, by the way she moved not just her feet but her hips, shoulders, arms, fingers. Even her face danced. We were like girlfriends listening to those tapes.

I would have flushed her ashes down the toilet in exchange for that shoebox.

Through talks with Dr K I began to face the memories I'd pushed away, and later, as part of my therapy, I was allowed to read the news accounts. I, Chizuru Akitani, half-Japanese daughter of Living National Treasure Hiro Akitani, had swiped the gold Morimoto (they never left out the name of the designer) letter opener from my teacher's desk and stabbed Tomoya Yu in the neck. Tomoya had bullied me, yes. Hurt my feelings. Touched me. But telling the story out loud was impossible. A part of my brain shut down when I tried. Some days, Dr K would only have to say the name 'Tomoya Yu' and I'd shudder, have to ask for a break.

If it weren't for Tomoya, I might have turned out normally. Not that I was normal. Most twelve-year-olds aren't. But this was Japan, where blending in is a necessity just like shelter or food. The biggest thing wrong with me was my mixed blood; I was *hafu*, a word that still has the ability to make me feel like what it suggests: that I am half a person. *Hafu* implied my Japaneseness was the only part of me that mattered, that there would never be enough. Classmates never let me forget that I wasn't like them; teachers attributed my positive traits – good grades, obedience – to my Japanese side, while bad behaviour was explained with a shake of the head that meant, What can you expect? She's a foreigner.

But I had remarkable parents. Early in elementary school, my white, light-haired mom was a source of fascination for the other kids. *Kawaii*, they'd whisper. So pretty – like a movie star! And my father's status got me respect. I didn't have close friends, but I didn't have enemies, either. Things had been okay. Not great, but okay. Tomoya's arrival during sixth grade was a contaminant. It changed everything.

My father arrived six minutes past noon, a year and twelve days after I was admitted. We met in the sharp-smelling visitors' room. Though Kawano was a detention and recovery centre, they were always bleaching things as if it were a hospital. He did not try to hug or touch me. We sat down, me on the red beanbag and he on the hard couch. I had fantasised about cuddling up beside him, sitting in his lap, even – I hadn't experienced physical affection from an adult since my mom died – but when we came face-to-face the idea felt absurd. The space between us was infinite. My mom was in that space. My *kireru*. My American half.

'You look different. Lost a little weight. That's good,' he said in Japanese, which we always spoke together. He looked the same; even the frowning shape of his thin moustache had not changed. A bad painting of a basketball, done by one of the older kids, hung on the wall behind him like an ugly moon.

'You must realise this is very hard for me,' he said.

I let my hair fall over one eye, a habit I knew he disliked. I should've known better than to expect him to ask how I was. 'I'm sorry I've made your life so difficult,' I said, using the most polite verb forms possible.

He nodded; sarcasm was lost on him. 'Now listen,' he said. 'A lot has happened, but in a way, it's for the best. Your mom never wanted to marry me. Said she didn't believe in the institution. Can you imagine? She only agreed so that she could stay in Japan after you were born. You were that important to her.' He shook his head. 'But it looks like she got tired of you, too.'

Harsh as my childhood may've been, I'd never been hit. But that's how I remember that moment – as if my father had reached back and slapped me. Was it true? Had she killed herself because of something I'd done – or hadn't done? I started to cry.

He shushed me, but I couldn't stop. Tears had always made Hiro mad. He'd raise his voice like a shield, as if his anger might protect him from witnessing something embarrassing. He couldn't handle earnestness or sentimentality. 'I've died before,' he'd say whenever my mom or I got emotional, referring to his famed childhood fever that had once led a nurse to pronounce him dead. 'It taught me that crying only gets in the way of getting better.'

There are a lot of things I never got to ask my father – if he felt responsible for what I'd done, how my mom's death had affected him – and that was the last time the questions were close enough to my lips to be asked. But I couldn't say a thing. Dr K, who'd been observing the visit through the big window, rushed in and suggested Hiro come back in a few days. My father, looking relieved at the suggestion, stood and walked out.

At Kawano they kept me busy, trying to distract me, maybe, or trying to figure me out. I took pleasure – my sole pleasure, in those days – in making it hard for them. I themed my Rorschach test responses; one day I'd do composers, another, kitchen appliances. I was tested so frequently I began to recognise the forms, and one day Dr K threw the cards on the floor. 'Chizuru,' he said, 'I promise you, from here on out, you'll never have to look at an inkblot again.' He kept his word.

It wasn't that I was mad, or even tired of being there. The place, after you got used to it, was okay. And it was all I had. Sometimes Dr K made me feel better; occasionally, I felt good. I had weathered a terrible storm, Dr K told me. It was his job to shore me up so I might one day sail again. I had to help him help me learn to captain my own vessel.

In those days I still hoped, more than I was willing to admit, that my father would rescue me. He'd bring me home, or at least use his connections to get me out before my twentieth birthday, when I would become a legal adult. The kids who were older when they committed their crimes had to stay longer, but I'd been under fourteen at the time of my *kireru*, which meant I could return home and be monitored in the Family Care Programme if my family wished.

'The laws are changing,' my father said when he returned two weeks later after a trip to Paris. He paced the visitors' room while I sat stiffly on the couch. 'Other kids, young kids, have done similar things. It's a goddamn phenomenon you've started. You leaving here would call more attention …'

It would not do to release me when the boy's family continued to suffer, he explained. Public opinion would be

13

against us. The press had jumped on my story, and how could they not? 'Mixed-race child of Living National Treasure snaps and kills her bully!' – it was all over the news. But my father was a powerful man. The same people who funded the Tokyo Symphony Orchestra owned the companies that ran the news-papers, and he knew them all. There had been news stories for three days, and now it was done. No one would print them. He'd done quite well at erasing his daughter, he told me proudly, as if he'd cleared a tricky rodent infestation.

The black organ woke up; it felt like being pinched from the inside. 'Aren't we lucky she's gone,' I muttered, and this time the sarcasm was clear even to him.

'Without my reputation, you would have nothing. You think it was easy to get this off the front page? Do you know how much apology money I had to give the Yu family?'

'Without your reputation, I might have everything,' I said. 'Like a mom.' I stood and kicked the beanbag. My foot stuck in it and I fell forward. I sank into the red plastic, punched it with both fists, and said what would be my last words to him: 'And a dad, too.'

After our blow-up, I refused to communicate with Hiro. It wasn't hard to avoid him. He called once, a month after our fight. Dr K told him to return when he was interested in the Family Care Programme, and he never came back.

Anyone was allowed to visit. Dr K made this clear. And I did have a couple of visitors over the years – my father's estranged brother and his skeletal third wife; an expat friend of my mom's named Lydia – but they were never the visitors I wanted and they didn't come a second time.

The person I wanted most to see, other than my mom, was Miss Danny. Miss Danny had been my English teacher at school and, for a while, I'd believed she was my friend. A grown-up advocate. I still believed it, despite her strange treatment of me in the weeks leading up to my *kireru*. When I remembered our jokes, the unmistakable affection between us, I could only conclude her coldness had all been in my imagination. She would come. She could adopt me! My father wouldn't mind giving up his burden. But Miss Danny never came. Dr K promised he would tell me right away if she ever as much as enquired at the centre, and as the months and the years went by, I stopped waiting.

Without a family member to be legally responsible for my rehabilitation, I had to stay. I kept up with school assignments easily. We didn't receive grades. I worked at my goal of Japanese illiteracy, which I knew would horrify my father. I was aided by the logistics of the language: you couldn't absorb kanji characters the way you could the twenty-six letters of the Roman alphabet. The written language was so complex the Ministry of Education had created a system dictating which characters students learnt and when. A publicly educated child couldn't read a newspaper until the end of high school. So my task was easy. I stopped reading Japanese books and refused to study new kanji. The bored social worker in charge of my lessons was studying to be an English teacher; her pronunciation and conversation skills were terrible, so we spent most of our time chatting in English and preparing for her Instructor's Exam. I tested myself once a year and watched my reading level drop. By the time I left Kawano, I struggled happily with the third-grade-level storybooks. I liked imagining the look on my father's face when he found out. Even then, I still thought I'd see him again.

I started helping out in the garden when I was fifteen. It wasn't much of a garden, five or six raised beds surrounded by a chain-link fence. (To keep out what, or whom, I couldn't guess. The facility was already fenced and secured.) Tam, the boy in charge there, was a ward of the state and deaf from birth. He was two years older than me, thin but muscled, and good company. When planting asparagus, he pressed the seeds into their grooves by applying pressure to my fingers with his. After doing this a few times, I continued on, Tam following me, poking each hole to make sure each seed sat at the right depth.

He showed me the long plastic container in the basement fridge where he kept seeds and bulbs. Some were flat and dark, others plump and white, still others pinky-red or striped or spherical or spiky. He planned to expand the garden. I plucked seed after seed from their compartments, rolled them between my fingers, smelled them, pretended to eat one. Tam laughed at my curiosity. I marvelled at the way those simple little packets contained life. Bury one and something would germinate. Hydrangea. Yam. Watermelon. Plum.

The feelings I developed for Tam were not like the crushes I'd had in middle school. There was none of the paralysing shyness, the embarrassment at not knowing what to say. We communicated mostly through touch. After a while, to kiss him felt not only natural, but necessary. The salty taste of those first, experimental embraces, so warm, so exhilarating, was the door to another world.

I talked to him while we gardened. He glanced at my mouth as I spoke, his wide-set eyes unblinking. He didn't nod when I talked; he shook his head. (It was a habit I picked up; as an adult, I still confuse people when I listen intently.) I spoke aloud the intimate details of my life: my parents, my town, the sweetshop, Motomachi Elementary, Tomoya Yu. Telling him about it helped me recall some of the painful memories, and when I cried or panicked as a new one surfaced, Tam shook his head and stroked my wrist. After we started lying together naked in the unused nurse's quarters, he would place his pale, thin palm at the base of my throat and listen to the vibrations as I talked. It seemed he understood more, or better, when he wasn't looking at me. He could write, but not well, and doing it made him frustrated and tired. Once, I got a book on sign language from the library. When he saw it, he slammed it shut and made an X by crossing his wrists. That was the end of that. So I couldn't ask him much about himself, but that suited us; telling him about me was enough for us both.

Nothing fazed Tam. He experienced life on a five-second delay. I was drawn to his constancy, punctuated as it was by the occasional burst of wild, barking laughter. I could never make him laugh on purpose, but I often did things he found funny. He was nothing like Ned Nickerson, the boy in the Nancy Drew books they gave me in place of English lit. I didn't know any real boys, just the sick ones at Kawano. When I was grown-up, I assumed I'd find a guy like Ned: tall, dark-haired, athletic. A banker or a lawyer. A man always ready to help.

Tam liked to pore over illustrations of the human body in Kawano's third-floor library. He whistled as he looked. It was a peculiar sound, full of trills and skips. Once I pursed my own lips to mimic him; when he looked up and saw me, he touched my throat and laughed so hard his notebook slid to the floor and he drooled. He flapped his hands like wings and tapped his temple: I was making the sound of a bird in his head.

It was always hot up there. The room smelled like old paper and information. One of Tam's favourite books was an oversized hardcover called *Jintai kaibogaku* – Human Anatomy. When he found an image he liked, he pulled out his notebook and sketched a copy. He liked the brain, with all its ridges, rivulets, and bumps, the best. Once he sketched the frontal lobe – centre of emotion, though I doubt he was aware of this – and then, with a few smart placements of gulls, sun, a boat, turned it into a seascape. He presented it to me with two hands. It was the only picture I taped to the cinder-block wall behind my bed.

As my bond with Tam grew, I became healthier. My biggest barrier to becoming 'sustainably functional' was major anxiety triggered by minor things: papers strewn rather than stacked, the smell of a certain cleaning solvent, drops of liquid spattering the table when someone ate noodles. I'd always bitten my nails but now I picked at and chewed my cuticles and the ends of my hair, too. The official line on me was generalised anxiety disorder and post-traumatic stress. Dr K said the last important hurdle was to face the memories of 'the event'.

'Your brain was too horrified by what your body was doing, so it created a special compartment for the memory,' he said. 'Think of it as a safe below decks. The bad news is, you won't be whole until you figure out the combination to that safe and face what's inside. The good news is that once you do, you can accept it and move beyond it. It's hard to stay afloat with too much cargo,' he added. 'You need to look at your freight head-on, become picky about what you carry.'

I remained under Dr K's care; he tried hypnosis and psycho-analysis and a puppet resembling Tomoya Yu, but I refused to recount the story of the murder. I could see it in my head. It played back at random moments: while brushing my teeth, or eating lunch, or cleaning my room. It never came while I was gardening. The scene appalled me. How could that girl be *me*? The words would not come. Putting words to the memory would make it true in a way I wasn't ready for. The words were in a cup in my brain that was full to the brim with darkness and saying them would make everything spill.

Still, I improved so much in my behaviour and anxiety management – Tam's calm was contagious; time with him was like resting in a warm bath – that by my sixteenth birthday, Dr K shifted focus to newer patients.

One day Tam wasn't at breakfast. Nor was he in the garden. I went to Dr K.

'Tamahiro's been transferred, Chizu. It's not Kawano policy to allow – such things.'

'Who saw us?' I grabbed at the nearest object – a stress ball made to look like a persimmon – and threw it against the wall. If only the black organ were so easy to massage, squeeze, remove! 'You didn't even let me say *goodbye*?'

He bowed his head and apologised formally, the way you would to a superior. 'Chizuru, I am so, so sorry. I couldn't stop it, but—' He looked up and in his eyes I saw something that eased my pain a little, my first glimpse of an adult humbled. 'I should have told you.'

The staffer who'd seen us wasn't technically employed by Kawano; she was a Christian missionary from Zambia and the only person in the place to find fault with what we were doing.

That evening, I sat *zazen*-style for seven hours in the garden. I wanted to convince everyone I'd come down with catatonic schizophrenia as a reaction to the trauma of Tam's departure. Really, it was a vigil. I coped with the emotional drain of Tam's loss by doing something physically demanding. Before the garden, I went down to the nurse's quarters where Tam and I had spent those intimate hours, but found the door locked. A plastic bag hung from the knob. Inside was a Bible.

In my room, I stared at his drawing of the brain-turned-seaside. Was everything an illusion? Or was the picture's beauty an accident without meaning – a spontaneous act on his part, something you could trace back to his morning meal, or a new prescription? From then on, when looking at images of the brain, I saw the ocean. My skull contained a sea. Memories and knowledge floated or sank or hung suspended, somewhere in the middle; there were periods of whitecaps and periods of glassy calm.

During the weeks that followed Tam's departure, I collected diagnoses the way other teenagers were collecting CDs. To get back at Dr K, I read the *DSM-III-R*, which was shelved near the books Tam liked to draw from, and when I came across an interesting disorder, I memorised the symptoms and acted them out. I accused Dr K of inflicting me with further post-traumatic stress so that he'd be able to publish a unique case study. The surprise and hurt on his face were gratifying, but when he turned from me without saying anything and walked away, head down, I felt sick with shame.

Dr K's next move saved me. He gave me Tam's role of lead gardener. I saw this as a trick at best, revenge at worst. After a few months of doing the bare minimum, unable to look at the weeds sprouting, let alone pull them, I asked myself – what if Tam came to visit and saw the garden so unloved?

The garden required constant attention, demanded I become part of it, grow attuned to its cycles and idiosyncrasies, to the habits of worms and slugs and delicate shoots. Weeding satisfied me like nothing else. What a thrill to pluck a patch clear, to turn the dirt and fill it with air, to witness the order of plants in rows, obedient and helpless, wanting nothing more than to flourish.

I began to think of the future. It started as imagining Tam's return but expanded beyond that to my possible release. In less than four years I'd be twenty. At the very least, I'd have to choose a citizenship – Japan didn't allow dual. Or maybe they'd take away that right. Maybe I'd be forced to keep my status as a Japanese national, give up my right to an American passport, and stay locked up for life.

I joined the morning exercise group and began to jog. I hated it. My lungs burned and the flab at my sides made the skin of my torso feel as if it might rip. I didn't like running with boys. I clutched the chain-link fence and puked. But I kept going. My body had betrayed me with its ugliness and heft and the black organ, and I wanted to punish it.

But the inevitable happened: I improved. I had never witnessed such straightforward progress in myself. How simple: the more I ran, the more I *could* run. I felt, for the first time, control over my body.

And my body began to change. My skin lost its waxy texture. I slept through the night and woke clear-headed. Still, I didn't notice the weight loss until Dr K mentioned it. 'You look like a different person,' he said one day. I ran to the mirror and pulled up my T-shirt. The frowns of fat at my waist had melted into soft curves; my belly button was visible. I had cheekbones.

I kept running. I was starting to love it in a way I had never loved anything, even sesame sticks, chocolate balls, and cherry-walnut frogs. When I ran I couldn't cry. I loved the feel of my heart thudding against my ribs, of using my body the way it was intended: sweat drying to cool me, lungs expanding, recycling what I brought them. I'd found a way to soothe that curdled feeling of anxiety; when I ran, the bad things fell away. It always began with a chase. And I found that my darkness could be caught, pinned, banished. After six months, I was running forty laps a day around the big dirt yard. Counting my steps let me go farther. The black organ disappeared for hours at a time.

Beyond the fence was a dammed river lined with trash, and a mountainside slathered with concrete that held up a road. I decided if I ever got out I would go to America, somewhere fresh and untamed and green, a place where nature, not man, ruled. I had a social worker send away for college materials and when I saw the photographs of California in the Stanford brochures I fell in love. I imagined weekends at the beach, Frisbee on the meadow with Ned Nickerson between classes in ivied buildings. No one would know about the previous version of me. This version.

I took the tests, wrote the essays. I applied to a few other schools because Dr K insisted. Getting into Stanford was like getting into Tokyo University, he said – impossible. I didn't care; it was meant to be. I had Dr K mail my applications from his posh neighbourhood of Aoyama. I didn't want admissions committees to know where I was living.

Stanford rejected me. So did Berkeley and UC San Diego. Then came a thick packet from Colorado. I'd been accepted at CU-Boulder, where I applied because I thought the 'C' stood for 'California'. They even offered something called a Friends of the Pacific Rim scholarship, meaning I'd only have to pay in-state tuition and that I'd qualify for no-interest loans and a work-study job as long as I kept up my grades. (I learnt later that the initial recipient of this scholarship, a basketball player from Singapore recruited to round out Boulder's dominant women's team, died a few days before my application arrived.

The scholarship had to be awarded to someone or the funding wouldn't be renewed – so it was offered to me.) But all I knew of Colorado was snow and mountains, and skiing seemed like a good way to break my runner's legs. I threw the packet on the floor and kicked it under the bed.

A few weeks later, days before my twentieth birthday, came my final hearing. My father did not attend; Dr K told me he was performing in Berlin. Hiro's absence sealed our *tegire* – estrangement. Literally, a severing of relations. That this was a form of the same verb, *kireru*, that now defined me seemed appropriate.

I would be leaving Kawano no matter what, Dr K explained, but it was up to the judge whether I would be released, paroled, or further incarcerated. Life in a detention centre, where juvenile criminals were often sent after age twenty, was awful. Your food came through a flap in the wall and you got cavity-searched weekly.

The judge eyed me, her face free of the white make-up female judges usually wore. 'You are an expense to this nation,' she said.

I kept my eyes on the grey carpet.

'Thus far in life, all you have done is *take*. *Take* from the reputation of our public school system. *Take* honour from your parents. *Take* an innocent boy's life. But what have you given back? You are lucky to live in such a refined, compassionate country. A less civilised nation might have you put to death for your crime. The court would like to hear you thank your father's country, the great nation of Japan.' She gave me a hard look. 'Now.'

I turned to Dr K. I'd been told that under no circumstances should I speak in the courtroom. He raised his eyebrows and nodded vigorously toward the judge, as if she were armed and demanding my wallet.

'Thank you very much.' I used the most polite form possible, the one recommended for greeting the emperor. When I tripped over the verb ending, the judge's mouth twitched into a shape that resembled a smile.

'Your mother was an American,' she said, pronouncing the word like she'd found something disgusting in her teeth.

'A Japanese may not hold dual citizenship. As the child of an American and a Japanese national, you must choose which citizenship you will take when you reach twenty years of age. I hear you have been invited to attend college in America. It is the *strong* opinion of the court that you should pursue this option. I spoke about giving and taking. The greatest gift you can give this country now is to leave. This means, of course, renouncing your Japanese citizenship.'

As I watched her mouth form these words, an iron door in my chest swung open and relief surged out. They wanted me gone as much as I wanted to go. Goose bumps pricked my arms despite my long sleeves, required in the courtroom. I clenched my teeth so my smile wouldn't show and promised I would go to America. I recited the words of contrition required of me as a criminal.

'You now move into the world carrying a burden of debt,' the judge said before ending the session. 'But I would not advocate for this outcome if I thought it uncarryable.'

I filled out the form that put an end to 'Chizuru' and turned me into Rio Akitani on 7 October 1996. The social security officer said I couldn't change my last name, but my given name could be anything I liked. I hadn't heard that term before, 'given'. My father named me Chizuru, 'a thousand cranes'. The choice pleased his parents and annoyed my mom. 'I wanted to call you Rio,' she told me. 'In Spanish it means river, and when I was little, the San Jacinto was my favourite place to play. It was a perfect name, too; the sounds work in Japanese. But your father wouldn't hear of it. It wasn't "traditional enough" for his parents. You'd think by marrying me he'd broken all expectation of being traditional! But it was the opposite. Like he had to raise you in a way that would make up for picking an American wife.'

Right before my *kireru*, a copy of *Rio* by Duran Duran appeared in my mom's secret shoebox. Anytime Hiro was sure to be gone awhile she'd lie between the floor speakers as if they were giant headphones. She loved the title track most of all. In those moments with her, I felt invincible. I'd wanted desperately to be Rio, and eight years later, I got my wish.

It wasn't easy. To be dumped into freedom, into a place where people spoke only English and I had to shop for and cook my own meals on weekends, decide for myself when to sleep and when to wake up. I was more alone than I'd ever been. But I knew I could succeed. Out of fear of trying anything different, I followed my Kawano schedule. Early to bed, early to rise. I went to class. I smiled when I was sad. I accepted every invitation. People were *nice*. My work-study job was manning the front desk of the MBA school's graduate dorm. It was mindless work, yet the students treated me with respect, as if having access to the mailroom and a telephone with the building manager on speed dial made me a peer in possession of valuable expertise.

Being half-Japanese didn't seem to matter much to people beyond the occasional 'Where are you from?' questions. Even the people who bluntly asked, 'What are you?' did so with genuine curiosity. In America, *everyone* was half-something. Or quarter. Or they didn't even *know*. I hung out with a girl named Leslie, who was Native American, Polish, English, Welsh, and German. She called herself 'a Heinz fifty-seven mutt'. I liked that people asked each other about their heritage – a pointless question in Japan. Yes, once in a while, usually at a bar, guys would ask if I was a geisha (or, more accurately, 'a gee-sha girl'), and once, a waiter brought me chopsticks with my poached eggs and toast. People assumed I was Chinese or, sometimes, Korean. But it didn't strike me as something to complain about – at least, not then. I only got annoyed if I corrected someone and they replied, 'Same thing.' That kind of wilful ignorance perked the black organ right up.

'Racism' was not a term used in Japan when I was growing up. This version of racism, which is of course what it was, felt quaint, naïve, compared with what I'd endured as a *hafu*. People in America may have been occasionally ignorant, but they were rarely mean.

I joined the Sole Train running club and explored the trails and forests. The beauty of the mountains, the way tiny wild-flowers sprinkled the earth in springtime, made me believe it was possible to forget where I came from.

I majored in biology and immediately entered the school's nursing programme. I had to be methodical in my studying to memorise names of muscles and bones and diseases and symptoms and spit them all out not once but seven months later, and again a year after that. It felt like tending a huge garden. I hung Tam's picture on the wall in my dorm.

Sal and I met on a hike organised by a mutual friend my first year in nursing school. He was getting his master's in applied math and came from Chicago. The Italian side of his family had lived there for generations. He claimed that in one part of the city, he had sixty-seven cousins within a two-mile radius. We walked among the trees, which were unlike any I'd seen, leaves shimmering like heat from a road. *Populus tremuloides*: quaking aspen. Their leaves were special, Sal explained. The stalk wasn't round, but flat where it attached to the leaf, and this flatness allowed easy movement. He demonstrated with his hand. In a breeze, he said, it's like confetti. A celebration. And when the wind blows hard, the leaves sound like a round of applause.

By the time we got married, I was pregnant. I graduated and passed the national licensing exam, so I could now practise as a registered nurse. I'd keep my promise to the judge; I'd make a career of caring for others. Of giving. But it was Lily who gave me real purpose. I was ambivalent about children, including the one growing inside of me, until she was born. When she arrived, I became ecstatic and obsessed. I worried she pooped too much or too little, whether the bars on the crib were too far apart so her head might get stuck or close enough together that she might wedge in her hand. I worried the dark rot inside me might have leaked into her. Any time she cried, I felt pain in my chest, certain that, if not for my genes, she would be forever happy.

But Lily was never sad for long, and when upset she became downright stoic. She channelled her Japanese ancestors before she knew of their existence.

Lily reacted to my over-worrying with fast-growing independence. She was an early walker and, once on her feet, sought out the most inaccessible places. Parenting was equal parts awe and terror, though I felt sure I was experiencing greater-than-normal extremes of both. That was fine. My wild love for Lily rooted me so firmly in the present that the past seemed inconsequential. My background could've been someone else's completely, the crazy story of a third cousin in another country.

Time passed. It was easy to forget. For a long time I believed I could.

I

THE NEWS of my father's second and final death arrives by FedEx.

I push open the front door and the smell of Sal's garlic marinara hits me in the face. 'That smells amazing!' I call as I kick off my shoes in the entryway. I'm lucky: my husband gets off work by four o'clock every day and he likes to cook. Sal sticks his head out of the kitchen and waves, a wooden spoon in his mouth. His dark hair's covered by a blue bandana.

Lily sits on the couch with her skinny legs tucked to her chest, arms folded around her knees. My origami daughter. A long rectangular box lies between her and the curled-up cat. As he's aged, Bagel's fur has turned dark brown in spots, causing him to look more like a cinnamon roll every year. He flutters his eyes and goes back to sleep, unimpressed by my return.

'From Japan,' Lily says, freeing her hands and picking up the box. She shakes it the way we do at Christmas and birthdays.

'Papers and something long. Like, a ginormous chopstick. Dad wouldn't let me open it. What'd you order?'

My appetite disappears like it's been vacuumed out.

I sit next to Lily, kiss the top of her peach-scented head. She nuzzles my shoulder. She is eleven, no longer a baby but not yet a young woman, and there's no middle ground between the two; being eleven means jumping from one state to the other at random. Some days – or moments – we encounter the curious, loving child; others, the surly, apathetic preteen. I take the box from her and, for the first time, find myself wishing for one of her apathetic days.

Red and green labels partially obscure the FedEx logo. The return address is in Japanese. On the packing slip, our address and 'Rio Silvestri' appear in block print. I stand, focusing on my name, the markered strokes of which seem to sharpen and rise off the surface of the box. This can't be right.

I left Japan as Chizuru Akitani. As far as anyone in Japan should know, that is still my name. Chizuru gave up her Japanese citizenship. Rio Silvestri is the new me, the American. That's how it works: no one in America knows about Chizuru, no one in Japan knows about Rio.

'Where you going?' Lily asks. I've crossed the room to the stairs that lead to our bedrooms. I take the steps two at a time, the box clutched in one hand. Lily yells, 'Open it here. I wanna see!'

I stop and give her a look. 'It's addressed to *me*.' My tone is sharper than I intend.

She's about to whine, then her face goes stony. 'Lame,' she declares, a word she knows I despise. She turns the television on.

'Hey,' Sal calls to her from the kitchen. 'Remember what we said about attitude?'

Lily keeps her eyes on the screen, feigning interest in a commercial for male body wash. Normally I'd ask her to acknowledge us, like the parenting books advise. But I can't do it. I can't do anything until I know what I'm holding. I speed-walk down the hall to our bedroom.

Maybe it's age, maybe it's something else, but I'm not as excitable as I once was. The black organ, soothed into submission by my running, retreated even further once Lily was born. It's still there, though, and I sense it now, just behind my heart. Sal avoids triggering it, either instinctively or by luck, but Lily's the opposite; she knows exactly how to piss me off. She also knows that if I have to leave the room while we're arguing, she's won. I'm happy to give her those victories. She will never see her mother out of control.

Downstairs, Sal says something to Lily that I can't hear. A second later he calls, 'You stockpiling ninja stars, Ri? I had to sign in three places before the guy would hand that thing over.'

Sal doesn't know all of me. Maybe this is true of all husbands and wives; surely there are inaccessible places in each of us. Places few would understand, and marriage, I've come to believe, is about finding someone who understands the right things without digging up the wrong ones. I've kept the promise I made to myself. Sal has never heard of Chizuru Akitani, the girl who snapped.

I lock the door and grab Sal's beard-trimming scissors from the mug on our dresser. The lightest pressure splits the brown tape sealing the box. Sal sharpens these scissors, along with the kitchen knives, every sixth Sunday. He draws a pointy blade on his calendar to mark the dates.

I lift the flip-top lid, which sucks upward the typed letter lying inside.

A lawyer gives assurance in clumsy English – *Mr Akitani's suffrage was not lengthy, he died in piece* – that it happened quickly. The lawyer manages to get the medical vocabulary right: cardiac arrest. I push out a long breath and sink onto the bed. I'm not in trouble. My father died, that's all.

I set the letter aside and, from the box, pick up a ten-thousand-yen note folded into a butterfly. I'm surprised he's hung on to it after all these years.

I lift the butterfly's wings and let them settle back into place. Hiro didn't trust banks. This peculiarity, combined with his absent-mindedness, meant money all over the house. Once, as a kid, I opened my origami box to find a stack of flat, smooth bills. I folded them into swans and placed them in the low alcove in the living room reserved for sacred objects. For weeks, no one noticed the equivalent of three grand sitting in plain sight. When Our Living National Treasure (in private, my mom and I often referred to him using this preposterous title, which we knew he was secretly proud of) was in a good mood, he might hand me a wad pulled from a sack of rice or the shoe cabinet and say, 'Look at this! A kid who's entertained by money without spending it.' Of course, when I was older, desirous of comic books and gadgets, he never gave me enough to buy more than a sticky bun.

I put the butterfly on top of the lawyer's letter and turn back to the box. Dividing it diagonally is the object Lily called a chopstick. My father's violin bow. I run a finger along the smooth Pernambuco wood.

During the periods he was home with us in Tokushima, on break from the orchestra in Tokyo, cleaning the bow was my weekly chore. I'd spend an hour – far more time than necessary – coaxing rosin from between the strands of Mongolian horsetail, polishing the pad and stick. He never said a word when I gave it back, spotless. As his trips grew longer and more frequent, and he began spending full weeks at the Tokyo apartment, I'd sometimes leave a bit of wax on purpose, to provoke an interaction. He got mad at my mom all the time, called his American wife 'my Western demon', but I had to work to get under his skin. If only I could raise his passion the way my mother did! Measured against ambivalence, rage seemed a gift.

What's he done with the violin? It doesn't seem right to separate the bow from its instrument.

In New York City, during my second and last childhood trip to the United States, I heard a fat man in a tux refer to my father as a 'super-auditor'. Like a chef whose sense of taste is so refined he can detect a dash of paprika in a gallon pot. It was true. Our Living National Treasure (or, more officially, *Jūyō Mukei Bunkazai Hojisha*, Preserver of Important Intangible Cultural Properties) was ultrasensitive to sound and heard music in the strangest places: the truck that collected burnable trash on its Thursday dawn rounds, but not the non-burnables truck on Fridays. He heard a backbeat as my mother washed dishes. But he was equally sensitive to that which did not resonate – what he called *sazameki*: the Din. The sound of my pen across a page sent him out of the room, but when my mom wrote, he relaxed. He assigned people musical intervals. Whenever I succeeded in irritating him, he whistled mine: the tritone, or 'devil's interval', that sonic argument one heard from an ambulance. The space between those notes, he said, had driven men to fight, to ravage, to kill. Mine was the interval that could start a war.

There's a sheet of notebook paper at the bottom of the

box. Japanese writing covers the page. My father's tiny, precise lettering.

Thanks to YouTube, I know I can still understand spoken Japanese well. But my ability to read kanji is gone. Even the third-grade level I left Kawano with has likely deteriorated from lack of use.

I stare at the page, willing the language to let me in. What is he trying to tell me? I have no idea how he's spent the last twenty years. I scan the letter but can only pick out a few characters – there are 'ten', and 'tree'. And the one for 'west' that looks like a bottle, and the name of our prefecture, Tokushima, and the crossed pitchfork, *shi*, that means 'city'. My father's voice echoes in my head: *You are Japanese. You must learn to read and write kanji like a Japanese; not carelessly, like your mother.*

Even in death, the man finds a way to point out my deficiencies.

I can't read his message, but really, it doesn't matter what the letter says. Even if it's a reproach – he reached out. Sent *something*.

Bow, butterfly, letter. This, according to the lawyer, is my inheritance. I can touch these objects, smell them, throw them at the wall. These things handed down have weight and shape. Fragility. My knee can crack this bow. The money will burn. So will the letter.

A state ceremony honouring my father will be held in Tokyo tomorrow. A more intimate funeral service and celebration of life, organised by his friend Leonardo Verutti, will be held in a week in the small city on Shikoku where I grew up, allowing mourners outside Japan time to make travel arrangements. The details of time and place are included along with a map of Tokushima Prefecture. I stare at the lines that represent roads and highways of my childhood, but cannot connect them to my first home just as I cannot make meaning out of my father's note. I've accomplished the goal that drove me for years: leaving that life behind.

But I don't feel proud. In our Pier 1 bedroom, surrounded by proof of my success, I feel like someone's pointed out a hole in my favourite sweater. I feel like what I am: a thirty-eight-year-old mother and wife with a retirement fund and a house in the suburbs and a Volvo. My life has been built for safety.

But it has to be like this. I know how it feels to be left, to be thought worse than worthless. No one I love will ever feel that way.

Three times, I've come close to telling Sal the truth about my past. The first was after finishing my first marathon, the Boulder Backroads. It was the race's inaugural year, and in commemoration, they promised any first-time marathoner a pine-cone necklace when they crossed the finish line. I hit a wall at mile twenty-one, and didn't think I'd be able to make it. My legs felt like they were made of wet sand. My thighs and nipples were chafed raw. My feet, I was sure, would look like pieces of pounded meat when I took off my shoes. But I thought of that dirt yard at Kawano, of the fence that kept us inside; I thought of how I already knew how to separate my mind from my body, and I kept moving. A group of bagpipers serenaded runners along the last quarter mile, and the crowd was buzzed and rowdy. It felt like a welcome-home party.

Sal and I had only been dating a few weeks. He was there at the finish line despite the day's heavy rain. I fell into his arms, crushing the pine cones between us, and he put a raincoat around my shoulders, pulled up the hood, wiped the water and sweat from my face. The bagpipes sang of mourning and joy. I looked up at Sal and felt something cave in my chest. But when I breathed in to speak, I couldn't gather the air. The moment passed.

The second time was the night before our wedding, the third when I found out I was pregnant. Each time, I psyched myself up. 'There's something I need to tell you about myself,' I'd rehearse. 'When I was twelve …' But no matter how much I prepared, I could never bring myself to start, and I'd retreat into frustrated, shamed silence.

I walk down the stairs, counting the rhythm of thumps and creaks. One, two, creak, four, five, six, seven, squeak, creak, ten, big creak, twelve, floor. 'My dad died,' I say.

Lily's eyes leave the TV.

Sal comes out of the kitchen, asks me to repeat myself. He hugs me tight. He knows my relationship with my father was strained, that I haven't spoken to him since I was a teenager. But he also knows that right now, this doesn't matter.

Lily asks, 'My grandpa? The one in Japan?'

'That's right, sweetie. That's what the box was about. His lawyer sent me some papers and things.' I hold out an arm and she comes to me.

'Did the lawyer send his chopsticks?'

I laugh. 'That was his violin bow. You know he played, right?' Last year, Lily went through a guitar-playing phase, and I briefly wondered if she'd inherited her grandfather's musical ability. But she didn't like practising scales and complained that playing a song wasn't nearly as fun as listening to it. I identified completely and was so relieved, I let her quit sooner than I probably should've.

'How'd he die?' she asks.

'His heart stopped.'

'Why?'

It's a good question. He was only sixty-four. 'I don't know.'

'Is there anything we need to do?' Sal asks. 'Clean out the house, meet with his lawyer?' He doesn't know everything, but he does know I'm the only child, that my mother is long dead. And I know he's not going to be happy about the idea whipping up like a summer storm in my head.

I can go. I want to go. Alone.

'It doesn't seem like there's much for me to do.' I add, 'But I think it would be good to attend the service.'

'We can pull Lily from camp, I guess. I don't know if they give refunds this close—'

I feel Lily stiffen under my arm. 'No,' I say. 'I'll go alone.'

Sal's surprised. 'Why wouldn't—'

'It's too expensive to fly us all there on short notice, and Lil would flip if she had to miss Reel Girls. Right?' I give her a squeeze and she nods. We've already paid for this two-week camp in LA that promises to turn young women into the next generation of movie directors. It will be her first sleepaway camp. When we told her she could go, she leapt around the living room, sang 'Let's Go to the Movies' to the cat. For days afterward Sal and I received spontaneous hugs. I was proud of her bravery, proud of us for raising a kid who wasn't afraid of new experiences, new people. When I was Lily's age, I was kept inside a locked room inside a locked building inside a barbed wire fence. Which was, I believed, where I belonged.

Sal brings up the idea of a family trip to Japan every couple of years. He's curious about the place – in his mind, it's all temples and bamboo and untamed neon. And he thinks Lily should see where her mother grew up.

It's not that I haven't thought about returning. I have Japan dreams in which I remember nothing visual or narrative – I just wake up with a sense of having been there. More specifically, having been there, running. Never toward nor away from anything I can identify – more like a sense of movement, of … covering ground. And I *am* curious: about how Japan has changed, how I have. What would Lily think of it? But every time Sal mentions going, I brush off the idea. *It's so expensive. I don't know who we'd visit. Lily's not old enough to enjoy it. It's crowded. It's the World Cup/Obon holiday/New Year's and a terrible time to travel.*

The real reasons are too big, too private. I might've run into my father. Yes, the chances were tiny, but it was still possible. He'd surely say something awful. Or maybe they'd connect my new name with my old one and turn me away at the airport, revealing my status – unwelcome, unwanted – to my husband and daughter. I might lose control, unable to face the memories. I'd have to explain everything. It wasn't worth the risk.

But now – now I can dip in a toe. The sentinel, Our (no longer!) Living National Treasure, is gone. The guard's left his post.

Sal nods toward the TV. 'Lil, go finish your show, honey.'

So far, Lily has been too young to care about where we vacation. Our summer trips to Chicago and her beloved North Avenue Beach thrill her. Other than the movie *My Neighbour Totoro*, which she loved as a little girl (and still does), she's shown no curiosity about Japan, or any foreign country. Still, I worry about what will happen when she gets interested. I don't want to keep Japan from her, or from Sal. It's only who I was in Japan that needs to stay secret.

I follow Sal toward the kitchen, past the puzzle table. The pieces on it are in a day-one array, separated into pre-assembly piles by type: edge, boot, perfect, different, and the uncategorisable ones Sal calls 'Lily pieces'. When I first met Sal, I assumed this taxonomy was universal. I'd only done a few puzzles in my life, and none as large as the ones Sal liked to pore over on weekends or while watching a movie. It wasn't until Lily came home from a friend's house complaining that the girl didn't even know what a boot piece was that I realised this was Sal's private language.

In the kitchen, Sal leans against the tile counter. I know what he's going to say. 'Why don't you want me to come?'

Bringing him with me would start a series of questions, beginning with *Why doesn't anyone at this funeral recognise you?* 'It'll be easier to deal with it alone,' I say. 'Anyway, I don't want a funeral to be your first impression of Japan.'

'Husbands go to their wives' dads' funerals. You need someone there for you.'

Sal prides himself on being a Good Husband, a bona fide family man. I usually love this about him. But not always. A few weeks ago, a planned community opened on the western edge of Boulder, near us – Tuscany Terrace, it's called. The streets have names like Chianti Circle and Gondola Way; two golden 'T's' are intertwined on the wrought-iron gate at the entrance. Sal mentioned offhandedly that it'd be an ideal place for a small ('but maybe growing?') family like us to live, 'just, you know, hypothetically'. Think of all the new appliances they stock those houses with; imagine a stainless steel fridge and stove, he said. Granite counter-tops! His interest in such a phony place annoyed me. I told him you can't buy into the neighbourhood of perfect lives. He laughed. That night in bed I imagined my body as a subdivision. Here was the community gym, here the in-ground pool. The girl who killed Tomoya Yu. Nurse. Wife. Mom. Runner.

'You *are* there for me.' I gesture at the kitchen island, where the wooden salad bowl, brimming with spinach and diced tomatoes, sits awaiting Sal's famous blueberry-mint vinaigrette. Every napkin in the house bears a stain from this dressing, and it's the only stain that doesn't bother me. Lily has adored Sal's 'blue stew' since she was a baby. Cauliflower, Brussels sprouts – she'd eat anything doused in it. Against our advice, she once put it on a stack of pancakes and ate the whole thing. I look forward to the day she admits how gross that was.

'You don't need to make a snap decision,' Sal says. 'This isn't the hospital.'

'I happen to be able to make a choice without debating every single option, making a pros and cons list, and checking a million websites,' I tease. But it doesn't go over as teasing. I touch his arm. 'C'mon. I know how I feel. It's not snap. It's *efficient*.'

He gives me a pointed look. 'If you go without me, we'll miss this month.'

Sal's wanted a second child for years. He joked about how if we had another one (in his examples it's always a boy) we'd only be point-five kids and a picket fence away from the American dream. Two months ago he told me that if we didn't start trying soon, he'd seriously regret it. So we did. Or at least, he thinks we did.

'I know. But it's only one month.'

From the living room, Lily calls, 'When are we eating?'

Sal grabs two forks and starts tossing the salad. Pieces of spinach fly out of the bowl. He doesn't look at me. I pick up

40

the spinach that's fallen on the floor but he keeps going, sending more leaves flying.

'Are you even *okay*?' he asks.

I wish it didn't have to be this way. I wish I could tell him. But you can't have everything.

'I'm fine,' I say as Lily comes into the kitchen. 'Really, truly fine.'

I come down to the computer after bedtime, sidle carefully past the puzzle table.

The new puzzle is a Springbok, as usual. Sal doesn't bring his hand-cut jigsaws home unless he's testing the difficulty level or there's been a mistake in the cutting. And Springboks are to him like eating a Hershey's bar even though you're an adult and have access to Godiva. They were his first love. He did these puzzles with his dad, who did them with his dad, and so on, all the way back to the Depression, when puzzles were a form of cheap, recyclable entertainment. At Sal's parents' place in Little Italy, there's a picture of Sal's great-granddad and a bunch of young men doing a puzzle on the front stoop of the Taylor Street apartment. Sal's dad swears that one of the men is Al Capone. To Sal, a place doesn't feel like home until it contains a card table with a half-done jigsaw puzzle on it.

I sit down and run a search for plane tickets. The screen fills with options. I can leave tomorrow if I want; I haven't taken a sick day in five years. Sal stays home with Lily if she's too sick for school, so I've got weeks of vacation time stockpiled. Two days from now, I could be in Japan. It makes no sense. There should be a spike-covered wall to scale.

My passport's in the metal box in the bottom drawer of the desk. I flip open its stiff blue cover. The photo was taken eight years ago at Walgreens in preparation for our first and only international family trip, to Cancún. My skin is unlined and my forehead shines. I've forgotten: my skin used to be oily. Now, if I don't slather on Oil of Olay, my face feels like a mask about to crack.

I'm getting older. Thirty-nine in September. And I want Sal to be happy, so I made a show of throwing out my birth control pills. He got choked up and for a minute I considered leaving the pills in the trash. But I didn't. Instead I remembered how awful it had been to run pregnant, how the morning sickness had kept me from exercising at all some days, and how after the first trimester, when the nausea finally faded, I'd had to wear an adult diaper under my sweats because I had to pee so much, often uncontrollably. Add to that the sheer commitment required and – I just need a little more time. Space to think. This trip can do that for me.

There's a creak at the top of the staircase. Lily. 'Mom?' she says. 'How come you're not sad?'

I meet her on the stairs. 'Sweetie, I am sad.' I lead her to her room. 'It's been a long time since I saw your grandpa. I guess I'm thinking about being a little girl, spending good times with him. I'm happy for those memories.'

I tuck her in and sit beside her on the bed. Bagel's in his usual position, spread-eagle on his back next to her pillow. He's slept with her since he was a kitten and Lily got her first big-girl bed.

She bites her lip, an old habit. Even as a baby, she fought tears. I touch the corner of her mouth and she relaxes.

'Is Daddy gonna die?'

'Oh, Lil. My dad was old and sick. Your dad is healthy and will live a long, long time. He'll still be around, bugging you, when you're as old as me.'

'I'll never be *that* old,' she says, grinning. I tickle her feet, grateful for my sweet, healthy kid, grateful she has a father who would never let anything take him out of her life.

When Sal and I started dating, I sensed he saw something in me that wasn't there. But eventually his belief overrode my knowledge and I became a cheerier, more carefree person. He seemed to be presenting a role and offering me the part. No doubt our attraction was real; I loved that he could pick me up and carry me, loved how passionate he got when he talked about building things, different types of wood, the miracle of laser cutters. We laughed at the same TV shows, liked the same bands. 'I want to create something good,' he told me on our third date. We were at Gino's, a pizza place where the chefs tossed dough into the air and the wine came in carafes. We still eat there. 'Normal. Happy. Quiet.' That was the night I fell for him, and the first time we had sex. I told him I wanted the same things he did. I felt like I was getting away with something, and said so when the wine was gone. Sal replied that that was what happiness felt like.

I let go of Lily's feet. She starts to bite her lip again, stops herself. She's wondering about something. 'I'm sorry I said "lame".'

I plant a loud kiss on her forehead. 'Thank you, Lil. That makes me feel good. I love you so much, you know that?'

'I know.' She begins to hum softly, a seemingly random tune. She has always been an unconscious hummer when she feels safe and content.

I back out of her room, pulling the door almost, but not completely, shut. She likes it that way and I do, too. That sliver between the door and the frame seems to grow narrower every week. Soon she'll be closing the door, making use of the lock.

A few years ago, I was training for the longest race of my life, a sixty-kilometre ultramarathon. I'd drive to Wyoming, stay overnight, to run it. The course was up in the Bighorns, and I wanted to train as often as I could at elevation beforehand, so I started a routine in which I'd go up to the summit at Pikes Peak and train for a long morning on both of my days off. This was a Saturday, one of my last workouts before the race. I was nervous about my performance at elevation – I didn't think my lungs were there yet – and eager to push myself. The night before, Lily had gone to her first sleepover. The two other girls involved were friends she'd known since kindergarten, and because she'd begged me for months to allow it, I was fairly sure there would be no middle-of-the-night call. And yet there we were: 5:00 a.m., hoodie zipped, New Balances double-knotted, Sal sipping coffee on his way to the studio to accept a shipment. The phone rang.

'Mommy, can I come home?' I hardly recognised Lily's voice. I put her on speaker. Sal set his coffee down.

'Of course,' I said, shifting my weight. My calves felt itchy. I wanted to run badly. 'Dad can be there in ten minutes.'

She sniffled. 'I want you.'

I looked down at my leg. It was bouncing. I put a hand on it and forced it to stop. 'I'm about to go out for a run, sweetie. I'll see you in a couple hours, when I get back.'

She burst into tears. 'You're always going for a run! It's not fair! Why do you always have to go for a run when I *need* you?'

Sal's eyes were wide. We both knew she was exaggerating; she was emotional and probably hadn't slept all night. She was clearly being unreasonable. And yet he was watching me curiously. He wanted to see what I was going to do. Which I would choose: running or my daughter.

But it wasn't a choice about that, really. Was it? Reality split for a moment; I was two equally rational people in one. Of course Sal could pick up Lily; he'd comfort her, put her to bed, and she'd sleep until noon. I'd return while she was still dead to the world. But then there was the me of this moment. Lily wanted me to prove something. I didn't like that. I had done everything for her, would do anything still, and I believed she knew that. At least, that's what I told myself when I said, 'Ten minutes, Lil. Daddy's on his way.'

Sal did not react. He just looked at me. 'She's testing you,' he finally said.

'Sure is.' I grabbed my water bottle and purse.

'But if you were about to do anything other than training, you'd be going to get her right now.'

He was right. I would have gone any other time, even if it had meant I'd be late for work.

I glance back at Lily's door. She hasn't had a problem with sleepovers in years. So quickly, it's gone from *I need you* to *Please, just one more hour at Dahlia's?*

The glow from the computer illuminates a corner of the living room. A beacon.

The website wants to know: one-way or round-trip? A one-way ticket, that open-ended dream, brought me to the US nineteen years ago. But it's not for me now. I need a day for travel and rest, one for the funeral, a few to get out and run. Yet five days doesn't seem like enough time.

I open a new tab. Hiro Akitani's Wikipedia page was updated with the information about his death immediately upon its announcement.

Little is known about Akitani's personal life. Rumours that he was the father of Chizuru A., the 12-year-old girl who stabbed a classmate to death in 1988, appear to be unfounded.[3][18] Throughout his life, tabloids tried to link Akitani romantically to many women without success. [5][11][12] Other evidence suggests he was possibly homosexual. [citation needed]

This last sentence is new, though forms of it have shown up before. The changes were made eight hours ago from the IP address 133.65.88.26. Undocumented claims show up all the time on his page. Two years ago, someone modified his bio to say that Hiro Akitani actually *had* died during his childhood illness, and been replaced by an alien impostor.

Edit this page. Click. *Your edits will be attributed to SalSilvestri1974.*

Let's see what the truth looks like. *Hiro Akitani is partially responsible for the death of his wife, Elena Akitani (née Brown), in 1988, and is survived by his daughter, Rio, whom he abandoned in a detention centre when she was 12, and a granddaughter, Lily, whom he never met.*

I close the tab without submitting the changes.

On the JAL webpage, I type in our credit card number. It's so easy. Those sixteen digits and a box containing a few mementoes are all I need. Denver, LAX, Osaka. I'll stay a full week, pay the change fee if that ends up being too long. My finger hovers a second before I click 'Purchase'. I imagine my father standing behind me, cradling his cracked turquoise tea mug. He's laughing at me because I waited until he was dead to face his beloved Japan – to face him. I hate that I care enough to conjure him. I know I shouldn't: it's been so long since the door between us hung open.

Still. There's something in his letter, the bow, that butterfly. An invitation. Even after years of estrangement, the old beast has raised its head and whispered, *Come*.

2

I PREPARE FOR THE TRIP by renting Japanese movies, including my childhood favourite, *Nausicaä of the Valley of the Wind*. Lily watches it with me twice, a surprise given that she hates subtitles and won't watch foreign-language films without English dubbing. Sal refuses to join us; he spends the three days before my departure upset that I'm going without him. But I catch him watching the movie from his desk more than once. He's too much a part of us to detach fully; once in a while our eyes meet over the top of his computer monitor. He makes a mock-mean face at being caught, then narrows his eyes to show he is still not cool with the way things are playing out.

The morning of my flight, I do the seven-mile run through Betasso Preserve, whose network of trails and aspens I can reach in ninety seconds from our back door and whose hills, sharp roots, and deer hideouts I know by heart. The hills on this loop

49

are killer, which I like. Hills demand everything and hills are ambivalent. I can get mad at a hill for being relentlessly steep and it doesn't care. Not to mention the up-and-down taps more muscles and helps me avoid shin splints by providing variation in how I wear myself out.

My lungs are huge and gleaming. The oxygen here is super-charged. The air smells of dew and tangy pine and earth. In the halfway meadow, a spray of violets has popped up. Something big is about to happen to me.

Before leaving for the airport, I fold my father's letter and put it in an envelope. The butterfly goes in my wallet; Lily asks for the bow. She puts it on top of her bookcase, where she keeps precious things: a piece from the first jigsaw puzzle Sal cut for her (a stegosaurus, made of smaller dino shapes), broken shells from Cancún, crimson lip gloss I've never seen her wear, a years-old participation certificate from Boulder Children's Theatre, a string bracelet I don't recognise. The bow bisects the space, creating an unintentional border between girlhood and womanhood. In front of it are the mysterious bracelet, lip gloss, and a photo of Lily and her friend Dahlia in a glittery blue 'BFFs 4-Ever' frame. Behind it are the shells, the puzzle piece, the certificate, and a key-chain photo of her and me on the biplane kiddie ride at Elitch Gardens.

Sal will take me to the airport. Lily is allowed to stay home alone for up to two hours as long as our neighbours Jill and Chuck will be home; she wavers between spending half an hour more with me in the car and the freedom of an hour in the house by herself. Alone time wins. I hug her goodbye, try to commit her sugary smell to memory. When I see her next, she'll be bronzed and half an inch taller, red glinting in her thick cedar-bark hair.

'Be good,' I tell her, tucking a long strand behind her ears. She automatically flips it forward. She has my eyes, almond-shaped and dark, and Sal's elephant ears, which she's recently decided are too long and must remain hidden at all times.

On the drive, Sal talks about his plans to do some rock climbing with Justin and E.J., guys from work. 'It's been two years since I went,' he says. 'My arms are gonna be like jelly after one ascent.' He's trying to be positive. I rest my hand on his thigh, lean over and kiss his cheek. It's extra-smooth, rubbery, a first-date cheek. He offers to park and go in with me but I say the kerb's fine.

I put on my backpack, which doubles as a suitcase. The roller bag at the back of the hall closet smelled like cat pee when I pulled it out, so I decided to make do with the pack. It's big enough to hold my running clothes and shoes – I never travel without them – an outfit for the funeral, and a couple of T-shirts and pairs of shorts. Sal slides it back off. 'I'm not saying goodbye over that thing,' he says, catching a tag hanging from one of the pack's zippers ('Stealthpack: 14+2 hidden compartments'). Instead of yanking on it like I would, he slides his Swiss Army knife from his back pocket and cuts off the tag. The pale green REI backpack was his Valentine's gift to me last year. He was excited about the number of hidden pockets. I played along, though I haven't done much hiking since college; I like moving faster than that.

When he hugs me he puts his hand on the back of my head, as always. My cheek hits below his shoulder. I can hear his steady heart.

'I'll be waiting,' he calls as I head toward the revolving door. I turn and smile. He's smoothing back his dark hair. I can feel my fingers getting tangled in those slippery waves, the same ones that crest on Lily's head and knot at the nape of her neck. Maybe I do want another baby. Or maybe it's easy to think that when you're heading into an international airport, blissfully alone. I blow him a kiss. I push the heavy glass into motion, sealing myself off.

No patients to intubate, no kid to pick up, no floor to Swiffer or peanut-allergy-friendly lunches to shop for. I'm ready for this. In a way, I've been waiting for it for a long time. Boarding the plane to Japan will set me on a singular path. Until I reach the immigration entry point at Kansai Airport, there will be no way to turn back.

Two hours into the twelve-hour flight from Los Angeles, once meals have been passed out and the lights dimmed, I ask Mariko, one of the flight attendants patrolling the back of the plane, to help me practise Japanese conversation. She takes the empty seat beside me and gives me a play-by-play of her life since boarding school in Tokyo. I comprehend most of it, with the exception of a few slang phrases. She's older than she looks – thirty-three – and married less than a year. 'I like being away from home,' she whispers. 'My husband is a good person, and I have many friends, but it's when I'm on my way to a foreign city that I feel most alive.'

My own speech comes slowly – I stopped thinking in Japanese years ago – but it comes. 'Tell me about a typical day,' Mariko says. 'Describe each small thing.' I tell her about my hospital, how Sal turned puzzle-making from a hobby to a career, Lily's desire for a smartphone. The logic of subject first, verb last shakes loose. Each time Mariko leaves to answer a call, I practise to myself: 'This is a magazine.' (This right here, magazine, is.)

'I need to go to the bathroom.' (As for me, bathroom, to go need.) I tell her how Sal proposed – with a gleaming gold, ring-shaped puzzle he'd cut himself – and she squeals, '*Romanchikku!*' And I remember: Japanese doesn't have a word for 'romantic'.

When Mariko asks what my plans in Japan are, I say I'm visiting my father, who's not well. I consider showing her his letter. But friendly as she is, I sense that I'm being held at a precise distance. Communicating in Japanese isn't just about the words. Interactions revolve around *honne* and *tatemae*. *Honne* is what you really think and feel; *tatemae* is the face you show to the world. While Mariko is remarkable for revealing any bit of *honne* to me, I am, for the most part, the recipient of her pleasant and patient *tatemae*. I must reciprocate, which means the letter's out of the question. The letter is all *honne*.

A chime sounds twice in the dark cabin. Mariko rises and, speaking English for the first time, says, 'Now you will sleep and I will work. Ah, I'm jealous of you! It's lucky to be bilingual. I practise, but my English is poor.' She takes something from her pocket and hands it to me: a holographic bookmark with a dolphin on it. 'For your daughter,' she says. I act appropriately grateful, but inside, I'm laughing; Lily finds bookmarks as useless as I do. They're never around when you need them and they never seem all that necessary anyway. Lily either leaves her books face-down and open, which drives Sal nuts – 'You'll ruin the spine that way' – or she dog-ears them. She got her bad habits from me. When I was her age, I'd mark my progress in the margins with a pencil: 'I'm here. I'm here. I'm here.'

I sit up straighter, drink the cabernet Mariko's brought me. I'm enjoying myself. In the air there's nothing to attend to, and the realities of landing, entering a new country, and busing from Kansai Airport to rural Tokushima Prefecture seem distant.

Worries about what I'll find at my father's funeral – a second wife; children, my half siblings – recede. The only sound in the dark, still cabin is the steady hum of air rushing by outside.

I fall in and out of sleep during the infinite artificial night. I dream again of Japan, of running up impossible hills and mountains without the slightest trouble. I come to – my legs are moving against the seat in front of me. Then I'm back on the bizarre terrain, bounding, flying. In this half-awake state I sense a tug on my abdomen. I'm attached to a tether. The tether is firm and gentle and it is drawing me toward Japan. It's a new sensation, and not uncomfortable. It feels like the plane is being not propelled but pulled, an entire island nation reeling me in.

The foreign passport-holder line moves slowly as it snakes toward the front. I take out my passport and customs form, put the passport and form away. It's too early to have them out. My mouth is terribly dry.

It's perfectly legal for you to be here, I tell myself. I'm an American. A tourist visiting Japan for a short-term stay of less than ninety days. Even if my name still was Chizuru Akitani, it's not as if I'd been barred from coming back. Still, I can't shake the feeling that in Japan, I am a bad person. A guilty person. The couple in front of me is arguing in German and does not move forward when the group ahead of them moves. I clear my throat, take a step closer to them. The gap grows larger. 'Excuse me,' I say a notch too loudly. Finally they are called.

And then it's my turn. A gloved hand beckons me to the farthest booth.

As I walk, the eyes of the other passengers and immigration control clerks press in from every direction. Walking is complicated. I'm moving too slowly, holding things up. No – I'm going too fast, giving away my nervousness. I push a smile at the serious young man behind the glass. No sound comes out when I try to speak. He tilts his head. In English he says, 'Passport?'

I fumble in my bag, check all the compartments. 'Sorry,' I say, unzipping a pocket the passport couldn't possibly be in. 'I just had it.' I check my pants. Riffle through the main compartment of my bag for a third time and find the blue booklet in the place where I first checked.

The clerk takes my documents without a word. His expression as he flips through the empty pages of my passport reveals nothing. I blurt, 'I should get out more, huh? Out of the country.' He holds the page with the faint stamp from Cancún up to the light. He sets the booklet down, flips to a brand-new page toward the back, and slams it with his stamp.

My heart feels like a racehorse let out of the gate. I rush past him toward the arrivals terminal. I'm in Japan.

There's a crowd outside the automated exit doors. Dozens of people hold placards, many printed with kanji I can't read. People glance at me and move on to the next face.

I have never had such freedom. I can board a bus to Mount Fuji and climb to the top, or take a bullet train to Tokyo and party all night in Roppongi; I can ride the escalator up one flight to departures and buy a ticket to Okinawa, Hong Kong, Paris. No one can stop me; no one would even know they should.

The currency exchange clerk gives me an assessing look, perhaps trying to guess which language to use. I greet her in Japanese and cash my traveller's cheques without a problem. Clutching my fattened wallet, I step into a convenience store.

A metal vat next to the cash register holds simmering *oden*. But *oden*'s a winter food. Apparently, the broth-soaked hunks of boiled potatoes, root vegetables, and nondescript white spheres are popular enough among travellers – as a welcome-home treat, or *sayōnara* last bite – to warrant a place out of season. It's been almost twenty years, but one look at the vat and I can immediately taste the tangy broth.

The refrigerator along the far wall is full of *onigiri* rice balls. There must be twenty varieties of the palm-sized triangles. I swallow hard. I imagine my teeth breaking through the lightly salted seaweed wrapper, plunging into the sticky, firm vinegared rice underneath. Then there's the filling: spicy chicken, tuna, roasted pork, or my favourite, the pickled plum *umeboshi* – its savoury pucker closes your eyes, makes you grateful to possess a tongue. I grab a chicken, a tuna, and two *umeboshi*.

I leave the store and wander the concourse. The riders in the seamless glass elevator appear to be floating on an open platform. An angular mobile a few hundred feet up slowly turns its limbs, which are a charged shade of orange I'm sure I've never seen before. Everyone I pass drags a spiffy suitcase and a distinct odour: tobacco, hair spray, warm rusty pockets of Chanel No. 5.

A balding man in a thundercloud-grim suit and gleaming shoes avoids my eyes as he passes. Steps later, I come across another man like him, and another, each identically dressed. Their faces wear the same tired expression, as if they've all tapped into the same pool of national weariness.

The airport feels alive, eager to help. A sign for long-distance buses points me to an escalator that begins to move when I step on it. Everything is automatic: doors swing open unbidden; luggage carts unlock with a touch. The walls are lined with vending machines offering hot drinks, cold drinks, dried fish in a gift box. One sells black hard-boiled eggs, a souvenir from the hot springs at Hakone. The machine announces its wares in English: LONG LIFE EGG.

As I near the doors that lead outside, a pair of miniskirted girls come in. Both look like they're wearing spiders for eyelashes. They are lovely creatures: impeccably accessorised, clothing tight in the right places, hair swept out of the eyes. The girls cast a collective glance at me. I become aware that I am a grown woman wearing a backpack. *Now* I remember how it feels to be female in Japan. These girls make me want to lock myself in a bathroom with a blow-dryer and a bag of make-up. I don't own a bag of make-up.

I say a silent thank-you that my daughter has grown up in a city where hairy legs and armpits don't merit a second glance; where a woman in a thrift store dress and Toms slip-ons is complimented on her style.

The humidity hits my arms and face before I reach the automatic doors. When they slide open, a bubble of heat engulfs me. I inhale the city. The dampness in the air magnifies the smell of exhaust and cigarettes. Betasso Preserve, with its sharp, sweet, piney oxygen, must surely be on another planet.

The coach-style bus to Shikoku waits at the last platform. I buy a ticket from a machine that speaks to me in British-accented English. As the ticket prints, an animated woman bows onscreen.

The bus is stuffy. Thick pink curtains and matching valances (a word Sal taught me; how charming I found it that his practical knowledge extended even to window dressing!) adorn the scratched Plexiglas panes. I sink into a window seat and close my eyes. All I've done is sit on planes or in airports for eighteen hours, talk to Mariko, and sleep, yet I feel like I've been through forty-eight hours on call. The backs of my eyes hurt. During that final shift before I left – two nights ago – a boy a year older than Lily was brought in with head trauma from a bicycle accident; he died before surgery started. His yellow Denver Nuggets T-shirt was sticky and dark with blood and fluids. Images like that get stuck in my head. It's the hardest part of my job. I can look at blood in a tube all day, but I'll never get used to it on a child.

The bus rumbles to life. There are only two other passengers, a teenager wearing huge DJ-style headphones and a middle-aged woman who has already managed to fall asleep. We pull away from the airport and crest a hill, which affords us a view of the human-infested landscape. Grey cubes tile the earth. Three hundred feet above the streets, a second society of gases goes about its business. White smoke billows upward and tangles with brown and purple soot-swirls from invisible chimneys. On the other side of the highway divider, a river of slow-moving cars flows into the city.

Where does Osaka end? A few hills and only the sharpest peaks have been spared the urban carpet. Who lives in those rust-stained towers? Am I like them? Every single one would know of my father's death. No. That's not true. There are so many of them that surely there are a few who wouldn't.

There's a trick to opening *onigiri*. To keep everything fresh, the plastic that wraps it is actually folded *into* the seaweed when it's made, so if you go about it wrong you wind up with green shreds stuck to your palms and a naked ball of rice. But fingers remember. Pull this tab upward, wind it to the left, drag it this way, tug, and voila! Plastic in one hand, immaculate treat in the other.

Crack of seaweed, the smoothness of the rice, and oh – that plum. Bright sourness hits my cheeks, bites the roof of my mouth. I smile so big that a glob of rice falls out and lands on my thigh. I can't remember the last time I ate something so *fully*. The Japanese food we get in Colorado is uninspired: pale tuna, salmon on weakly vinegared rice, frumpy rolls of cream cheese and neon imitation crab. Moist *nori* that clings to your teeth.

I take another bite, savouring the long-lost flavours. On top of being delicious, the *onigiri* is comfortingly ugly. Last week, Sal convinced Lily and me to attend the Tuscany Terrace neighbourhood association's dinner: a 'B-B-Q Nite' in which no grills were lit. Instead, waiters carried trays of food in combinations surely dictated by dartboard throw (who eats pickled peppers with cantaloupe?) and salmon cakes topped with something a server described as caramel foam but looked like dirty soapsuds. We sat for a while with another family whose kids, twin boys a couple of years younger than Lily, shared their Goldfish crackers with us. 'You can't trust pretty snacks,' Sal said. 'It's like wave-particle duality. They can either look good or taste good, but never both.' The other couple had smiled politely. Their kids – Maxwell and Arwin, home-schooled – kept applying crackers to their mouths. We left early, stopping at 7-Eleven for a pint of Phish Food. I look forward to telling Sal about *onigiri*'s perfect, tasty plainness.

The bus makes three stops before leaving the suburbs. Five people get on at the first, two at the second, and a man with a cane and a Yomiuri Giants cap hobbles onboard at the third. Small wooden houses separated by rice paddies fill the space from the road all the way to the mountainous horizon.

Reminders of my old life are everywhere. The recorded female voice on the bus advising passengers to keep track of their belongings has the same singsong lilt as the one on the special Tokyo bullet train I rode with my father when I was still small enough to sit on his lap. (Nozomi, that train was called – 'hope'.) The man in the Giants cap, across from me and one row up, opens a Tupperware of *yakitori* chicken kebabs. The incredible smell, charred and peppery, summons the anticipatory tingle I had as a child before summer festivals and fireworks. The man eats slowly and wipes his mouth with a green handkerchief between each bite.

The outer suburbs drag on. It seems the buildings are not built on solid earth but upon other buildings. Maybe it won't end. Maybe all of Japan has been taken over by sprawl.

The highway rises higher and higher, and then I see it. The bridge. They built this enormous suspension bridge, spanning the Naruto Strait and its dizzying whirlpools, three years before my *kireru*. It was the first connection between the mainland and Shikoku. I've never crossed it, but I've thought of it often. This is where my mother died.

The bridge is not as high as I imagined. The pasty concrete posts and barriers make it hard to see the water. I never found out whether she jumped from here or from the observation deck below us. Did she dive or simply step off? Was she scared? The metal and asphalt where she last stood rush by, eight feet beneath me. Hard as I try, I can't connect her to this place.

The rowdy forests and endless coastline of my youth were no dream. There: the sea's appeared in the distance, and beyond it, the purple outline of taller mountains. Shikoku is as rural as ever. The island's resisted the big-box growth of Honshu. Expanses of rich green rise alongside the highway. We pass fewer cars, and the ones we do see are rusted, out of date, faded from summer sun. Gas station signs are as shabby as the vehicles they serve. 'Shikoku is old Japan,' my grandfather used to say. And by 'old', he meant 'real'.

Grandfather Nao, or Ojīsan, as I was made to call him,

was Hiro's father. He and my grandmother lived in a draughty wooden house with spiders in the corners (Grandma refused to disturb them; they were lucky) in Ehime Prefecture, and on our rare visits my father and grandfather would greet each other civilly, like business associates, while my grandmother bustled about, wiping imaginary dirt from spotless surfaces. She rarely spoke to my mother and me but favoured us with secret smiles. I liked going there. Hiro may have played to a crowd of ten thousand at the Great Hall of People in Beijing, but confronted by Ojīsan, he was a child. I didn't know the details of their relationship but I did know that at my grandparents' house, the pecking order was more in my favour.

Grandfather Nao had been a young man during the war. He believed in order and respect and duty. Outside his and my grandmother's house, the Japanese flag – 'maru', Ojīsan called it – flew on a splintering bamboo pole, and each night before dinner we stood before it and listened to the national anthem crackle from tiny speakers wired to the record player. Though he never said anything, I could tell Hiro hated this ritual.

I was nine or ten during our last visit. Upon our arrival, Ojīsan announced we would all climb Ishizuchi-san, the tallest mountain on Shikoku. It had been named a special historic site because of its role as a hideaway during the war, and it was affiliated with the eighty-eight-temple pilgrimage, which Ojīsan had completed in his twenties, after the war. We had learnt about the pilgrimage in school, though I'd never been to one of the temples. The idea intrigued me – all that silence, all that peace. But we weren't an outdoorsy family.

'Chizuru needs to feel what it was like,' Ojīsan said, and I was happy to be singled out, made important enough to mobilise the entire family. I had never climbed a mountain.

It was left to my father to coordinate the trip. This must have been some kind of punishment from Grandfather Nao. Ojīsan was the organised one; he always knew what time the train was coming or how long it would take us to get somewhere. I sensed a fight brewing; Hiro was too unreliable for the task. The weather was awful: cloudy and damp, and frozen fog hung all the way down to the top of the grass outside. I heard Hiro grumble to my mom, 'Ridiculous. Have you ever climbed a mountain you couldn't see?'

We prepared all morning. My grandfather grew eerily calmer as the delay progressed. Something was wrong. By the time Hiro had found the maps, packed supplies, and loaded Grandfather Nao's old green car, his T-shirt had dark spots under the armpits. Finally he called, 'We're ready. Let's go.'

Grandfather Nao strolled out to the car, looked at the sun, which strained weakly through clouds overhead, and said, 'No.'

'No?'

'It's too late,' Ojīsan said, and turned back toward the house.

My father stood very still, a bead of sweat rolling down his temple, his skinny arms trembling. His left shoulder fell noticeably below his right, as it always did when he wasn't paying attention to his posture. I waited for him to explode, but nothing happened. I ate a second helping of each dish at our early dinner, having already forgotten that I cared about climbing anything.

On the train ride home, I asked my father, 'How come Ojīsan never comes to your concerts?'

'He doesn't like music,' my mom said. She was sitting between us, her hand on my father's knee. I offered him a shoulder rub, something kids did for teachers at school, something my mom loved, but he shook his head.

Didn't everyone like music?

'Not everyone,' he said.

'I like your music,' I said.

My father stared out the window. There was nothing out there but rice fields and a few uninspired windmills. Not a single billboard, which were fun to look at when we took city trains.

'I like it too, sweetie,' my mom said. She put her arm around me and moved her other arm around Hiro and suggested a game of no-hands rock, paper, scissors. Instead of throwing one of the three signs with your hand, you counted off and shouted your pick. She'd made up the game in New York, the story went, because Hiro had practised violin so much his fingers were never free to play the normal way. ('And how else do people make decisions, if not *janken*?') We played her game the rest of the way home. Though it was a game of chance, it seemed to me Hiro came out ahead.

It's past ten when the bus pulls into Tokushima Station. 'Hotel Up?' I ask a man piloting a minivan cab. Ten minutes later he deposits me at the entrance of a fifteen-storey concrete cylinder.

I picked Hotel Up for its view of Tokushima, went all out and booked a junior suite on the top floor. Sal doesn't know. To me the expense is justified: I want to put distance between the city and myself – to be in a place where I can look without being seen.

The suite is done up in busy black and white and there are so many mirrors on the walls I get dizzy. But the enormous bed with its topping of whipped-cream pillows is perfect. I flop onto my back and sink. The funeral is tomorrow at 2:00. No need to set an alarm – I asked for a wake-up call when I checked in.

I have directions printed and will walk the five blocks – two north, three east – to the funeral home. I won't run into family at the service: my father's parents would be over a hundred years old, and my mom's family – well, even if they were informed of my father's death, none of Elena Brown Akitani's remaining relatives would care to make a trip from Texas to pay respects to the man who stole their cowgirl and turned her into a fool.

These thoughts drain into the mattress, past the box spring, through the white carpet, down to the building's foundation and into the earth. There is no black organ, no Sal or Lily, no hospital, no immigration counter. There's only the single thought, playing on repeat: I'm here. I'm here. I'm here.

3

THE FUNERAL HOME is a dark marble cube. My silhouette's reflection in the stone is anonymous and unassuming. Shadow self, are you ready? The silhouette straightens her back, lifts her chin. A figure passes behind and I turn, embarrassed. Count on me to get caught checking myself out before a funeral.

A woman a head taller than me, with deep lines around her blue eyes, stands behind me fussing with her hair. The wine-stain birthmarks covering her cheek are unmistakable.

'Miss – *Danny*?' I say, and balk at the absurdity of calling her that as an adult.

Her mouth hangs open. 'Chizuru?' She inhales sharply as if she's trying to suck the name back in, and then she's engulfing me in a hug. 'I hardly recognise you,' she says, pulling back. Her dark curls are streaked with grey. A red shawl covers her shoulders, and pale stone bracelets – one yellow, one blue – encircle each thin wrist. What is she doing here? Ah: she loved my father's music. Used to tune her blue boom box to the classical station during class, annoying the vice-principal whenever he passed in the hall. Once in a while, a performance of Hiro's would come on, and kids would giggle and watch me to see how I'd react. 'What a *talent*!' Miss Danny would say, except instead of 'talent', she'd use the Japanese version of the word, *tarento*. This added to my discomfort, as if I were responsible for her corny language-mixing and poor pronunciation. I couldn't look too proud, but I couldn't seem embarrassed of my father, either.

'It's a surprise to see you,' I say.

'And you as well. I'd say I'm sorry for your loss, but ...'

'Yeah. We hadn't been in touch.' I lower my voice. 'And I'm not Chizuru any more – it's Rio now. Rio Silvestri.'

Miss Daniela Townshend: my English teacher during that terrible year, my last in Japanese public school. Miss Danny, the only teacher who didn't pretend. Didn't pretend to like Japanese food, didn't pretend to be helpless in a foreign country, didn't pretend that bullies didn't exist. Miss Danny, who I fantasised would rescue me from Kawano and adopt me. I never thought I'd see her again.

'Rio Silvestri – what a name you've taken. Have a look at you. Grown-up and lovely.' Danny touches my jawline gently, raises my head up to look at her. Her fingertips are warm.

'I can't believe you flew all the way from New Zealand for this,' I say.

'Oh no. I live here.' She reaches for the door.

'Here?'

'Well, Tokyo. I returned to Auckland briefly, ages ago. But Japan got its hooks in, and I wound up coming back.' She steps inside. 'You're not alone, are you?'

I can't believe she's been in Japan all this time. Longer in total, now, than I lived here. 'Actually,' I say, 'I am.' I follow her so closely I step on the back of her heel. I don't want her to get away. 'Sorry,' I whisper. If she'd been back in New Zealand while I was at Kawano, it made sense that she wouldn't have visited me.

Inside, the smell of incense is strong. Pews line the dim wood-panelled room. There must be seventy rows of seating, and it's filling fast. Up front, a carved wooden crucifix sits propped on an altar beside a portable Shinto shrine with an urn inside. Lavender smoke curls out of a gilded box.

I don't recognise any of these faces. He was my father – it's basic, true, and in the circumstance, completely unsayable, because who would believe it? I have to act like I've never spoken to the man in the urn, never yearned for him to push my swing at the park, never prepared his breakfast or cleaned his bow. What a relief, what luck, to find Danny here. She knows everything.

Despite my dismissal of anonymous sources on Wikipedia (CITATION NEEDED), the lack of an obviously grieving family still comes as a surprise. It's been twenty-odd years since my mom's death and my extrication from my father's life. But I see no woman at the centre of attention, no children looking shredded the way they do at St Mary's when they're told their daddy or mommy isn't going to wake up. My father's parents, as I expected, must be dead, and if he hasn't remarried, this makes me the closest kin in the room. I like that that's my place here, even if it is a secret one.

'Let's sit in the back,' I say. As with my suite at Hotel Up, I want to be somewhere I can see without being seen.

Danny smooths her hair. 'Um ...'

'Were you planning to meet someone?'

'No one particular, really. Come along, then.'

Danny leads the way through clusters of mourners. She's wearing a gold tunic dotted with sequins, and billowy white pants.

Near her, I am pleasantly inconspicuous in my grey pant-suit. Most of my clothing is like this: simple, neutral. Stuff that doesn't draw attention to itself. I grew up acutely aware of how other people looked at me, of the lack of sameness they saw between us. I aimed to close that gap and blend in. Danny, on the other hand, makes foreignness work for her. She reminds me of Lily's director at the children's theatre, Rachel Stein. When she started going grey, she grew more forceful, as if all that melanin had been holding her back.

Danny is tall, but she's smaller than I remember. More angular, too, where in my memory everything about her is round: full-moon face, pear-shaped body, that comforting, stout personality.

We take seats along the back wall, which is covered with thin, rust-coloured carpet.

This place is buzzing like a cocktail party. Men and women laugh, hug, mingle. The crowd is comically diverse. In the aisle near us, a lady in a sari pinches the cheek of an albino boy in a tux and exclaims, '*Mon dieu, petit fromage!*' Who are they? Which Hiro Akitani did they know? Some people show the same face to everyone; others, like my father, are gemstones, constantly turning to display the most advantageous façade.

I touch my purse. My father's letter is inside. I want it to contain a happy message, something that explains why he left me at Kawano, something that explains him. A gesture, finally, of love.

I whisper to Danny, 'How's your kanji?'

Her eyes are trained on a group of people up front. She doesn't move her gaze when she responds. 'Kanji? Fair, I suppose. I passed the JLPT *ni-kyu* last year.' She finally looks at me. 'Took four tries. You'd think living here for years would've made it easier. But reading's never been my strong suit.'

Ni-kyu is the second-highest level.

I hope the service is quick. Danny won't be able to say no to a coffee. We'll find a quiet place. She'll read the note aloud, the way she used to read from works of literature each Friday during English class. She said it was important for students to hear the rhythm of a master even if no one (except me, though I often feigned indifference; understanding English wasn't cool) grasped the meaning. I remember one story in particular, about a classroom of kids on Venus about to see the sun after years of rain. As a prank they lock the class outcast, a girl somehow different, in the closet. The students are then swept up with excitement as the sun comes out; they play outside for an hour, relishing the warmth and light. Only once the rain starts again do they guiltily remember the girl in the closet. At the end they let her out but you know it's too late; she missed her chance to see the sun and she'll never get it back.

I cried when Miss Danny finished that story; I couldn't help it. Tomoya Yu puffed out his cheeks and fake-sobbed, making the rest of my classmates giggle. I knew that if that story had taken place in Miss Danny's room, I would be the girl they locked in the closet. Chubby, with the double-lidded eyes and not-quite-black hair – I was the one somehow different.

A priest appears at the front of the room and welcomes us. The mike on his lapel isn't working. Everyone in the room leans forward. Smoke from the shrine drifts out from behind his heavy white robe, making it look like his back is burning.

The man's voice needs oil. He reads a passage written by the Dalai Lama, then a verse from the Bible, then a Cherokee death prayer. With each selection, small clusters of guests exchange glances. They're probably wondering, *Where's the Shinto prayer and chant? Isn't this guy Japanese?* But my father was always fond of foreign things. This affectation seemed to bolster his patriotism and fuel his desire for me to be as Japanese as possible, as if that could make up for what some might consider his disloyal appetite. He performed abroad at every opportunity and was rarely home on weekends or holidays. Other kids' fathers were gone a lot, too, salaryman slaves, but this was different. My father was an artist, a dreamer in the fullest sense of the word. Even when he was home, he was gone. My mom excused his oddness by reminding people of the fever, but I never bought the justification. My father was as self-centred, prideful, and charismatic as they come. I knew this before I knew words for it in any language.

I've heard the story so many times it's in my bones. How, at age seven, not long after his first public performance in Sapporo, little Hiro fell ill. At first it seemed like a bad flu, but his temperature got so high his mother swore the damp red cloth she applied to his forehead sizzled on contact. My grandparents rushed him to the local hospital, where the doctors tried to control the fever with pills and an ice bath. They failed.

Hiro slept through most of this. What he recalled most vividly about the experience was the iridescent *tennyo* – garden fairy – dancing on his chest in the hospital. The *tennyo* wanted him to come somewhere – 'a bright frog kingdom with a tickly breeze' – and asked so nicely that he agreed.

The nurse in the room declared him dead. But when the doctor arrived, Hiro came back. He sat up and told the room that he'd gotten all the way to the shining castle, but stopped, because the *tennyo* said he couldn't bring his violin. The nurse fainted.

When it was over, Hiro's left arm had no feeling from the elbow down. The fingers did not respond when he tried to wiggle them. Reflex tests failed to produce movement. Hiro would not play his violin any more, the doctors told my grandparents. But just as they had underestimated the severity of the illness, the doctors underestimated Hiro.

'You're wrong,' my grandmother recalled him telling the doctors, to her horror. 'I'll play my violin. I've already played on the stage in Sapporo with Shinji Okamoto.' The specialist smiled kindly at my grandmother, who was so polite that, two years later, when Hiro gained enough control of his left arm to hold the violin and enough control of his fingers to find the strings, she did not report it. She didn't want to embarrass the doctors. My father liked to tell how he used an abacus to exercise his fingers and regain the nimbleness needed to navigate the neck of his instrument.

Up front, a small Italian man, weeping freely, tells how in Napoli my father played his favourite violin – the Busano that was now gone from this earth, cremated with its master – for a Gypsy woman who later found God because of the experience. This must be Leonardo Verutti. My father was that good, Leonardo tells us, eyes shining. He channelled the divine.

I believe him. Any passion my father felt, he bottled, to be poured into performance. The women who loved him wished they didn't. This included my mom and me. We wanted to believe he played for us. But he didn't play for anyone but himself. This single-mindedness meant my father needed protection. He'd walk outside barefoot without noticing he was standing in snow. One morning he put the entire bowl of rice I set out, chopsticks and all, into his violin case.

Despite all this, I'm surprised he's taken the Busano with him in cremation. The thing was carved in Venice in 1730 and worth half a million dollars. My father loved to show it off. I had no idea of its worth until my first trip to New York: Hiro and I came across a young guy playing Max Bruch's Second Violin Concerto in the subway. My father stopped, closed his eyes. He loved the romance of that piece and to hear it played on a poor-quality instrument hurt his ears. He grimaced and walked right up and put his hand over the kid's fingers. Try it on this, he said, and opened his case. The guy shrugged, picked up the violin, and began to play. His mouth fell open. A huge smile spread across his face and his whole body began to sway, as if the Busano were a beautiful woman with whom he knew he'd only have the pleasure of one dance.

But my father must have figured the Busano had fulfilled its earthly duties by belonging to him. He was Hiro the Hero, a Living National Treasure. In 1975, a year before I was born, NHK broadcast a series called *The Akitani Odyssey*, which was so popular they aired it twice annually until I was in fourth grade. He was also a spokesperson for Yakult, the mega-company responsible for drinkable yogurt; a rail line; and a mediocre baseball team. Sterling Parnassus and Olivet Lineze wrote works for him. There were rumours, of course, that he only got so much attention because of his disability – he never regained full range of motion in his left arm – but they were wrong: he won the Avery Fisher Prize and countless orchestral seats and solos based on blind auditions. It was undeniable. Hiro Akitani was the best.

Danny sniffles through the ceremony, blowing through an entire pack of tissues in under forty minutes. They accumulate in her lap like snow. Twice she breaks into full-on, shoulder-heaving sobs. I've seen people handle death in every way possible. There is no normal. But I wish I could do something, express something, more along Danny's lines. He was *my* father, and I sit here dry-eyed, not crying but not wanting to be outdone.

The priest rolls in a projector screen so we can watch a presentation from Leonardo's laptop. The lights dim and reveal the first image: my father as a uniformed high school student, solemn and slender. Then comes him playing violin on a European sidewalk, eyes on a yellow-haired toddler clapping beside him. His elbow is cocked at the odd angle he used to compensate for his limitations of movement. The strange posture became his trademark – Yakult did up his silhouette for their products so they could invoke his image without paying for a photograph. His critics (they were rare, and mostly German) went so far as to allege he'd never have become a master without the lucky accident of his posture. Yes, they said, adorable, chipmunk-cheeked Hiro Akitani *did* perform Paganini at age six (a piece of information included in his every introduction), but his execution? Cute, sure, but virtuosic – no way. He skipped the harmonics altogether and the tone quality of the half-sized violin was tolerable at best.

Now I do cry, as my good memories of him, none of which appear in the slideshow, surface: the trips when I was small, when I cherished long international flights because they guaranteed our time together; and his laugh, an enormous, bursting sound that made people jump. But I'm really crying because coming has made it clear: my father's death has nothing to do with his presence. There's not a single photo of his family, no acknowledgement of me or my mom. We've been edited out.

Danny's face is a mess of permanent blotches and fresh pink ones. She blows her nose so often and so thoroughly it's a surprise there's anything left inside her. The priest tells us to go in peace, and she stands without a word. We flow out of the funeral home amid the other guests.

Outside, the air is warm and heavy, hemmed in by low-hanging clouds. The damp street smells of gasoline and plum blossoms.

'Do you have time for lunch?' I ask Danny. When she doesn't respond right away I lamely add, 'No pressure.'

'I don't think so, dear. I've an appointment across town.' She pulls a case from her purse, removes a business card, and passes it to me like it's a cigarette, not formally, with two hands, like you're supposed to. 'Ring me up and we'll get together another time.'

I take out the envelope containing my father's letter and remove the paper. It's folded in a neat square. 'Just a coffee, or a quick snack? I wanted to ask if you'd help me read this. It's from him.'

She takes it warily. 'I suppose I could do,' she murmurs, turning it in her hands. 'If we're quick.' She doesn't unfold the letter. Instead, she turns down a side street and starts talking about her life. I have to jog a few steps to catch up.

'Up in Tokyo now, Asakusa, the old teahouse district. Used to be rather seedy but they've cleaned up the river and built a darling park; the neighbourhood children bring their boats to sail there ... never had children myself; well, never married, either, but that's no prerequisite. To each her own, and besides you know how Japanese universities demand your heart and soul in exchange for tenure ...'

She chatters on and on; it's more like a recitation than a conversation. But that's fine. I can ride the wake of her energy. Besides, it's nice to think that this is a woman who knew me well, and who still, clearly, feels comfortable in that knowing. She knows more about my past than anyone, even my family.

Her voice hasn't lost its music. My father had to explain accents when Miss Danny first arrived at my school; panicked, I told him I'd lost my ability to understand English. He said New Zealanders had the loveliest accents in the world. 'I could listen to a Kiwi lecture on politics – or, dear god, *economics* – all day and hear nothing but melody.'

Danny walks slowly once she hits her stride; now I need to slow down, shorten my steps so she can keep up. We pass a comic book store, a stand selling fried octopus balls, a hundred-yen shop. Though she's aged, the jittery girl who stood at the blackboard during my sixth-grade English class, scrawling verb conjugations and passing out illustrated home-made bingo cards, is still visible. Her face is the same, memorable but not beautiful: short-lashed eyes set close, lopsided lips, and of course, those birthmarks. More than half of the right side of her face is covered by the burgundy blotches. Still, it's a face with *promise*. When she smiles, everything balances out and she becomes, for seconds at a time, pretty.

At the corner a young man with spiky hair offers us packets of tissues advertising an English-conversation school. Danny takes one; I refuse.

'There's this study that proved people will take anything that's handed to them,' I say.

'Useful for the loo,' she says. I forgot; in this country, a girl has to carry her own.

We walk on. Danny plays with her bracelets and asks difficult questions. When did I last see Hiro? So he never met his grand-daughter? What's *she* like? What made me decide to attend the funeral?

I don't mind answering her. It's been so long since I could talk about my father with someone who knew him. With Danny, I can drop *tatemae* and reveal *honne*. I find myself explaining why I've come: to satisfy my curiosity about who he became, to see where I grew up, and something else I only realise as I'm talking, that I want to know more about that girl who spent her first twenty years in Japan, the girl I thought I could – should – leave behind. Danny coos and nods.

'Remember how you used to read to us in English?'

'The students despised it. All but you, Chizuru.'

'Everything you did impressed me. You were always travelling, learning, curious.'

She points to the window of the ramen shop in front of us, where bowls of dusty plastic noodles languish behind a pane of glass. 'This place is meant to be good,' she says.

The faded, threadbare *noren* hanging across the doorway is about as appealing as a dishrag. 'Are you sure?' I ask. A block down there's a brightly lit area that must surely contain a nicer restaurant. But Danny has already ducked past the curtain, eliciting a call of welcome from inside.

The place smells like pork grease, but it's clean and invitingly lit. Danny orders a bowl of plain noodles. The chef repeats the order – to his stove, since there's no one else in the kitchen. A steaming bowl piled high with green onions appears on the orange tile counter before we've settled onto our stools. Danny puts the letter down. I unfold it, smooth it with my palms, and set it in front of me like a meal. 'I can't wait a single second longer.'

'Right.' She slides the letter toward her bowl. I slide it back. 'Away from your soup.'

Our shoulders touch when she leans in. She smells grassy. 'Let me read it to myself first, to get the translation smooth.'

As she reads, her mouth moves. She pauses, licks her lips. There are tears in her eyes. 'This isn't easy to read,' she says. I don't know whether she's referring to the content of the note or Hiro's minuscule writing.

She reads the Japanese aloud:

'"*To my daughter: When you were born, your name was 'one thousand cranes'. That was not good enough for you?*

'"*Using the Internet, I found a photograph of my grand-daughter on the stage in Colorado. She has my charisma, it is obvious. If you haven't yet please tell her about me and what I have accomplished. Children need a good example.*"'

Danny squeezes her eyes shut and pops them back open. 'You practically need a magnifying glass. He had a stroke ten years ago. He stopped performing three years later, after a second one.'

I know about the second stroke, the one that stopped his performances, but not the first. 'What else?'

'"*I didn't leave you money. Don't be offended. Money doesn't help and anyway, I found something better to do with it.*"'

'That's all.' She folds the letter before I can reach for it, violating the paper with a new set of creases. 'Did you understand everything?'

'That's it? "Children need a good example"?' I open the letter back up. There are so many characters on the page; they couldn't all go by that quickly. At the funeral she'd said that reading wasn't her strong suit; maybe she's right.

She shakes her head, covers her eyes with her palms. 'It isn't easy to read,' she says again.

'What about the butterfly that he sent? Or the bow? He doesn't mention them?' I picture Lily's bookshelf, the divisive piece of wood among her things. Half of an X. I'll have Sal take it off.

With one chopstick, Danny swirls her soup into a whirlpool. The broth creeps up to the lip of the bowl. She pulls out the chopstick and looks right at me. The noodles keep spinning. 'That bow,' she says. 'I thought he burned it.'

'Because of the violin? Me too. I used to clean it for him. Must be his way of telling me I'm not done with my chores.'

All these years, and his last effort is to make sure I know his opinion hasn't changed. I fold the letter properly along its original creases, sharpening them with the edges of my thumbnail. The cook asks what I'll have. I shake my head. Noodles seem so base, so crude, so far from the nourishment I want.

Danny lays her hand on my mine. 'I'm sorry it's not what you expected.'

I want something to hold, so I grasp her fingers. 'I thought I'd finally get some sort of answer. And here I find what amounts to another fuck-you.'

Danny pulls her hand from mine. Her arm hits her purse, and a book falls out and hits the floor. She picks it up quickly. There's a temple on the cover and the pages, fringed with Post-it notes, have separated from the binding. She shoves it back into her purse.

'Is that the Shikoku pilgrimage?'

'It is,' she says reluctantly. 'Putting boot to trail day after tomorrow.'

'You're going to *walk* it? The whole thing?' The pilgrimage – the same one my grandfather hiked – consists of eighty-eight temples and takes a couple of months to complete. I can't imagine her getting through a quarter of it. The landscape's steep and mountainous. You have to carry a pack. Pilgrims sleep on floors, in tents. The hike to the shrine at the top of Mount Ishizuchi, would-be destination of the failed trip with Ojīsan, would have wiped out a fit twenty-year-old.

'You reckon I'd drive and miss the suffering?'

Whatever age has done to her body, it has not affected her spirit. During English Club meetings all those years ago, she told us of her weekend adventures: cycling fifty kilometres to try a specialty noodle, catching the Wakayama ferry for some obscure festival. She was in constant action: studying Japanese, researching a trip, grilling us kids about some cultural nuance only grandmothers understood. It was impressive – and intimidating – that this foreigner could know my country better than I did. I guess by now, she probably does. I don't like how this makes me feel. Jealous of the time she's been able to spend here, possessive of what was once mine. A latent sense of ownership bubbles in me like hunger.

'My grandfather did it once, after the war,' I tell her. 'Said he wanted to thank God for keeping him alive in battle, but in doing so he almost died anyway, hiking for so long.' It would be a challenge, not knowing where you're going to sleep, going without a shower after a day in the island humidity. I'd miss my king-sized feather-top mattress and on-demand hot water. Or would I? There's something to the idea of just *going*. Becoming portable. The pilgrimage might be like running one endless hill.

'The university needs their guidebook updated and I volunteered for the job. Trail conditions, accommodations, shops along the way. They're covering the cost of equipment, offerings, *minshuku* room and board – not an opportunity to pass up.'

'You're not worried about safety?'

She raises a ladle brimming with broth to her lips, slurps, and laughs. 'This is Japan.'

'The mosquitoes out there are the size of plums.' I can picture the huge ferns towering over me, the ancient cedars growing straight up, determined to find light.

'And I taste *awful*.' Danny sucks a couple of springy yellow noodles into her mouth.

'How long is it, total?'

'A nudge over a thousand kilometres.'

Six hundred miles. My toes itch at the idea of setting a goal distance so big, even if I wouldn't technically be running the entire thing. My longest race was the sixty-three-mile Pikes Peak Jamboree two years ago. The pilgrimage isn't a racecourse, obviously. Ideally, it's the opposite. Still, I can't help being drawn to the idea of a set route and length, an attainable goal with a start and a finish line.

'You'll be heading back soon, then?' Danny asks.

'My flight back isn't until Friday. I thought I'd get out in nature myself, go running,' I say.

Mouth full, she replies, 'The trail around Bizan is perfect for joggers.' Mount Bizan is the centrepiece of Tokushima City, more hill than mountain. The kanji for Bizan means 'eyebrow', because that's what it looks like. It's got a tramway that brings tourists to the top even though it's only a thirty-minute walk up.

'Thanks for the reminder,' I say. Maybe I'll hit the beach, see how far I can run along the sand without man-made interruption. It's possible the shoreline hasn't changed much from my childhood, hasn't been built up beyond recognition.

Danny slurps her soup loudly. I turn away. I want to ask her why she never visited Kawano, but I don't want to embarrass her. I need to bring it up in a way that's not accusatory, that highlights my curiosity, my detachment from that time – a question full of implied forgiveness. Here's someone who was there: that year, that month, that afternoon at 12:12 p.m., the event my father and his family referred to afterward as 'Chizuru's difficulty'. Danny seems to think that since I've grown up, lost weight, married, I've forgotten.

I draw a pair of disposable wooden chopsticks from a cup and pull them apart. They don't split evenly; the one in my right hand gets the top. My father would call this bad luck.

'I'm late,' Danny says, rising.

'Wait. Can I walk you to where you're going?'

'I'll taxi-*suru*. It's too far.'

This is happening too fast. 'Can we meet tomorrow? Please? We've barely had a chance to catch up.'

She drops a few large coins on the counter. The sound of metal on porcelain nips my eardrums. 'Why don't you come by tomorrow evening? Seven o'clock. Hotel Sakura, near the tramway station. We'll have a send-off dinner for you. And for me.'

4

BACK IN THE COLOURLESS SUITE, I strip. My suit, blouse, bra, and underwear go into the plastic bag provided for dry cleaning. I ball up my pantyhose, which reek of incense, and throw them in the silver wastebasket. The dry, cold air blowing from a vent near the bathroom door glances off my skin in a way that does feel *conditioned*, as if it's been trained to ignore what goes on in this room.

Throughout college and nursing school, I saw a therapist. Sofia was a thin-haired Polish woman with a hacking cough and, if the extra sessions she allowed me to schedule each semester were an indication, a soft spot for me. She always had green grapes on the table, even when they were out of season. I liked her.

There were bad times – when I slept through my organic chemistry final thanks to a recently upped dose of Prozac and

Professor Glick wouldn't let me make it up, or when Freddie Ng told me he wasn't into Asian girls – that triggered the black organ and made me so angry it took a ten-mile run to regain control. After I flushed the Prozac, Sofia urged me to try other meds, but I refused.

'What's *under* the anger, though?' Sofia would prompt in these sessions. The answer was fear, of course. I pictured an angry grape with clenched fists hovering over a wide-eyed, finger-biting grape, berating it. I tried hard during those times to be like everyone else – to kick my feelings in the ass and act normally. But sometimes I could only sit still and breathe while the black organ kettled inside of me.

As I've aged, though, my feelings have mellowed. I have plenty of energy, which running tames. But I also crave relaxation far more than I used to. I don't know how the second-career nurses at the hospital do it. They're almost always women with grown kids and I want to say, *How could you spend twenty years raising children and have strength left over to go to school and begin again?*

And I'm not scared like I used to be. I am nurse, mom, wife. Minor upsets bounce off these walls. My father's letter made me mad, yes. It hurt. And that funeral service: What else had they cut from that curated version of his life? But it isn't fear under the anger now. It's disappointment. We could have salvaged something, he and I.

The bathroom floor is heated. I run the shower, and within seconds, steam fills the glass stall. Next to the stall, a floor-to-ceiling window frames the sun as it slips behind the layered hills west of the city. A few miles away, the edge of an S-shaped tower glints pink. I take the tiny bottles of juniper-scented shampoo, conditioner, and body wash Lily gave me for my birthday and after washing myself in bubbles that smell like home, I sit on the shower's marble floor under the water. There's something rebellious about sitting in a shower. It isn't like a bath, that constancy of the water on skin, the feeling of being softened, like a grain of rice. I bring my knees to my chest and let the hot spray pound my back.

The sun disappears, leaving the hills in darkness against a purple sky. The bathroom and me are now visible in the glass. I rise in the shower, my left knee popping twice, and watch droplets slip down my body.

I like the arch of the tendons behind my knees and the definition in my thighs and calves, the result of running forty miles a week for over a decade. 'You have that *line*,' my co-worker Maya said once, pointing to my leg. My belly's still flat, though it's gotten softer over the last few years despite the crunches I do at the end of my runs. My right breast has been larger than my left since Lily was born. My face is my face, my hair my hair.

It's been nearly seventy-two hours since my Betasso run. I can't remember the last time I went so long without the catharsis of sweat, the rhythm of my heart telling me, *I've got this. I'll take care of you. Just go.* I don't like how I feel when I haven't run; it's like my brain and my body are fused. As if a body is all I am. It makes me feel claustrophobic. By using my body, I can escape it. I can leave the black organ and my head behind.

I wrap myself in the plush hotel robe and pick up my little bag of clothes meant for the dry cleaner, catching its reflection in the mirror: things worn-out. I twirl the plastic, trapping air inside.

The hallway is empty. I jog to the gold trash bin at the end of the corridor, drop the bag of clothes in, turn, and take off. My toes grip the bright carpet. I love sprinting down hotel hallways:

the endless doors, the dense padding underfoot, the mental release of following a pattern: *red diamond, yellow square, 808; red diamond, yellow square, 809.* After five lengths there and back, my body's at a comfortable distance and I feel better.

I've run four marathons total, and two races that qualify as ultras: the 60K trail run in Wyoming and the Jamboree. Training for an ultra is different from training for a regular marathon. Instead of building up to longer distances, ultra training utilises intervals. The same way sprinters build up speed, ultra runners build up stamina. You can't run sixty kilometres non-stop. No one can. So you have to build in periods of walking.

It took me a long time to give in to the fact that I would have to walk briefly in order to run farther. The hardest part was intellectual; an ultra is so physical, the reason I had gotten into running in the first place. This was about getting my mind to a place where it knew when to listen to its body but also when to pat its head like a good child. In the midst of running these long distances I sometimes wondered if this was what my father felt when he played, what my mom felt when she painted. Maybe I wasn't completely uninspired. Running was my art. I, pumping through a hill, was a solo violinist, and I played surrounded by an orchestra of trees. It was a silly thought – I never told anyone about it – but I liked thinking it.

Though it's the middle of the night in Colorado, I call Sal.

'I thought you'd call earlier,' he says. 'How was it?' His sleepy voice is right there and real; I can feel the flannel sheets he put on the bed the night before I left, smell his thick-sweet night-time breath.

I tell him about Leonardo Verutti, the slideshow, the cremation of the priceless violin. 'My hotel room looks like a Eurythmics video.'

'Did you know people there?'

'No one from my family. But my elementary school English teacher was there.'

'Really? The Australian one?'

'Danny's from New Zealand.'

'Same thing, right?' He laughs.

I flop back onto the bed. 'Yeah. And I'm Korean or whatever. Close enough, right?'

He sighs. 'Babe, I'm sorry. It was a joke. I said it without thinking. You seem tense. I wanted to make you laugh.'

'It's important where people come from, Sal. It's who they are.'

He's silent for a moment. 'I know. I'm sorry. Please – tell me about seeing Danny.'

'She translated my father's letter. All it said was that he hadn't left me any money.'

'What? Are you serious? That's fucking shitty.'

'Nothing I shouldn't have seen coming.' It's embarrassing that I wasn't better prepared for this.

'You couldn't have known, Ri.' When I don't respond, he says, 'Family's like that. They know all the vulnerable spots. I moved across the country to get away from mine, and I don't even have much beef with them.' He yawns directly into the phone. 'You there?'

'I'm tired.'

'Ready to hop a plane back home yet?'

'I just got here.'

'But what'll you do till Friday, all on your own?'

'I'll figure something out.' I stretch my right leg, flex my foot so the quad tightens. I lower my leg slowly, then do the left.

'Well, if it matters, I miss you. Plus, we have Silvestri number two to make.'

I don't say anything. The round pink case with my pills inside is on the nightstand. It may as well be dancing and making a *shh* gesture at me.

Sal asks, 'Is it like you remember?'

I don't know how to answer. 'It feels … familiar. But not familiar.' I roll over on the bed, stick my feet in the air. 'I ate an *onigiri* yesterday. A rice ball covered in seaweed with stuff inside. It was so *comforting*. It's the opposite of those soapsuds sandwiches at the Tuscany Terrace thing. Not a work of art, but so good.'

'That reminds me, I ran into Ken and Lisa, the couple we sat with that night, at the climbing gym. They're gonna buy there.'

'The ones with the twins?'

'Yep. Put an offer on one of the cul-de-sac lots this week. They were nice, don't you think? Probably make good neighbours.'

They *were* nice, and their kids were sweet if a little dumb, and I wouldn't mind if they lived on my block. As long as my block was not a street that wormed through a faux-Venetian subdivision. 'They were like animal crackers,' I say, 'but people.'

He laughs. 'C'mon. You know, you never like people when you first meet them.'

He's right, but that doesn't mean I'm not right about people 90 per cent of the time.

He continues, 'Those houses have the extra bedroom downstairs, they said, which is great since they want another kid. Put the boys on the first floor, then have their room upstairs next to the baby's. And when the baby's older, they can switch it up so the kids are all upstairs.'

I can't look at the pills and talk to Sal about this at the same time. 'Go back to sleep before you wake up completely. I'll call you tomorrow.'

After we hang up, I sit on the edge of the bed and stare at a black-and-white chequered mirror across the room. It reflects two other mirrors, which reflect other chequered patterns. I can't tell what angle I'm seeing anything from.

This is how Sal thinks of me: as someone who'd be pleased to live in Tuscany Terrace. As someone who will come right back simply because I'm on my own. He thinks I can't have fun without him. That I don't take risks. But I'm not like him, not as predictable. He's the guy who comes to a complete stop at an empty crossroads in the desert.

Okay. I don't take risks. Coming here is the biggest risk I've taken since flying to the US twenty years ago. But that pre-Rio person – Chizuru Akitani – still exists. Danny remembers her. Danny, who is about to become the most improbable person to ever undertake the *hachijūhakkasho*. To follow a designated path, but to live each day undesignated. Just her and the trees and the earth. The hills will be gruelling.

That's it. I can run here. A path through the forest – or at least partially in nature – where a member of my family has gone before. How long would it take me to run the entire thing? Could I do it alone? I know so little about the pilgrimage, which is supposed to be a part of me as an *awakko* – a child of Tokushima. Now that I've seen it, I can't push the vision from my mind: Danny and me among the thick Shikoku forests, visiting temples, splashing our hands with blessed water, sunlight streaming through the ferns and casting itself upon us. Me running and running and running. The past trampled into the dirt far behind, forgotten.

The next morning, I toss my belongings in and zip up the pack, put it on. It hangs comfortably from my shoulders. I am compact and conveniently packaged, like an *onigiri*.

The elevator goes straight down, no stops. I step out into the high-ceilinged lobby. On my left, a string quartet sits bowed over their instruments, weaving Vivaldi among smartly dressed businesspeople. Suitcases glide along the marble like obedient pets. No one is about to do anything crazy, except me.

The piece is 'Summer'. Silver streaks the lead violinist's long hair. She'd know my father. I could say, 'Ever meet Hiro Akitani, Living National Treasure?' and she might say, 'We competed for first chair at Juilliard.' Or maybe, 'I spent a night with him in Vienna. Where do you think this grey came from?'

The wild end-strings of 'Summer' soar over the lobby. Each member of the quartet sways; the female violinist plays with her eyes closed, wearing a small, private smile, as if she can feel the sun on her face.

Hotel Sakura is two miles away. The walk will take me half an hour. It's cooler than yesterday. I feel more excited than I have in a long time. I walk so quickly, I begin to skip, bounce into a jog. People smile at me.

Hotel Sakura's got a giant pink cherry blossom on its façade above the entrance. It creates a flowery shadow on the sidewalk that I step on to get inside. I'm seven hours early for dinner. I can't wait to see Danny's reaction when she sees me ready to hike. This is the kind of thing she would do.

Danny's in the lobby, sitting cross-legged on an overstuffed couch. Her red shawl is draped over a workout top and track pants. Shoes on the couch! Affection wells in my chest at her disregard for manners.

There's a worn red hiking backpack on the floor beside the couch. She doesn't notice me until I'm right in front of her.

'Were you leaving ... now?' I ask.

Something like fear crosses her face, then disappears. 'You're early.'

'I'm coming with you,' I say.

Danny stares, then laughs so loudly that a few people turn and stare.

'I'm serious. I want to come. I've got some time before my daughter's back from camp. I need to push myself. Do something risky. Like you're always doing.'

She looks at me – really looks, like she's reading a book.

'You don't want me to?'

'It's not that.' Her voice is gentle. 'Dear, it was nice seeing you and having lunch yesterday. But this pilgrimage ... this isn't just a hike. It's spiritual. Personal.'

'Of course. I could use some ... awakening, myself.' I can't bring myself to say the word 'spiritual'.

Danny closes her eyes. 'This is sweet. But it's been a long time. In a way, we hardly know one another.' She must see the hurt on my face. She pats the empty space beside her. I sit. 'I know what you should do,' she says. 'Go up to Aomori. The fertility festival's happening. Big phalluses getting lugged around, young men in diapers. That'll take your mind off things.'

'It'd only be for a couple days. After that, I'll start running the trail. I'll make it as far as I can, then turn around and run back. I'll catch you on my way out. If I leave without doing something big, I'll regret it. It'll be like the Japan part of me will have disappeared completely. And I promised myself it wouldn't.' I cringe at the childish whine in my voice.

She's watching my face carefully, as if she's familiar with every expression. 'Promises,' she says quietly. She twists the bracelets on her left wrist. 'Fine. Let's give it a try. Might as well set out now if you're so keen. I was about to go buy a few supplies on the way.'

'Really?'

'I had a premonition that I wouldn't be alone for long.' She doesn't look happy, but I don't care. She won't regret this. 'Singletons always meet people on the trail. I didn't realise one of them was going to be you, before I even began.'

5

BEFORE WE LEAVE THE HOTEL, Danny drapes a strand of heavy shells around my neck. They look like blackened chestnuts and clink dully when I move. 'For protection,' she says. I like wearing them. The weight feels important.

We take a cab to the edge of town, near the spot where the Yoshino River empties into the ocean. A sign proclaims the convenience store on the corner to be a 7-Eleven, but it is nothing like the place where Sal and I make ice cream runs in Boulder. There's no layer of cigarette butts at the entrance here, no Smurf-coloured puddle on the counter by the Slurpee machine. Instead of a scruffy kid playing with his cell phone, three fresh-faced clerks shout greetings.

We're here to pick up snacks for the trail. There are enough inns and restaurants near the pilgrimage path that we don't need to buy a lot. Danny's friend En owns a 'pilgrim shop', where we'll head next, to buy other supplies. Here, though, I need to get a phone – something basic that will let me call home. And I'll have to buy a water pouch at En's shop, maybe a hat, but other than that, I don't need much.

Someone had fun arranging these aisles. Chocolate bars are stacked next to feminine products; motor oil is shelved above toy cars. A wire bin brimming with plastic bottles blocks my access to the prepaid cell phones. GOLDEN TIME WHISKEY reads the sign over the bin. A cartoon gerbil winks from inside the 'o'. I pick up a bottle.

I pay for the whiskey, a box of granola bars, a Calpis soda, and a disposable cell phone with an international plan the brochure describes as 'heartful'.

'What does "heartful" mean?' I ask the girl behind the counter.

She repeats the question to her co-worker. 'He studies English conversation,' she says.

'It translates as "good feeling", "lots of spirit",' the English student explains.

The employees singsong thanks as I step outside to wait for Danny, who's deep in thought in the baked goods section. The sun is high, the air heavy with river smell. I unscrew the Golden Time's plastic cap and turn on the pink clamshell phone. When Our Living National Treasure was out of town, my mom would pour a little whiskey into her evening tea, throw on an old T-shirt, and paint in her underwear. Her paintings in those days were abstract, slashes of colour amid a generally gloomy background. In New York, where she met Hiro, she used to paint portraits of what she called 'the nothing people'. People who weren't anyone important. She gave away every painting she made, so I only knew these works from photographs. She painted one self-portrait that I know of, though I'd never have known that's what it was without my father to identify it. The image was of a black square on a background of navy blue. It took a second before you noticed there were two different colours on the canvas.

During my father's trips, we'd let the house get messy. Takeout containers piled up. The day before Hiro came back we'd turn up the music and clean. Mom put the whiskey away in a crate with her canvases.

Here's to you, Mom. The liquor hits the back of my throat and I cough. The Calpis makes for a bad chaser, but I don't care. I am being irrational. A group of teenagers come out of the store, see me, and start whispering as if they've just spotted a celebrity. I laugh. One girl looks back, notices me laughing, and throws the peace sign. I throw it back.

A smiling purple gremlin with big eyes appears top left on the phone's display. This, apparently, indicates good reception. I take out Danny's business card and send her a text: *testing!* Through the window, she pulls out her phone and checks it, looking confused for a second before she sees me waving. I walk into the parking lot and dial home, half expecting an error message, a request for more money, or some other obstacle. But the line buzzes, and there's Sal's voice in my ear.

'Danny's doing this cool research trip,' I tell him. I describe the pilgrimage, the way the monk Kobo Daishi, also known as Kūkai ('he of sky and sea'), circled the island ordaining eighty-eight temple sites, how the path he took became sacred, and how every year thousands of people take a month or two off from life to follow in his footsteps. Pride creeps into my voice. 'And … I was thinking I'd do a part of it with her while Lily's at camp. Hike with her a bit, then run some.'

'You, hike with another person? I can't even get you to do the day trip up to Blue Lake.' There's hurt in his voice. After

Lily was born, hiking or running became something I did alone. I'd always preferred it that way – I dislike shifting my pace to suit others, and my breathing gets messed up if I have to make conversation – but then it became a rule. Home had once been a respite from the chaos of work. A baby changed that sanctuary into a cluttered box where, just as at the hospital, I was constantly *needed*. The forest asked nothing of me.

I take another sip of whiskey, Calpis. 'I know. I probably won't stay with her long. It's just ... nice to talk to someone who knew me when I was little.' Sal sighs. 'Let's go to Blue Lake when I get home. We'll skinny-dip and howl at the moon. Lily can stay with Dahlia.'

'Does this mean you're changing your ticket?'

'I'll probably have to. Extend it like three or four days, to give myself time to get back to Osaka. We're pretty remote here.'

'I wish you'd talked to me before – ugh, hold on, Lily wants to talk to you.'

'Hi, Mom!' Lily's voice is a rocket, fast and direct, straight to my heart. 'How was Grandpa's funeral?'

I've done my best to tell Lily nice stories about her grandparents. Sal knows – or thinks he knows – how much I leave out, and he plays along in front of Lily. He'd hate that I've fooled him, too.

'The service was nice. It made me sad. But I'm glad I went.'

'I guess I'm not sad because I never met him ... but I am still sort of sad.'

'You are?'

'Yeah, I don't know. Like, when Scott G's grandma died last year, he cried in class and missed like three days of school.'

Hearing that, the distance I've created between Lily's version of her grandpa and reality strikes me as cruel.

'It's normal to feel sad, Lil. Death is a hard thing. It takes time to deal with, even if you never met the person.'

'Yeah ... So wait, where are you? I hear bells or something.'

I'm outside a 7-Eleven, sweating in the shade, drinking whiskey, about to undertake a pilgrimage. 'I'm in the city I grew up in, called Tokushima. It's a little bigger than Boulder, and just as pretty.' I look out across the water and into the dense forest. Danny and I will soon be among those trees. 'There's a wide river, and people picnic along the bank and hang out under the bridges when it gets too hot. The mountains here are lower, greener. Jungular.'

'That's not a word.'

'It is now. Picture Chautauqua Park, only more like Cancún. Very humid.'

'It was suuuuper muggy in Cancún,' she says. I've never heard her use the word 'muggy' before.

'You remember that? You were only three.'

'I have a good memory.'

'You certainly do. So, guess what? I'm going to have an adventure. Me and a friend are going to hike around some old temples. Actually, she used to be my teacher.'

'Hiking with your *teacher*?'

'You like your teachers.'

'Yeah, but ... Wait ... Oh my god, so yesterday? Miss Dirmiggio made us all stay after the bell because Roni threw paper at Jaylen but wouldn't admit it and so the rest of us had to stay after until some people's moms started knocking on the doors so she had to let us out.'

'Wow.' I close my eyes and lean against the side of the building. The concrete is hot on my back.

'*And*, I got a five on my book report, which is cool, but I should have gotten a six, Sawyer got a six, and her drawings weren't that good.'

This teacher doesn't believe in letter grades or percentages. A six means perfect; I always think of figure skating in the eighties. 'Maybe you should've upped your degree of difficulty.'

'Are you gonna be back by the time I'm home from camp?'

'Absolutely. Sweetie, I have to go. Let me talk to Dad.'

'I think he's mad.'

'I'm not mad,' I hear Sal say as he takes the phone from her. 'Your mom's changed her plans and I have to catch up, so I'm a little frustrated, that's all.' With me he is all practicalities, so I know he's seething. Bagel got a tick but Sal removed it without a problem. He changed the oil filter on the Volvo and put on new wiper blades. Though I know he's avoiding his feelings, I like when Sal talks this way; his voice is like a rope whose strength is hidden until it's pulled taut.

'I miss you,' the whiskey and I say.

'So come home.'

I have nothing to say, other than 'I can't', which feels true but I have no idea how to explain 'I can't' to him, so instead I count the seconds of empty air and wonder how much this is costing.

'Don't waste your phone card, or whatever you're using,' he finally says.

A rusty mint-green car with two surfboards on top idles beside a boxy van. A man emerges from the car in a wetsuit. He waddles over, his hands cupped. '*Ohenro-san?*' he whispers. Am I a pilgrim?

'Just a sec,' I say to Sal. I give the man a questioning look. I'm not wearing the traditional white costume. He points to my beads.

'*Osettai.*' He opens his palms to mine, dropping two plastic-wrapped rice balls and a few coins.

Homemade *onigiri*! I am overwhelmed by love for him, the way his boards are tied to his car with what appears to be clothesline. I toast him my thanks. He gives me a thumbs-up and goes back to his car.

'Sorry about that. Hey, remind Lily about being nice to everyone, will you?' Sometimes my daughter looks familiar to me in an uncomfortable way: not like me at all, but like Harumi Yonezu, or one of the popular girls I knew growing up.

'I told her she needs to come home with at least ten new Facebook friends and she said, "Dad, people don't use Facebook any more. It's for little kids."'

'It's begun. We have a preteen.'

'I swear, kids don't grow a little every day. They save it up. One morning you wake up to a brand-new, much older kid.'

I promise to call when I can, and warn him about the lack of reception we're likely to have in the mountains. He says he's going to map the pilgrimage on Google Earth and get an idea of the terrain. 'So I'll know what to expect when *we* go.'

I am so grateful that he isn't pushing this further, that he's cutting me some slack. 'You're good to me,' I say.

'Because I love you,' he says. There's defeat in his voice. I feel the familiar surge of having gotten away with something.

En's shop stands alongside the Hotel Islander in a seaside strip mall. It is obvious which does better business. Rust stains the hotel's pink concrete face. The sign flickers and the 'I' is burned out.

'Used to be posh,' Danny says sadly.

'Hotel slander,' I say. 'Ha.' The place looks like someone came along after it washed ashore and hung an OPEN sign as a joke. But En's pilgrim shop is doing well, if the umber-stained bamboo exterior and gleaming cross-hatch door are any indication. Traditionally, the door would have been made of wood and paper, but here, a metal and glass replica slides in a greased track. It reminds me of the gate at Tuscany Terrace.

A recording of bamboo flutes plays as we cross the threshold. Judging by the variety of supplies available, the transformation from human to *henro* is as much a matter of appearance – and cash – as spirit.

'*Dani-san!*' A tall, thin man springs out from behind a counter of polished grey stone that reflects the overhead lights. His skin is so wrinkled it's hard to make out his eyes; his head's covered with sunspots. 'And what did I tell you?' He speaks with a thick accent that swallows the vowels. 'I knew you would not be making the trip alone.'

Danny hugs him over the countertop. 'It's true what they say – En-san is always right.'

'Rio …' he repeats after I introduce myself. 'Interesting name.' He peers at my nose. 'Freckles!' he cries, stepping back.

'Irish mother,' I say. After nearly twenty years in the States, I'd forgotten about people like this. They look at you like they're trying to get you in focus and failing. I'm short, with a small nose and fine bones; there's no doubting I'm East Asian. I used to stand at the bathroom mirror and pretend I was someone else, a stranger giving me a quick passing glance. Did I look Japanese enough?

'Ah! So, you are *hafu*,' En replies, nodding. 'There are many foreigners making this pilgrimage nowadays.'

'Rio's not *hafu* – she's double,' Danny says, patting my shoulder. Her hand is reassuring. She can still make me feel safe.

En runs down the list of the things I need to buy: the white cotton coat and loose pants to symbolise the purity of the journey, a sedge hat to keep out rain, a stamp book, a sutra book, name slips, a water pouch, candles, incense, a mosquito net, a portable stove, and a walking stick.

'I'm more of a minimalist,' I say, eyeing the green price tags with all their extra yen-zeros.

'A walking staff is crucial, to show respect for Kūkai.' He holds up a polished length of wood; silver bells tinkle at the top. 'Never let it touch a bridge. Kūkai once had to sleep beneath a bridge for shelter. You must not wake his spirit.'

'I prefer to find one on the trail. One that doesn't make noise.' I've seen Danny's deluxe model and already dread the constant jangling I'll no doubt be hearing from its fat bells.

'Ah, but the bell directs one's attention to his task.' He lays the stick on the counter. 'And of course, *hakui*,' he continues, throwing one of the white jackets around his shoulders with a flourish. This is the traditional *henro* costume, a spotless coat with half sleeves and a rope that ties at the waist.

I gesture at my T-shirt and baggy running shorts. 'I have walking clothes.'

'You wear *hakui* out of respect for the trail. White is the colour of the funeral shroud. In modern times, it is more like a reset button. You're here to reset your life, yes? Throw away the past?'

I slip on the coat and catch my reflection in the mirror. I look like someone else.

'Plus, it identifies you as a pilgrim. Good for collecting *osettai*.' He adds, '*Osettai* is a tradition we Japanese have. You must always accept a gift. Americans love gifts, right? So you understand. *Osettai* is an investment for the giver. Like buying stocks.'

My hand instinctively covers my heart. If the black organ could speak, it would reply, *Is that so? Japan sure is unique! Tell me more about your fascinating traditions.* But I can keep it quiet. I can give this old man, who seems to accept Danny's pure foreignness more than he accepts my mixed blood, a patronising smile instead.

Danny grabs a pointy sedge hat from a rack on the wall and holds it out. 'Whinge all you will, but *this* is a necessity. Saves you from sunburn. And rain.'

I put the hat on. Beneath its wide brim I feel protected, a turtle in her shell.

I buy the *hakui*, along with the hat and a water pouch. At the register, I open my wallet and remove the flattened origami butterfly. After unmaking each wing and finally the body, I smooth the bill on the counter with my palms. But when I remove my hands the bill curls into a deformed version of its previous shape. En grimaces. After a couple of attempts to crease it so it lies flat, he sticks it under a stack of guidebooks on the shelf behind him. 'Money is money,' he grumbles, handing me a few coins' change.

Danny rushes to the counter. 'Was that the bill from Hiro?'

'Yep. Good riddance, *sayōnara, dōmo arigatō.*'

She opens her wallet and removes a ten-thousand-yen note. 'Here, En. Why don't you trade me?' She takes the crimped bill. 'Just in case.' She thinks I might regret my decision to get rid of it. I wish she'd mind her own business.

En tosses two packs of dried squid on the counter and announces grandly, '*Osettai.*'

'Thank you,' Danny says. 'These will come in handy on the trail. Speaking of which, we should get started.'

En spreads a newspaper over the counter. 'First we must be certain it is a good day to begin a journey.' He finds the Shinto calendar, with its shapes and colours that indicate the best and worst days for anything: signing contracts, travel, business matters, technology, weddings. He taps today's date and the symbols printed there. 'Yes – quite auspicious,' he says, satisfied. He glances at the section below: the weather forecast.

'Typical late summer weather. Hot, not much rain. But—' He points to the blue area representing water. 'You must remember to pray at Ryozen-ji for protection from typhoons.'

Typhoon season in Shikoku doesn't start until late fall, but I don't want to argue with En. Arguing would make me seem like a foreigner, and if that's how he sees me, I refuse to do anything to prove him right.

Danny's not paying attention. She's absorbed in the page opposite. Photographs of three smiling children take up the left column.

'Earth to Danny?' I see a word I recognise, three simple syllables. *Ki-re-ru*. Danny quickly folds the paper and says brightly, 'That settles it. We're on our way.' She leans forward and rests her arm on the newspaper.

'What was that?' I whisper.

'Beginning with Ryozen-ji?' En lifts his palm in the direction of the first temple, not far up the road.

'Yes,' Danny replies. 'Temple number one. We're so thrilled. Truly thrilled.'

She's babbling. 'Isn't it supposed to be lucky if you do them in reverse order?' I ask.

En claps as if I've told a wonderful joke. 'Twenty years ago, that was the fashion. So many people were doing the temples in reverse order that the end became the new beginning, and then to get the feel of going backwards, people had to go back to the original way.'

'Brilliant,' Danny says.

'You know the old saying,' En says, looking at me. '"The reverse side also has a reverse side."'

We say goodbye. En bends down below the counter for a moment, and while he's out of sight I snatch the sheet of newspaper. Danny motions for me to put it back. I dart outside; she follows me out and plucks the page from my hand. A corner rips and remains between my thumb and forefinger.

'What does it say?'

'Rubbish and more rubbish.'

There's a photo of a woman with a tiny nose and big rectangular glasses above the column with the *kireru* headline. 'What does it say?' I repeat.

Danny looks at the sheet like it's a shot she must administer. She begins to translate the Japanese:

'"*This current epidemic of child-against-child crime is a national disease traceable back to the 1988 case of Chizuru A., who killed Tomoya Yu, a boy in her class, by stabbing him with a Morimoto letter opener. Several cases occurred afterward, but by now, the phenomenon was thought to be long over. Sadly, her disgusting legacy lives on.*"'

Tomoya's face, the steep angle of his brow, his swingy haircut and his coat, from the same company as the other students' but made nicer-seeming with careful pressing, comes to mind unbidden. His eyes, when they landed on me, like two hawks, prey in sight, settling on a branch. 'Current epidemic?' I whisper.

'There've been a few incidents. In Nagano a few weeks ago, a teenager sliced up a kindergartner with a samurai sword and left the head on a fence post. Another knifed his teacher in the arse when he gave him a failing grade.'

I take a few steps, sit on the asphalt. It burns at first, then settles into a roasting heat on my thighs. A heat that could absorb me, absorb all of these kids' lives and deeds. A fire that could burn itself out and leave standing, among the ashes, the boy I killed. 'Keep going. Read more.'

'There's no sense in it.'

'Please. I have to know.'

Danny looks at me, looks at the paper. '"*These children should be put away for life. Once a killer, always a killer. There is only so much one can do for a child, even one's own. Some creatures are beyond repair.*"'

I kneel and cover my face. I feel hyper-visible, like this recurring dream I have where a plane is falling out of the sky, heading right toward me, and no matter what I do I can't get out of the way. 'She's saying this is happening because of me.' I point at the smaller blocks of text beneath the article. Each has a photograph beside it. 'People's responses? Do they think it's my fault, too?'

Danny stuffs the paper into a trashcan. 'It's rubbish and I refuse to read another word.'

I glance through the window at En, who's dusting his counter with a small hand-held broom. He is focusing much too hard on ignoring us. He would remember Tomoya Yu's death. He would remember the story of the half-breed stabbing the beautiful rich boy in the neck with the fancy letter opener.

'You're *fine*. It's nothing to fret over. That writer has no power over you. She won't hurt you.' Danny's eyes are hard and dark like the prayer beads. The words sound like a promise; in my ears, *She won't* becomes *I won't let her.*

A typhoon was forecast the day Tomoya Yu showed up at school. The storm swung north, eventually making landfall in Kagawa Prefecture, but I never shook the sense that disaster befell us anyway.

It was customary for a parent – usually the mother – of a new student to pay a visit to the school in order to grovel to the principal, vice-principal, teachers, janitors, tea ladies, and so on. This implied the parent's trust in, respect for, and – most important – deference to the school's authority.

Tomoya's mother arrived during lunch, seemingly unaware that she was interrupting student cleaning period as well as the meals of those she meant to impress. Not that it mattered. The senior teachers, even Principal Doro-doro (his eyes were too close together, like the cartoon character), bowed to her. Her choice of arrival time allowed us to view the spectacle as we performed our daily duties.

Smooth black hair hung razor-straight along her powdered jawline. Her lips, coloured a deep red, smiled up toward her pretty eyes and perfectly shaped eyebrows. She wore a navy-blue sweater set and khaki pants. Her pointy, low-heeled leather shoes clicked through the perfectly conical, Fuji-shaped dust mountain I'd spent five minutes sweeping up. Her shoes matched her gold-buckled purse and belt. She wasn't from here, in the best way possible. Unlike my mom, who wasn't from here in the sort of way people whispered about.

Tomoya's father came to school at the end of the day; rumour had it he held a high government post. We watched him stroll down the hall with the principal, who, though he was taller, seemed to be the smaller man, his shoulders hunched as he walked half a step behind his guest.

6

RYOZEN-JI IS ALL WORN STONE and dark, weathered wood. A pond with a fountain sits in the middle of the grounds. Goldfish swarm near an old woman tossing bread. She pinches off a piece and holds it out. A white-and-orange-spotted fish jumps fully out of the water. As it does, she drops the bread. The fish catches it before splashing down.

A lichen-covered stone, taller and a little wider than a person, stands in the early afternoon sunlight. I run a finger over its face and its cut lettering. The stone is smooth and cool. I know some of these kanji. The number one – a flat line – and the collection of strokes next to it that means 'temple'. Farther down, I recognise another, a bisected box. *Sun.* This is where so many have begun their journey – or, twenty years ago, ended it. I wonder what these strangers were looking for, and how many of them found it. Grandfather Nao stood here long before I was born, before Hiro touched a violin. Was he happy? Solemn? Was he strong and fit, with a full head of hair? Maybe one day, Sal and Lily will come here and wonder who I was – am – now.

I'll ask Danny about Kawano soon. Today. Whether she knew I was there, if she thought of coming. I don't need an apology. I just want to know.

'All the temples on the pilgrimage have a legend associated with them except this one,' Danny says, reading from her book. 'Apparently, being called number one is sufficient.'

Two men in *hakui* stand beside the washbasin smoking cigarettes. They nod at us.

Danny's visited a handful of the pilgrimage temples before and knows what to do. She leads me through the steps: Pour water over your hands. Light three candles to cleanse the body, mind, and spirit. Ring the bell. Clap your hands. Recite the temple's sutra. The sutra is spelled in simple hiragana characters, which are familiar to me, but I can't read them fast enough and end up mumbling under Danny's expert chant.

The next temple is a kilometre down the road. At one intersection, there's a wooden sign with a pilgrim painted in red and an arrow pointing us to our destination. According to Danny, the first five temples are located along this paved road.

'When does it actually become like hiking?' I ask.

'You'll be in pain soon enough.'

I hear the temple long before it comes into view. It sounds like the drone of a large insect. As we get closer, I realise it's not a new type of cicada, but the sound of a large group chanting.

An enormous tree rises from the middle of the courtyard, its branches like an umbrella over the grounds. It's as if the stones, bushes, the temple itself, dropped from those limbs.

'This is *chomeisugi*.' Danny reads from her guidebook. 'The Cedar of Long Life, over a thousand years old. Those who touch it will live deep into old age.'

I place my hands against the immense trunk. It's warm, like a body. 'Aren't you going to touch it?' I ask. Danny smiles and disappears around the other side of the tree.

Fat roots push from the earth. I balance along one like it's a beam. At the end is a small statue wearing a red bib. Two crescents arch across the statue's stone face to form eyes. The ears are overlong; the earlobes grow out of the jaw.

The statues are called Jizo. I remember a ceremony when I was small, for Carla, a friend of my parents who'd had an abortion. Jizo, my mom told me, takes care of babies that don't get to be born. Where do they go? I asked. They stay in heaven, she said. Jizo makes sure they get another chance. I wanted to ask more: What did the babies do while they waited? If they had a second chance, did they get the same parents or different ones? And if you were a second-chance baby, would you know?

'Legend says a pregnant woman who had miscarried several times came here to find Kūkai and get his help with her pregnancy,' Danny says. 'She walked the route backwards and met him here, right as her labour pains were beginning, and bore a healthy baby girl.'

'I almost had my daughter in the woods,' I say. Lily came three weeks early. I was out on a trail walking our dog when my water broke. The dog, a Lab-collie-boxer rescue named Snafu, had sniffed my wet knees and licked them while I called Sal. A guy Sal worked with took Snafu when Lily was born. I didn't trust the dog. I didn't trust anything that had been rescued.

'We'd been throwing around names. For a girl, we both liked Sadie, Madeline, and Lily. So I'm standing there, dripping, freaking out. I look up and the first thing I see is a patch of corn lilies. I knew then it would be a girl, and it was. That was almost twelve years ago. September twenty-fourth.'

Danny claps in delight. 'There are always signs if you look for them. My mum saw a fortune-teller when she was pregnant with me. He told her I'd travel far, find raging success, the usual sort of thing. But he also predicted there'd be a problem with my head. Mum was terrified I'd be born with a dented skull, something dreadful. I came out with these birthmarks.'

'She must've been relieved.'

'At first. But when they didn't fade, well – you know what kids are like. In junior high I tried hiding them with make-up but it made things worse. You should've heard the names they conjured up.'

'Such as?'

'Giraffe. Jigsaw. Others a bit more obvious. Arse-face. Cheek-shit.'

'Cheek-shit?' I clear my throat. 'Sorry – I shouldn't laugh.'

She waves this off with a gesture like batting away a spider-web. 'All in the past. Character-forming.'

'That's one way to look at it.'

'I've named them. Part of the process of owning them was giving them an identity. One I controlled. Like naming a pet.'

She points to the long, curved mark running the length of her jaw. 'This is Boomerang, or Boomie. Above Boomie is Starla, for her shape, and this' – she touches the amoeba-like blotch on her neck – 'is Frank.'

'Hello, Frank,' I say, bowing. 'Pleased to make your acquaintance.' Danny steps around the tree. The Jizo look like children waiting quietly to be adopted. When would they get their chance? Had some of them already gotten it?

Chūzetsu – 'abortion' – is one of the names Tomoya Yu called me. I can still hear his thick voice; he always seemed to have a cold, so that when he inhaled before speaking there was a small *click*, like a safety let off a gun. I wonder if Danny remembers this, if she remembers that first time he chose me. She saved me, that day. Saved me and cursed me.

After lunch was cleaning period, the twenty minutes when students swept, emptied trashcans, replaced toilet paper, or hid out in the stairwells. The day was overcast, the sky like concrete. Dull light came through the courtyard windows. The hallway reeked of KLEEN, a pink liquid disinfectant that came in twenty-gallon jugs. I hated the stuff. It stank like rancid roses long after it dried.

Kids worshipped Tomoya's hip clothes and big-city accent; he never touched a rag. Instead, he chose a daily slave to do his assigned chore. Whomever he picked rolled their eyes and pretended to give him a hard time, but you could tell they were pleased.

I was wiping down Miss Danny's blackboard, my regular task. Tomoya walked up and stood inches from my face. It was the first time he had spoken to me.

'Hey, Potato,' he said.

I ignored him and pressed harder on my cloth. The eraser was huge and flat with layers of felt attached to one side. I liked to remove every last chalk smudge from the slate. It made sitting down to our English class, the period after, full of possibility.

'I said, Hey, Fatty Potato!' he yelled, leaning in to my ear. 'Your turn to do my floor.'

I shook my head, not meeting his eyes. Miss Danny was

allergic to the chalk dust and if I didn't clean her board she'd sniffle and sneeze through class.

'It might help you lose weight,' he said, and snickered. He inserted a pencil into the sharpener attached to the wall and began to turn the crank. 'Walking to the candy store doesn't count as exercise, you know.'

When I turned toward him again, I saw the group of kids gathered in the doorway. 'I have to finish this board,' I said. I concentrated on scrubbing a sticky spot near the chalk panel where I had just removed a piece of gum.

From the corner of my eye, I saw his right hand come toward me. It held the freshly sharpened pencil. I flinched and raised my arms. The eraser slipped from my fingers, hitting Tomoya in the chest and sending a cloud of pale yellow dust into his face before landing on his new bright-white sneakers.

Chalk dust floated up from the floor and clung to Tomoya's legs. He staggered backward and blinked. Then he inhaled, and there was that *click*, a quick, deep intake of air meant to propel a string of insults. But instead of speaking, he began to cough.

He bent over, gasping and wheezing. The back of his neck turned pink. More kids gathered in the doorway. When Tomoya stood, tears ran down his cheeks. Someone laughed, and the whole group began to laugh along.

'Shut up!' Tomoya gasped at them. He stepped toward me, put a finger to the side of his nose, and blew. A string of mucus landed on my forearm. It was warm, then cold. I started coughing. The black organ needed air, needed to breathe. My fists clenched so tightly against the swell of it in my chest that there were pink fingernail marks in my palms for half an hour afterward.

'TOMOYA YU!' came a shrill female voice. Then Miss Danny, my hero, was there, her hand on his arm, pulling him toward the door. 'What has come over you, of all the filthy, disgusting ...,' she went on in English, gesturing with her free hand and bellowing. It was hard enough deciphering her New Zealand accent in class, but when she was upset, it was impossible for the other students to understand her.

She switched to Japanese. 'Is there another school shirt in your gym locker?'

Tomoya nodded.

'Good. Take this one off.'

He no longer looked like the kid who bossed everyone around. He shook his head.

Miss Danny repeated herself.

Slowly, Tomoya unbuttoned his shirt and removed it, which left him standing in a too-short undershirt with a yellow stain across the front. His belly was visible.

She tossed his shirt to me and said, 'Wipe off with this. He can explain the mess to his mother.'

I dabbed at the snot as she led Tomoya into the hall.

'She got his shirt,' someone whispered. 'How embarrassing!'

'What did she say, Chizuru?' Harumi Yonezu, a pretty girl on the volleyball team, asked. 'In English, did she say anything *bad*?'

I translated every word, adding more than a few of my own, for my rapt audience. Other than Miss Danny and my mom, no one had ever listened to me so carefully. But as I spoke, acceptance humming in my chest, I was aware of Tomoya's glare from the hallway. He stood facing Miss Danny, whose back was to us, but looked right at me. It was antagonistic to stare back, but I couldn't help it. I dropped his shirt on the floor and kicked it under a desk. Someone picked it up with two fingers and giggled.

'Nasty!' someone else cried, and the shirt got tossed around before winding up hanging partially out of the trash bin.

While this went on, the others also watched Tomoya, but they had less to lose. He wasn't looking at anyone but me. And that's how it began. They all knew Tomoya was a shark; circling back, he'd target the one who provoked him. He'd target the easy prey.

This road is killing me. It's asphalt, grey, boring. Hot. The low-lying scrub provides no shade; the top of my head is baking under my hat. How much of the pilgrimage is like this? I gaze at the distant forested hills, so lush, so silent. Why couldn't we start there? Cars honk and drivers shout '*Ganbatte*' – 'perse-vere!' – as they roll past. We come upon a middle-aged couple in full pilgrim regalia, leaning on a guardrail. He's fiddling with a digital camera while she talks on a cell phone. Neither glances up as we pass.

Danny reads from her book at each stop. This temple was built to aid fishermen and ease childbirth; this one cures diseases of the abdomen and eyes.

The air is wet and smells like motor oil. My hair sticks to my neck. There's a raw patch on the arch of my left foot. Walking with a pack apparently rubs my feet differently than running. Though she doesn't let on, I can tell from the dark rings under Danny's arms and the slowness of her pace that she's looking forward to stopping as much as I am.

It's past five o'clock when we turn off the highway and the landscape clicks into place. The Yoshino River plain is dense but wide-open, and whirring with frog and cicada song. The world here comes in every shade of green, bushes like limes and trees so dark they're blue. Our path is no longer paved smooth; this new dirt trail is soft and uneven. Walking it fills me with a sense of purpose. Something shifts within me.

Danny throws her arms upward. 'There's a healing energy here.'

My journey is not easy, but I am making it. Every step feels like a small victory – over pain in my neck and shoulders, over fatigue, over what we saw in the paper. I am a pilgrim. For the first time since Lily was born, I feel as if there is some movement in my life, not just lateral motion but expansion.

'Still a hummer, I see,' Danny says.

'I wasn't humming.'

'I remember when you were a student, the classroom would be quiet, everyone working on an assignment, and there you'd be, tuning up in the front row. Didn't even know you were doing it.'

So it's true: Lily *does* get the habit from me. She'll hum and hum and hum while playing a game, in bed, reading a book. It's endearing, but only to a point. A few weeks ago while she and Sal were doing a puzzle and I was trying to read, she started up. She never hums a real song, which makes it impossible to tune out.

'Lil. Please stop,' I said.

'Stop what?'

'You're humming.'

'No I'm not.'

'Yes, you are.'

A minute passed. *Humhumhum*. Sal and I stared at her. She looked up, still humming, and burst out laughing. 'I'm totally humming!' she shouted, delighted. 'That's crazy. I can do something and not even know I'm doing it.'

Sal said, 'She gets it from you.'

'Me? I don't hum.'

'Yes, you do,' Sal and Lily said together. 'You do it when you're happy,' Lily said. 'We like it.'

I tell Danny this story and she says, 'I'm glad you're feeling happy.'

The washbasin at the fifth temple, Jizō-ji, is in need of repair. A few shingles cling to the roof and one of the wooden supports has rotted through. Tied to one of the beams, a tin cup holds narrow strips of coloured paper – *osame-fuda*: the name slips pilgrims customarily carry on the trail.

It's nice knowing who's been here before, leaving a trace for a stranger to come. I regret not buying slips of my own. 'What are these different colours?'

Danny flips through her guidebook. 'White means you've walked the pilgrimage four or fewer times. Green, between five and seven; eight to twenty-four is red; silver, up to forty-nine.'

I hold up a thick slip of gold brocade. 'Does that say eighty-three years old? Can you read these kanji for the name?'

'Takaro Sakabuchi. Eighty-three! I'll be – old as boots and gone 'round over sixty times.'

I wonder what Takaro's feet look like. Maybe he hikes barefoot, like the Ute tribesmen who always win the cross-country races outside Boulder. I return Takaro's slip and pull out a white one. The pilgrim's information is written not in Japanese script, but in roman letters: SHINOBU OEDA. AGE 20.

'Shinobu – a woman.'

'So young, and trekking on her own,' Danny says. 'I love to see kids following tradition. A lot of my students get so obsessed with Western culture they forget their own.'

'And here we are – two *gaijin* on a Japanese trail, following Japanese tradition.'

She fixes her gaze on me. 'You really feel like a *gaijin*?'

'My passport says I'm one. I look like one.'

'But what about in here?' She taps her chest.

'I feel like an outsider pretty much everywhere,' I say.

I stand in the doorway while Danny clears space in the eight-mat room she's booked at a *minshuku*. I am brand-new after taking a bath.

Danny's lavender yoga mat covers a third of the space; baggies of herbs and tie-dyed cloth occupy the rest. The books stacked beside her pilgrimage guidebook are familiar from St Mary's waiting rooms: *Healing from Within. Fatigued and Fabulous. Soulwork It Out: Loving Your Pain.* This last is one of the most popular books for our patients with chronic pain.

I nudge a pile of clothes out of the way and sit on the tatami, the mat's smell of rush grass strong in my nostrils. 'You're sick.'

Danny continues arranging. I'm about to repeat myself when she speaks, her tone as even as if reciting an address. 'I get a bit tired. It's been on and off since the melanoma.' She makes melanoma sound no more serious than hiccups.

'God, Danny. Melanoma? When?'

'Ages ago.' She pushes back her curls, revealing the hairline along her neck and a scar like a starfish. 'Surgeon botched it.'

I lean in for a closer look. The skin is dark and puckered. Danny flinches. 'Sorry.' I pull back. 'How long ago?'

'This one? Six years next month. And this one' – she pulls up her T-shirt sleeve, revealing a nicer-looking scar, though long – 'ten years ago.' She flourishes her fingers. 'Lentigo maligna.'

'You did chemo both times?'

'Nine months the first time. Then seven. I told the doctor, if it ever comes back, that's it for me. I'm not going through that again.'

'And you've been easily fatigued ever since.'

'The occasional spell. But these things happen as you get older. You're too young for it yet.' She smooths a square of purple silk and clears her throat, but doesn't say anything more.

'This isn't related to menopause. You're what, fifty? When was your last check-up?'

She says, more forcefully than necessary, 'Fifty-five. And I know how to take care of myself. I have a system.'

I make her sit still while I check the map of birthmarks and moles on her neck and shoulders for irregularities. Danny stiffens at my touch. I'm used to poking, touching, palpating bodies, but for her it's obviously a rare and intimate feeling. I try to appear casual. 'I've done a million mole checks in my day. Seen everything,' I tell her. She relaxes her shoulders, but only slightly.

Most patients have the same 'never again' attitude toward chemotherapy. But every time they relapse – and with melanomas it happens often enough – they go back for another bout. Suffering has a way of slipping from memory.

'I know what you're thinking. But I don't want to be one of those people with three appointments a week, going from one place to another only to hear them say they can't help me.'

I pull up her shirt, check her lower back. A few odd spots, but nothing alarming.

'Have you always bruised easily?' I ask, examining a line of light blue marks on her hip.

'Suppose so. Probably deficient in zinc or some such.'

I let her shirt down and ask brightly, 'So, you set up house in every room you stay in?'

'It's a little ritual. Gets me comfortable.' She tugs the drawstring of a silk purse, dumping its contents onto her cloth: stones, shells, and a piece of melted red plastic. It's like Lily's bookshelf collection. A little sand sprays across the wood, lodging between the boards. Those tiny grains trapped in a groove make my skin crawl. I want to gather them and return them to the beach, to do my part against entropy. I look at the ceiling. It looks like cardboard; water stains darken one corner.

'Where do you get this stuff?' I ask.

'Oh, anywhere. You're walking on a road covered with stones and suddenly – pop! – one catches your eye, like it's been waiting for you to come along. Any time I've done something special that I want to remember, I pick one up. Later, I can pull them out and remember better times.'

'Interesting.' I hear Lily in my voice. She only calls things 'interesting' when they are clearly otherwise.

Danny sucks in a loud, long breath. Something riffles in one of her nostrils.

'Need me to grab your tissues?'

'Nah. Whatever it is, it's way up there.'

I press my fingertip into a crevice in the wooden floor, bring up a few specks of sand. I have to get out before she breathes like that again. 'I'm going to get some air,' I say, standing.

'Suit yourself.'

The street is deserted. A single streetlamp casts a lemony circle onto the road. Moths flurry around the lamp's bulb. Beyond the light, pieces of concrete separate the pavement from the rocky riverside. I scoot over this makeshift wall, pick my way past a thorny bush – looks like barberry – and stand on the spongy bank of the Yoshino River. It's not the most beautiful body of water, half-dry in some places and edged with scrub or litter in others. During the week-long summer holiday of Obon, people float paper lanterns down it to honour the dead. Sometimes the surface disappears altogether and the river becomes a glowing road. Downstream, low-level government workers stay up all night, using long wooden poles to fish out the lanterns so they won't pollute the sea.

Once, I saw one of the river lanterns catch fire. The paper was so thin, the entire thing seemed to disappear in a single flash. Grandfather Nao called it a bad omen. Secretly, though, I found the boldness pleasing among so much uniformity.

A tiny wave splashes up, soaking the tops of my shoes. The cold wet seeps through the material. I take off my shoes and socks and stand barefoot in the river, letting the water numb my sore feet. Overhead, stars prick the night sky. The moon hasn't risen yet; looking at the horizon is like gazing at a blank movie screen, waiting for the show to begin.

After the eraser incident and Miss Danny's humiliation of Tomoya, I enjoyed a few days of quiet celebrity at school; no one offered friendship, but there were smiles of acknowledgement on faces previously closed to me.

The drawings started a week later. Tomoya called the comic 'The Adventures of Fatty Potato' and circulated it among the sixth-grade homerooms. No one came out and told me, but eventually one of them grew brazen enough to leave a copy on my desk.

Fatty Potato learns to eat through her asshole, the caption said. *This way, she can eat twice as much. The shit comes out her ears.*

In the days that followed, I skipped my usual trip to Ame-Ame, the sweetshop. At home I stayed in the bathroom, which had a door that locked, and made my own drawings as revenge: graphic depictions of the horrible things I wanted to do to Tomoya Yu. I refused to eat dinner or respond to my mom. Being a tattletale was worse than being a fat *hafu*.

But my mom found my drawings. She insisted on speaking to my teachers. This level of bullying was not right, she said. These kids ought to be suspended. I heard her arguing with my father. He was dismissive. Discipline didn't work like that in Japan.

My mom made rash decisions. As soon as Hiro left for Tokyo the next day, she dragged me to see the vice-principal, Miura-san. We sat down across from him in his office, and in her stumbling Japanese, my mom explained that I was being teased. Miura-san listened, expressionless.

My face burned. The shame of being bullied was nothing compared with this. My mom deserved a pretty daughter, one who danced lightly with hair that flowed like water, a thin-limbed girl everyone could celebrate.

When she was done, Miura-san looked past her and said, 'There is nothing we can do about children teasing one another. It is a natural thing every child must endure.'

The colour rose in my mom's cheeks. Miura-san avoided her eyes. I could see that her beauty embarrassed him.

'That's ridiculous. This is worse than teasing. She comes home crying. She draws violent pictures.' To my horror, she produced my latest work, an image of a well-dressed boy's head exploding. It had taken a long time to sketch every bit of brain material.

Miura-san looked impassively at the drawing. There was an international school in town, he said. Perhaps I would fit in better there.

'She fits in fine here!' my mom yelled in English. Fear flickered across Miura-san's face and was quickly replaced by annoyance.

'We will investigate the matter,' he said, rising and looking at his watch. 'In the meantime, I'm sure your daughter will do her part to solve the problem.' He gave her figure a nod. 'As you have obviously done for yourself, Mrs Akitani.'

He addressed me. 'There are a number of sports clubs available after school. Perhaps you'd like to try volleyball? Or swimming – well, maybe not swimming, yet.' He looked pointedly at my gut. 'Perhaps badminton.'

Later, after the humiliation had worn off, I would have given anything for the presence of mind to spit in his face. Or blow my nose so it landed on his suit. As it happened, I stood there, processing his words. I heard the meaning under them: *This is your fault.*

My mom shot out of her chair. In English, she yelled, 'Don't you give her health advice. You reek of cigarettes, disgusting old man. And when was the last time *you* put on a pair of running shoes? Or god forbid, a bathing suit?'

This time he held her eye. His response came in Japanese. 'I have no problem fitting in, Mrs Akitani. My suggestions are meant to help Chizuru. As they say, when you point one finger, you leave four others pointing back at yourself. Now, if you please, I have a meeting to attend.'

At home, my mom went to bed with a headache. I ate dinner alone: a can of sweet red bean paste and a box of digestive biscuits.

My feet are used to the water, and the comfort of that initial chill is gone. Now, the sand and pebbles along the riverbank bite at the tender pads of my toes. It's completely dark. Time to get back. The moon pushes up behind the trees, an eerie red hump. Persimmon moon, my father would have said. Quick to ripen, quick to rot. Sal would say, *It's just the light getting distorted through the pollution and atmosphere.*

Holding my shoes, I step out of the water and wipe my feet on a clump of weeds.

The sound of voices comes from somewhere near the road. A flashlight beam zigzags and lands on me.

'*Konbanwa!*' a young man calls out. A long blade flickers in his hand. He lowers his voice. 'It's a girl, alone.' From the dark comes more laughter; at least two others are up there. I hold a palm toward the light: four teenage boys, two smaller than the one standing, and a pile of half-crushed beer cans. A metal canister of glue or paint sits on a rock between them. Local kids getting high are nothing to worry about. What I don't like is that knife.

The one who called out takes a couple of steps toward me, tripping over a bush but catching his balance. He's got the pocket-knife in one hand; in the other, a hefty metal flashlight. I think of Tomoya sharpening his pencil. *If I stabbed you, would you pop?*

'Hey, are you a foreigner?' the kid asks in Japanese. 'Come play with us.' Then, 'Yuu speak-a Engurish? Sexy lady! Harro, do you come here oaf-ten?' His eyes are glazed and puffy.

My chest pounds. To my right is a tangle of bushes too thick to push through; behind me, the water. Unless I make a dash for it, there is no way around him.

Loud and confident is how I need to be. 'There's a cop up the street,' I shout in Japanese, putting on the local accent En spoke with yesterday. 'You guys should watch out.'

The boy's eyes flicker up to the road. His friends hear me and scramble to cover the glue.

'Let's be friends,' he says, gesturing with the blade. He begins to laugh hysterically.

I sprint toward the road. The kid with the flashlight falls into a thorny bush. Pebbles and sharper stones dig into the balls of my feet. 'RAAR!' I growl at the other three, baring my teeth and spinning my shoes by their laces. I scoot over the wall. Thirty metres across the road, at the entranceway of the inn, I bend over to catch my breath. Hoots of laughter ring from the beach.

'We want to be friend! Pretty lady, Japanese-speaking foreigner! Are you a demon? RAAR!'

Danny's mouth hangs open; her upper lip twitches when I tell her what happened. Her horror is so touching that I begin to laugh.

'No, really! That's awful. Shall we call the police?'

'The kids are harmless. I think seeing those *kireru* stories in the paper has me on edge.' After seeing that newspaper, the police are the last people I want to call. I sit shivering in the warm room until Danny orders us a pot of tea. I enjoy her fawning. It's like I'm her favoured student again.

'You'll be pleased to hear that I steamed my face in the bath and got my nose all cleared out.'

'Good to know,' I say, pouring the tea. It's a caramel-coloured *hōjicha*, meant to put us to sleep. The room fills with the sharp scent of roasted leaves.

Danny takes a sip and grimaces. 'Harsh. But good.' She continues, 'We forgot to pray for protection from the seven calamities at the first temple.'

'Which calamity do glue-sniffing teenagers fall under?'

'Demons, dear. Demons.'

We both laugh. 'Remember that name card we saw earlier?' I ask. 'A single female *henro* – it can't be easy.' The bitter tea is starting to soothe my stomach and calm me. In Colorado I drink coffee, mostly because everyone else does. Maybe I should switch.

'Yes, let's send positive thoughts to that young woman,' Danny says. 'Shinobu.'

I raise my teacup. 'To Shinobu's safety, and our own,' I say.

'*Prajna Paramita Hrdaya*,' Danny sings, raising her cup. 'The heart sutra.'

'*Jai guru deva*. The Beatles.'

Danny pushes a stack of books against the wall. She unfolds a leg and presses her palms and belly to the mat. One arm goes out in front of her, the other straight behind.

'Teach me that stretch?' She shows me how to position my leg so that the IT band is completely at rest. I dig my thumb into the muscle and let out an involuntary groan; I could sit like this all night. 'You do yoga?'

'Absolutely,' she says, bowing head to knee so her thigh muffles the words. 'But let's change the subject.'

'Yoga's too personal?'

'It's – well, there are things I want to say. And it's difficult to get that perfect moment, isn't it, so you just have to jump in.'

I think immediately of Kawano. 'I feel the same.' I switch legs, dive into the pain of the stretch.

'I wasn't pleased that you asked to join me. But at those temples today … I saw that I need to let go of how I thought things would be.'

My quad tightens, gives a little pulse. I breathe into my gut and keep my eyes on my knee. There it is: she didn't want me to come. I've missed her signals, chosen only to focus on what I wanted to see and hear. Chosen to perceive her non-stop chatter as an effort to connect rather than a way to fill the uncomfortable silence. She invited me for a dinner she planned to skip.

I look down at the tatami, dragging a fingernail perpendicular to the weave of the mat. The sound is like a zipper. And that's how I feel – unzipped.

I prop my head on my elbows so I can see her. Her face is still flush with her thigh, nose to kneecap. 'Why didn't you visit me at Kawano?'

She shudders.

'Seven and a half years,' I say. My dumb voice breaks on the word 'years'.

She's silent for a long time. Finally, she releases the stretch, sits up, and says, 'I tried, but they wouldn't let me.'

'What do you mean?'

She won't meet my eyes. 'It was just – the rules at the time.'

She's lying. Oh god. The realisation is suffocating: she didn't come because she didn't want to. I'm too humiliated to say anything more. The shame of those days at Kawano comes rushing back. Of course she didn't want to come. Who would?

'I understand,' I say.

Danny smiles weakly. 'It was all such a long time ago, wasn't it? And look at us now. Look at you.' And she does look at me, deeply, with something like love. Love and sadness, like she's staring at an image of someone she's lost.

It was a long time ago. She's gently reminding me of that. I shouldn't have gotten so annoyed with her sniffling earlier. She's human just like me, and has handled things so far with a lot more grace than I have.

'Yes,' I say. 'Look at us now.'

7

IN THE MORNING, we get up with the sun and have breakfast at the inn – fish (head still on) and rice. Then Danny and I pick our way along a rutted gravel road beset on both sides by grasshoppers. They land in our hair, on our arms, our bodies. Somewhere nearby, the stream that feeds the river makes a trickling sound. Insects click past our ears.

After the awkward conversation with Danny last night, I'm not in the mood to talk, or do anything other than walk. Luckily, Danny seems to be in a similar frame of mind. I'll stick with her another night at least, before I start running. I want to make sure she's not going to collapse in the middle of nowhere. You can't stay hydrated on stubbornness.

We spend less than ten minutes at each of the three temples – just long enough to go through the ritual of water, candle, bell, sutra, stamp. Danny's anxious to reach the tenth stop, Kirihata-ji, the Temple of Cut Cloth. It's popular with women, and she wants to 'soak up the energy' and talk to female pilgrims to get their perspective on the journey.

'The books on the subject are all written by men,' she says. The bells on her walking stick jangle with every step. 'Female points of view aren't represented at all. There was a time when temples didn't allow women on the grounds, period.'

My mom hated the misogyny she witnessed in Japan. She'd ranted to Hiro, who only shrugged, about Miura-san ogling her in his office. It didn't seem like a big deal to me at the time – I'd have loved to be thought pretty like my mom was. I noticed the stereotypes when I got older, for a different reason: people were always surprised when they learnt that Tomoya's killer was female. As if a girl couldn't feel rage, couldn't be brutal. Girls were supposed to be tiny pink blooms of *yamato nadeshiko*; killing was only tolerated as a part of a man's nature.

The path curves gradually uphill and brings us out of the river plain to a drier, exposed landscape. The road follows an embankment brown with dead grass that stands unmoving in the hot air. Snack wrappers and ripped plastic bags dot the weeds. Ivy grows around an abandoned white sedan, its hood dented under the weight of a metal sake barrel.

I want to throw Danny's walking stick into the weeds. Maybe if I concentrate, I can turn the maddening tinkle into something musical. Even the mindless driving beats of 94.9 the Pulse, Lily's favourite radio station, would be welcome. Lily will be at camp by now, having her own adventure, caught up in the excitement of new friends and boys.

Boys. It's already started. Last month, Lily asked me what a cunt was. A month before that, I found a note in her underwear drawer that read, *I want fulk David Z.* When I showed her, she looked at her lap, teary, and said it was part of a game. Did she know what that word meant? 'Something dirty boys do to girls?' I was appalled. You see stories these days about nine-year-olds in Denver giving blow jobs in school bathrooms. Sal was less concerned. 'Imaginary play is normal, remember? And how great is it that she thinks "fuck" has a silent "l"?'

It's called the Temple of Cut Cloth, Danny says, because it's here Kūkai met a girl who brought him food and water for seven days while he meditated; in her free time she wove beautiful cloth. She gave him two lengths of this cloth, one for leggings and one for a new robe. She told him she was the illegitimate child of a man cast out of Kyoto; her mother had fled to Shikoku when she was born and left her near this temple for protection. Kūkai carved a statue for her, shaved her head, and ordained her as a nun, after which she attained instant enlightenment.

'That's why it's popular with women?' I ask.

'Quite a crock, don't you think? A girl sitting around all day sewing, never complaining, does whatever a man asks of her!'

When the path becomes too overgrown to follow, Danny leads us toward an embankment where we're to pick up a trail into the forest. Vine-strewn trees grow from a slope so steep it's like a wall. But after gazing at the jungle for a few seconds, Danny raises her stick and points.

The trail is a narrow mud rut the width of a single shoe. We step like tightrope walkers. Cicadas pulse around us. Up ahead, steam rises from a frond in direct sunlight.

'No more than a minute or two of this,' Danny manages between heavy breaths. I focus on my body, listening for the rhythm that will kick-start the endorphins of a runner's high. But at home, I don't run with blistered feet and a pack pulling me backward.

'One last bit!' Danny gasps. 'Just three hundred and thirty steps.'

I look up, and up: a stairway of stone climbs the last, steepest part of the slope. Wooden crutches lay scattered alongside the steps.

Danny stops, puts her hands on her knees. 'Walking the pilgrimage is said to improve one's luck in health – ever heard it called "going to the Shikoku Hospital"? This temple's supposed to do miracle cures on diseases of the legs and eyes.'

'Twenty kilometres a day wouldn't make your health any worse. Do blisters count as disease?'

The stone underfoot is rounded and shining; the pocks and cracks have been buffed by the weight of visitors. I count each tap of my rubber soles. As difficult as this is physically, it's a relief to be in nature. I wipe sweat from my forehead and keep an eye on Danny. She's got endurance. She stops halfway up for a minute's rest, and again a minute later, but her determination never falters; if she wants to turn back, she gives no indication.

My mom's visit to Vice-Principal Miura was common knowledge by the time school let out on Friday, despite her coming in midday, during class. Kids whispered she'd tried to seduce Miura-san to get me protection, but he had turned her down. *Gaijin* women smelled bad.

On Monday, I suffered through homeroom, which I shared with Tomoya. His dagger glare had sharpened over the weekend. There was a fresh sheen of meanness to him, like a new skin. When Sumamori-sensei called my name from the roll, Tomoya squeaked, '*Hai! Minikui desu!*' – Yes, I'm ugly. The blood rushed to my face and I stared at the surface of my desk, which had been carved up by students before me. *Fuck you! Akari is sexy. Junko + Taro.* The teacher ignored Tomoya and repeated my name; I opened my mouth to respond but couldn't produce more than a whisper. Sumamori-sensei was hard of hearing. He called me, angrily this time, and before I knew what was happening all the rage boiling in the black organ made its way up my throat to my vocal cords and I screamed, 'I'm HERE!' The class giggled, Sumamori looked annoyed, and Tomoya smirked. When the bell sounded, I didn't try to outrun him. Instead, I walked the way I'd learnt: head down, shoulders hunched, eyes to the floor.

He fell into step behind me. 'Want me to pull down my pants? I'll show it to you.' He poked a finger into the back of my skirt and pushed at the thin wool. 'I know you wanna see. I know you're dirty.'

He slowed down as we turned the corner. Miss Danny stood in her doorway; by that time Tomoya was on the other side of the hall, as if nothing had happened. As I approached Miss Danny, the black organ shrank. She turned her smile toward me and I approached her gratefully.

But Miss Danny was looking beyond me, at Ikemi Takara, the pigtailed choirgirl who'd sung the school song during morning assembly.

'Brilliant job, Ikemi,' Danny said, beaming. I kept my eyes on her face; with each step, pain beat in my heart, until the point of panic – she must see me now, she must – when she dropped her eyes to me.

'Shirt tucked, Chizuru.'

Numb, I shoved the tips of my shirt into my waistband and kept walking. Miss Danny usually greeted me with a soft pat on the back, a word of praise. She never gave me a hard time about uniform code. The button-up sailor top only came in two sizes and was not long enough to stay tucked into my special-ordered 'big size' skirt. She knew that. I felt the black organ developing weak spots, like a balloon worn thin from too much inflation. These places glowed red. I moved through the halls with my hand on my chest.

Miss Danny's coolness continued throughout class. No slang or jokes directed at me, no smiles. I scoured my memory of the week before and recalled nothing – no forgotten promises, no screw-ups, nothing out of the ordinary – that would have driven me out of her favour. I raised my hand, volunteered for board activities. She ignored me. Toward the end of class, she stumped the class with the conjugation of 'dive' and as my arm shot off my desk, she said tiredly, 'Chizuru, since you were raised speaking English, it's not fair of me to always call on you. Besides, no one likes a show-off.' A couple of kids snickered. I tried to smile, but found my facial muscles uncontrollable. I rocked in my chair.

She must have heard about my mom's visit. Was that it? Was it humiliating to be associated with me? Or maybe I'd stopped being useful as a language helper. Her Japanese was improving and she no longer needed a translator; when she spoke to kids, she used Japanese so she could practise. I'd been a crutch while she got used to Motomachi Elementary and Japan.

A week later, my mom was dead. Miss Danny invited me into her empty classroom my first day back at school, closed the door, and hugged me. She held me for a long time without saying a thing. I wanted to keep my head pressed against her belly forever. I could hear her heart pounding and her blood swishing. Her stomach growled. Then the bell rang and she released me and ordered me to clean her chalkboard. Other kids came in to sweep the floor and wipe down desks. Miss Danny never touched me or acknowledged my mom's death again.

Danny's back sways as she stomps up the last few stairs. I should stop thinking back to those days. The memories make the determination in her shoulders sinister, her kind words double-edged. The point of this pilgrimage is to be in the present. Still, the more I think about it, the more I'm sure that there are definitely lines in the letter that Danny didn't translate completely, or at all. She's keeping something from me. I've been over it in my head. Even if she summarised some of it, there's got to be more.

At the top of the staircase sits a boy, head buried in sunburned arms, his thick legs half-covered by green cargo shorts. 'I feel like crying, too, after that climb,' I say, but then I notice the energetic tapping of his sneakers on the stone and the headphone cord snaking over his tie-dyed T-shirt sleeve.

He glances up. His chubby face is burned as well; his nose is red and peeling. An image of John Lennon's face covers his chest, along with the words YOU MAY SAY I'M A DREAMER BUT I'M NOT THE ONLY ONE. 'Please excuse me,' he says in English, yanking on his earbuds. His voice is breathy and high and determined. 'I am so happy to see you on the pilgrims' trail'.

He asks where we're from, looking hopefully at Danny, whose answer visibly disappoints him. 'And you?' he asks me in Japanese, faltering as he gets a closer look at my face.

'I'm American,' I answer in English. 'But I grew up in Japan.'

'That is very cool!' he says. 'May I speak to you in English?'

'You already are.'

He laughs. 'Oh! Yes! I want to ask you if I may continue.'

'Of course.'

'Your English is quite good,' Danny says.

'That is your opinion, truly? How grrreat!'

'You sound like a commercial for breakfast cereal,' I say.

'The Frosted Flakes?' he says. 'I love those. I watch the commercial online.'

It feels good to laugh. 'You must be studying English very hard,' I kid.

'From when I was young, yes. It is necessary for my dreams.'

Before I can ask what those might be, a bus roars up a narrow side road, scattering a flock of pigeons.

The boy's expression darkens. He takes one step back, and another. 'Another cheating group.' He runs toward the trees behind the temple.

The bus opens its doors and within seconds, the grounds swarm with *henro* in full regalia. Most of them are older, past retirement age. Many of the women carry umbrellas. Bells tinkle on their walking sticks. Ant-like in their efficiency, the pilgrims form a line at the washbasin, and from there each visits the *hondo*, prays, claps, takes a few pictures, and scurries back to the bus. I want to yell: *You missed the climb up the stairs.* Men puff on cigarettes as they go about their sacred tasks. Someone mentions a typhoon. Danny approaches a tiny lady with white hair who inches back every time Danny speaks; finally, the woman bows and hurries away. Danny talks briefly to two more women.

As quickly as they arrived, they pack into their bus and disappear. A tendril of smoke rises from a cigarette butt on the ground near the bus stop.

Our friend emerges from behind the temple looking pained. He joins us at the washbasin. His wavy bangs, a puff in the humidity, fall to one side. 'They act like this is a drive-thru for food,' he says bitterly, pulling out a flat, palm-sized phone hardly thicker than a playing card. 'I *hate*.'

'Funny, isn't it,' Danny says. 'Retirees, in such a rush. That last woman said she'd joined the tour because her husband didn't want to do it alone. Another because she's praying for grandchildren. The first lady was interesting, though. Said all she'd done in life was raise kids and keep house. She wants to do something extraordinary before she dies.'

'Is that a phone?' I ask the boy.

He pinches the device between two fingers and holds it toward the sky. Perspiration dots his forehead. 'Always roaming or searching,' he says. 'The phone is much like me.' He drops it back into one of the many pockets lining his pants. 'It's not the way of the road,' he continues. '*We* are the true pilgrim. On foot, like the hobo. Like Kerouac. You know Kerouac? *On the Road*?'

'I haven't read it, but—'

'Have not read? Oh my god!'

'It is a bit like cheating,' Danny interrupts. 'But they seemed well-intentioned. And if you're too old or sick to walk, what choice have you got?'

The boy pulls a dog-eared paperback from another pocket and opens it to the middle. The pages are a collage of neon: yellow, orange, pink, green; more sentences have been highlighted than not.

His lips move as he traces two fingers over a line of text. Dirt is packed under his boxy fingernails. His cuticles are ragged and pink.

'Kerouac is wise. See, everyone wants to be' – he points to a spot on the page – '*a mad one*. But when shove comes to push no one wants to be *mad*.'

Danny approaches the washbasin first, lifting the metal cup

from its hook and dipping it into the bowl of water cut into the stone surface. From the structure's roof, three white cloths dangle like bats.

'Are you walking because of this book?' I ask.

He turns solemn. 'I am a wandering student. I failed five times to pass the examination for becoming a lawyer. You call it "the bar". So now I am like samurai, roaming and searching.'

'A Jack Kerouac samurai?'

'Yes, like this.'

Danny offers him the washbasin's long-handled cup and he passes it to me. 'Ladies are first.'

The brittle bamboo handle is split down one side. I dip the thin cup into the basin, pour cool water over my left hand, then my right.

'The Japanese bar!' Danny exclaims. 'That's one of the most difficult exams in the world.'

The boy blows a chunk of hair off his nose. 'That is true. No one passes on first attempt. Four is typical. But my father is tied for a record. He passes after two tries. But some never pass … they give ten years to studying. And then? They are thirty years old with no career. And no wife.'

'But you'll try it again?' I hand him the cup.

He doesn't respond until he's washed both hands and swished and spat a mouthful of water into the dirt. 'Recently, things changed. In Japan, there is now new test and old test. Old test is far more difficult. But anyone can try. But to take new, more easier test, we must first attend law school for three years! This is a swindle to make more lawyers in Japan, and give money to universities. I think if I can't pass old exam like my father, I don't deserve being a lawyer.'

'When's the test?' I ask.

'I passed first portion in May, many complex questions about our six codes of law. So eight days from now, I will take last portion, essay and interview.' He wipes his mouth on his sleeve. 'It will be my final attempt. That is why I walk like this. I did not start at Ryozen-ji, temple one, like you. I began near my grandmother's home in Kōchi Prefecture. There is a temple very good for scholars. So I have met many pilgrim. All have the different story. One man tells me his wife died so he wants to walk until he dies, too. Another guy, he did by bicycle the first time. His friends say it is too easy way, and he got angry and did again, by walking. He became addicted to collecting temple … *go shuin*?'

'Stamps,' Danny says.

'Addicted to collecting stamps, so he has gone in the circuit eleven times!'

'Pilgrimage addiction?' I laugh.

'It is big problem. The way of life on pilgrimage is simple. You must eat, walk, sleep, pray, only. In our normal life this is not the case. Some people become addicted, the same like they escape to pachinko machine.'

'What happens if you don't pass the exam?' I say.

'There is a second option. I have made a promise with a woman in America. Miss Linda.' He smiles as the name crosses his lips. 'I could find a job there if my English improves. It is dangerous in the US,' he says, glancing at me grimly, 'but I don't care. It is the centre of the world.'

'Where does this woman live?' I ask.

'Bedford, in Ohio state.'

I imagine tree-lined suburbia, a Costco, something as edgy as a skate park. Tuscany Terrace coming soon.

'Cleve-land is near. The location of Rock and Roll Hall of Fame. Membership costs only fifty dollars per year. There is a problem of American crime there, but my girlfriend tells me not to worry.'

'Japan's not that safe, either, you know,' I say, and recount the night of the glue sniffers.

'You should *not* walk alone at night,' he says. 'Even in Japan, it is not safe for woman.' He asks if Danny and I met on the trail.

'Believe it or not, Danny and I have known each other since 1988. She was my teacher.'

'How amazing! I see my schoolteachers sometimes, shopping or walking around, but I am shy and never say hello.' He asks when I left Japan, why I came back – was it for the pilgrimage? I answer the first with the standard 'I moved to the States for college', but I'm not used to the second question.

'My father passed away,' I say.

He hangs his head. 'I am sorry.'

'We weren't close. He was complicated.'

'I understand. My father—'

Danny interrupts. 'Complicated? The man made the Tokyo subway system look simple. Musicians – all artists, really – are that way, don't you think?'

'A musician?' the boy asks. 'With a group?'

'Orchestral, actually.' I can already tell what's coming. 'He was a classical musician.'

'A violinist,' Danny adds. 'One of the best.'

Recognition crosses the boy's face. 'Your father is not Hiro Akitani, the famous player? Recently I read of his death.'

'My friend talks too much.' The black organ whispers, *Danny's laying claim to something that's yours.*

He gasps. 'I have seen his documentary film many times! He was a sickly child who became a great musician and played on the world stage. Very inspiring!' He hums the chunk of Paganini that backs the film's opening credits.

'Don't tell me they're still showing it on TV.'

'My mother owns. She has much pride about Hiro Akitani because he lived in Tokushima also. Were you born there?'

'I was born in Tokyo, but I grew up in Tokushima.'

'Ah, but why would anyone move? Tokushima is such a … countryside place.'

'My mother liked it – the beach, warmer weather, more relaxed people. More "Japanese", she said.' I check to make sure he's catching all of my English. He nods along, his gaze angled downward in concentration. He's older than I had first guessed – in his early twenties, maybe. I continue, 'My father had a place in Tokyo where he spent a lot of time, when he wasn't abroad, so I don't know how much it mattered to him where I grew up. He liked having a home base on Shikoku. People there didn't make a big deal about him.'

'Yes. Tokushima people are like this. They respect hard work number one. Image is not so important.'

Danny adjusts her pack. 'We should get a move on.'

'May I join you to the next temple?' he asks.

'Sure,' I say. 'Join us as long as you like. Practise your English.'

Danny shoots me a look that surely means, *Are you kidding me?*

'Truly?' he asks, glancing at Danny, already aware that she's the party pooper of the pair.

'Well—'

'I will leave anytime,' he says. 'You could' – here he searches for a phrase – '*kick me out* when you want. And I can carry stuff. I can totally lend you my hand!'

I think of my father's letter. 'That would be fun,' I say.

'Or you two could team up, and I'll go ahead on my own,' Danny says.

The boy looks puzzled. 'But you are too old.'

Laughing, I say, 'Really, though, once I leave, it'd be good to have someone else with you.'

'I don't understand the universe,' Danny says.

'That means yes,' I tell the boy.

He throws his hand to his chest, his fingers framing the word DREAMER. 'You're so cool.' He pats at a few pockets of his cargo pants before finding the one that holds his name cards. 'My name is Shinobu,' he says, holding a card to Danny.

'*You're* Shinobu?' Danny snatches it.

'We saw your name a few temples back,' I explain. 'We thought—'

'I know, it is terrible,' he says miserably. 'You think I am a girl.'

'I go by a boy's name,' Danny says. 'And I think "Shinobu" is rather nice.'

'Call me Shin.' He spits in the dirt. 'Excuse me.'

'How about Shinny?' I ask. He snorts, shakes his head. I like teasing him. He takes it so well, as if he's trying to acquire a sense of humour as well as a second language.

Danny doesn't look particularly pleased or displeased. She looks distracted. She turns away from us and pulls a green bottle from her pocket, throws back a pill. 'And then there were three,' she says.

8

WE NEED TO STOCK UP on drinks and food before heading deeper into the mountains. The walk from temple eleven to twelve is known as 'the pilgrim's downfall', an elevation gain of eight hundred metres. Danny's excited. 'Now the true suffering can begin,' she says.

'Are you sure we have time to get there?' I ask. 'It's thirteen kilometres straight up and it's already past lunch.'

'We'll get there,' Danny says. 'Shinobu can handle it, right?'

He agrees gamely. But when Danny turns her back, he grimaces and mock-salutes her.

He prefers me – because I'm from America, I guess, but also because Danny is so brusque; even her whisper has the force of a yell. And she stands too close during conversation. I don't remember this about her. I wonder if it's a habit she's developed or if I simply never noticed. At the last temple I watched

Shinobu take a step back from her as she talked; a few seconds later, she took one forward, and so on, until he bumped into a tree.

Shinobu's a funny kid, part old soul and part right-out-of-the-packaging. He's made good on his word to carry many of Danny's things, asks thoughtful questions about our lives and my family – he is especially delighted by stories about Lily – and speaks positively about nearly everything. He is, well, *heartful*. He keeps one earbud in at all times, music piping in, while the other dangles unused. At the temple after Kirihata-ji, Danny whispers, 'Hasn't he learnt manners? He might as well have both of them in – at least I'd know when he was listening to us.' When I ask him why he listens to music in only one ear, he looks shocked and responds, 'I don't want to miss your speak, of course! That would be very rude.'

Our ascent is slow. Though the grade isn't steep, the path winds lazily around trees in a series of switchbacks. The humidity is choking. There's a dull ache under my left kneecap. I cross directly through the brush between switchbacks. Danny and Shinobu dutifully follow the path. Shinobu! Leave her behind and walk with me. I have something for you to read.

'The path is made this way to make a person think about life,' Shinobu says when they catch up. 'In life we must make long detours that seem unnecessary—'

A bird sings overhead. Shinobu tugs his earbud out and freezes. 'Listen! It's *uguisu*. This bird is well-known,' he says, eyes on the canopy. 'The great poets mention him.'

'Where?' I follow his gaze.

'You will not see *uguisu*. He is secretive and small, with boring colour. But loud! So it's better to listen to his beautiful song.' He puckers his mouth. 'Hoooo-ho-ke-kyo!'

'It's a bush warbler,' Danny says.

'You know *uguisu*?'

'You said yourself they're famous. Mentioned in haiku, considered a sign of spring?'

'Yes. But we learn this in elementary school.'

'I don't remember learning that,' I say.

'Why are Japanese people so astounded when a foreigner demonstrates the slightest knowledge about their culture?' Danny asks. 'I've lived here twenty years and people still applaud when I use chopsticks.'

'Foreigners have evolved different brains. They can't grasp such delicate concepts,' I add. 'It's like how Japanese intestines are longer because they eat more vegetables.'

'That is – no! I mean ...' Shinobu says, tugging at his ear. 'It's nothing about intelligence. You see, to Japanese such facts are ... natural. I'm surprising you think detail of culture like *uguisu* is interesting.' He turns to me. 'You are correct about intestines. Everyone knows this fact.'

A bend in the trail affords a view of the foothills and, in the distance, water. Shinobu and Danny bicker over whether foreigners can truly absorb Japanese culture. I look south. The Pacific Ocean is a blue plate with nothing on it.

Soon the growl of cars travelling the seaside highway reaches our ears; the noise is harsh and out of place. As we near the road and get a wider view of the sea, Shinobu points. Surfers in black wetsuits bob among small waves that draw them not toward the shore, but parallel to it. The effect is eerie. 'A powerful storm must be near,' says Shinobu.

He's right. The tide is coming at an angle.

'Still a ways off now,' Danny says. 'The surfers know. They wouldn't go out if it was too risky.'

We find the convenience store, a mom-and-pop operation on the ground floor of a two-storey apartment building. Under the dirty striped awning, a long icebox displays fresh fish and, beside them and their unblinking eyes, strawberry Popsicles. The place is empty. Danny calls hello. Footsteps sound above us. 'Coming,' a woman yells through the ceiling.

The store is packed floor-to-ceiling with crates, boxes, and shelving units. Danny has to turn sideways to scoot down an aisle and reach the counter. There are a number of important facts to collect: the quality of pre-packaged meals and rice balls, the brand names of energy drinks, trail mix, whether the place sells alcohol and cigarettes.

Shinobu stays up front with me. He plugs his phone into the electrical outlet powering the icebox. I don't dare take out the letter. Danny keeps looking back at us.

Shinobu taps a newspaper headline. 'I love baseball, but my team is worst in Japan. The Ham Fighters.'

'The Ham Fighters? You were born in Tokyo, right? You should be a Giants fan.'

'The Giants always win. And their fans are no good. They don't care about the team, only winning.'

'Fair-weather fans,' I say.

'Ferry?'

I explain the term.

'Yes, exactly!' he says, pulling out his phone. He types something and shows it to me: FARE WHETHER FANS. I take the device and correct his spelling, marvelling at how much lighter his phone is than the iPhone I left at home.

'But,' he says, pointing to the back page of the newspaper. 'We, ourself, don't have fair weather.'

A large typhoon has formed off the coast of Shikoku. Its

projected path is a cone, the centre of which holds Shishikui – exactly where we stand. Rain is expected as early as tomorrow. En was right.

'But it's only June,' I say.

'They come earlier every year. It is the inconvenient truth.'

My laughter seems to release his; he's relieved he got the joke right. Danny peeks around a corner at us from the back of the store, where she is arguing with a middle-aged woman in a fuchsia sweat suit.

A long green school bus pulls up, throwing us into shadow. A choking heat radiates from the vehicle. The driver leaves the bus idling and jogs in, yells for a pack of menthols.

A foot above our heads, faces crowd the half-open bus windows. I look away out of habit, as if these children might be able to see back in time to the unpopular kid I once was. One shouts, 'Where are you from?' to which another kid says, 'She can't understand you, dummy.'

I remember my elementary school bus. The cool kids sitting in the back, where you got bounced around most, the windows that pinched your fingers and never opened wide enough, the vinyl slippery seats and the anxiety that accompanied trying to find someone to share with. 'Partner up! Two to a seat,' the teachers would yell as we boarded. No one wanted to share with me. I took up too much space.

Danny comes out of the store, scribbling something in the margin of her guidebook. 'Look at the way the water's moving out there,' I say.

The bus driver walks past, rubbing his nose with two fingers. He looks as if he's been pulling the bus rather than driving it. He glances at us, hesitates, and speaks with reluctance. 'Do you have somewhere to stay during the storm?'

'We're on our way to Shōsan-ji,' Shinobu says.

'On foot? Impossible. The trail's insanely steep and it'll be dark before you're halfway up.' He claps his hands. There's authority in his voice. 'Get in. I'll take you. *Osettai*.'

The struggle on Danny's face is clear. What's worse, to turn down *osettai*, or to cheat and get a ride during the hardest part of the hike?

Then I remember: *Partner up. Two to a seat.*

'Kūkai will forgive you,' I whisper, and push her toward the bus. The kids go silent as we step inside.

I drop into a bench seat up front and pull Shinobu down beside me. A group of girls in the back call out to Danny: 'Hullo! I am fine thank you.' A burst of giggles is followed with, 'This is a pen. That is not a pen. That is a clock. Do you like pen?'

I take out my father's letter.

'I can guess your secret,' Shinobu says to me.

'Sorry?'

'I remembered a story. About the daughter of Hiro Akitani … but her name is not Rio. It is Chizuru.'

I stop breathing, then force myself to say, 'What? What are you talking about?' I can't tell what he's thinking. He doesn't seem upset, but I can't risk angering him. He might refuse to translate the letter.

A smile or a grimace – I can't say which – creeps over his lips. 'You *are* she. The first *kireru*.'

What game is he playing? And is it possible to play along? I nod slowly. 'That was a long time ago.' I try a joke. 'You scared?'

'Not scared. Honoured. You made justice. Killing that boy was good. To very many people …' His breath comes quickly; his face is red. 'You are a hero.' He types on his phone, holds it out to me. 'See? Your fan club.'

I hold the hot little phone in my palm. My twelve-year-old face. A school photo I haven't seen in ages. It was taken a month before I took the letter opener from Danny's desk. The last picture of me from 'before'. They must have included it in the yearbook – an oversight, surely. I never received my copy. I wonder if they included Tomoya's photo and what, if anything, they said about him. Did I kill him before the yearbook deadline?

Across the aisle, a girl younger than the rest sits alone, tugging at the laces of her untied shoe. She bites her lower lip as she carefully crosses two loops – bunny ears, we called them for Lily. But when she pulls, the laces fall loose.

Frustration slides from her face when she notices us. She stares for a moment before tucking the shoe underneath her body and spinning toward the window. Slowly she rotates her head forward and watches us from the corner of her eye.

'*Nan sai?*' Shinobu leans over and asks her age.

She raises her hands to her face, the pointer finger of her right hand pressed to the spread palm of her left. Six. Her fingers are ringed with plastic jewellery.

'Six? I thought you were twenty-five!' Shinobu says.

The girl presses her lips together in an attempt not to smile.

'How did you find this?' I whisper. I've searched my old name plenty of times – in Japanese and in Roman letters – and never come across this site.

'It's a social site, members only,' Shinobu says. 'Like Facebook.'

I scroll down the page, past advertisements for sex dolls and acne medication. There: Tomoya's face, his perfectly straight teeth, his pointy chin. I have not seen that face in twenty years.

It doesn't look menacing anymore. Tomoya just looks like a kid.

A digital 'X' marks the picture, and a skull-and-crossbones is superimposed over Tomoya's face. Farther down the page is a message board. One post, from 'Ayumi', is in English: WE HONOUR U CHIZURU! I click on the pink unicorn icon next to her name and skim her profile: Location: *Gunma-ken*. Age: *12*.

Lily will be twelve next month. Does she have access to this kind of thing? I try to imagine Ayumi's mother. Does she work? Is she married? Likely she has no idea what her daughter's going through. Would I know if Lily was being bullied? Or if she was bullying someone?

'Let me see that shoe,' Shinobu says to the girl across the aisle. The girl glances at me, then back at Shinobu. She sticks out her foot.

'A butterfly is about to land,' he says, forming a loop, which he flutters.

'I know about the butterfly,' she says suspiciously.

'Of course you do! But have you heard about the ferocious hawk that wants to gobble it up?' He forms a second loop; it attacks the first. '"Caraw! You look tasty!" says the hawk. But the butterfly is smart. She goes behind the hawk, like this, and shoots under him—' He tucks the second loop behind and under the first and pulls the bow tight. 'Boom! He's trapped. But you know what? They travel to many interesting places together, and end up the best of friends.'

She watches him, rapt. Now she tugs the bow out. 'The butterfly is smart ...' she mutters as she positions the loops. When a neat bow forms between her fingers she looks up with an astonished smile. She turns and presses her face to the window.

'Children and elderly love me,' Shinobu tells me.

'This is sick,' I whisper, still holding his phone.

'Some journalists call it evil, but I disagree. You stood up. You fought the Man.'

'Don't say that. I would give anything to change what happened.'

'You ran away from Japan to America after *kireru*. I see. It's perhaps funny then. Because no *kireru*, no America. And then you have no husband, no daughter.'

I remember every day that the two best things in my life came, indirectly, out of that tragedy. But that doesn't mean I wouldn't take it back if I could. A good life lived with a secret was nothing compared with a good life lived without one. But I didn't – don't – have that luxury.

'Your husband must be good man,' Shinobu says. 'Good at understanding people.'

'He doesn't know,' I say.

His mouth falls open. 'He does not know … Chizuru?'

'No.'

'I am shocking! How—?'

I take my father's note from my bag. 'I need your help,' I say, unfolding it. 'Would you read this to me? It's important.'

Delight spreads across his face. 'You are unliterate!'

'Illiterate. Too many years in the US.'

'I can help you. Who from did you receive this?'

'My father.'

'Oh my god! The writings of Hiro Akitani. A treasure!'

'Shh.'

He gathers himself. 'I think this is important for you.'

'Please – keep this between us.' I nod toward the back of the bus.

Shinobu points at me. 'Ah, *yappari*, I knew it. What is the deal with – do I say this slang correctly? – you and Danny-san?'

'I don't know what you're talking about.'

'There is tension.' He plucks the note from my fingers. 'And now there is this.'

The bus hits a bump and we both brace ourselves on the seat in front of us. 'We haven't seen each other in twenty years. It takes time to get used to each other.'

He squinches his eyebrows together and says softly, 'I am crying bullshit.'

I laugh and the girl across the aisle squeals, then covers her mouth and laughs, too. The bus chugs up the narrow road, which is so steep we're leaning back in the seat. It's like being on a roller coaster, simultaneously dreading and craving the top of the hill. The driver was right; there's no way we'd have made it before dark.

Shinobu reads the Japanese easily, the awkwardness of his English speech gone.

' "*To my daughter: A thousand cranes, that's what I imagined when you were born. Beautiful, with so many worlds in you. Danny tells me your name is Rio now. Why? It's kind of ugly, isn't it?*

' "*I've had two strokes since you left. I can no longer perform, but if you can believe it, that's fine with me. I'm going to have my last one soon and then I'll die.*

' "*My lawyer sends this because I don't want Danny to know about the bow. I told her I donated it – keep this to yourself. You used to love cleaning it. Sometimes I'd get it dirty on purpose. Maybe your daughter will like it. Have you taught her how to make origami butterflies?*" '

I close my eyes. It's like my father's sitting next to me. Shinobu even sounds a little like him.

' "*I assume that Danny has called and told you everything. Please be kind to her. How was I to know she'd never get over that tiny, hardly memorable affair? People's emotions and attachments are a mystery. She's been of help to me, at least.*

' "*On the Internet, I saw photos of your daughter, Lily, on the stage in Colorado. She got her charisma and talent from me. She looked happy and she must have gotten that from you.*

' "*They say you know you're old when you start regretting things so I guess I am old. To be honest, I had no real desire to contact you until now. I was never meant to be a family man. It's no excuse, but I am still giving it. I should've died when I was a child, but I was too stubborn.*

' "*I didn't leave you any money. I don't think it helps so I gave what was left to the tsunami relief effort. Those poor suckers! See you in the next life. There is one, don't you think? Hiro.*' "

The seat in front of us has a rip in its covering. I stare into the gash as we climb and bump into the mountains. Shinobu is speaking, but I can't focus on what he's saying.

He pats my shoulder. 'Danny and your father ...' Shinobu says, awe in his voice. 'You did not know.'

'I did not know.' I am waterlogged, sinking, with how much there is that I did not know.

The bus grinds to a halt. The driver whistles. 'Door-to-door service. How's that for *osettai*? Feel free to take a few of these little worms with you. Ha-ha!'

Danny rushes up the aisle, calling out goodbyes to her new friends in the back of the bus. I shove the letter in my pants pocket. When she passes us I can't help but lean away.

The girl across the aisle holds out a hunk of purple plastic to Shinobu. A ring. He gives her his pinky and she slides the ring on above the knuckle. She points to me. Shinobu passes the ring over and I put it on. I watch the way it breaks apart the late afternoon light and scatters it against my wrist. Shinobu tugs at my arm. I get up to face Danny.

9

THE LAST THING THAT HAPPENED before my *kireru*, before I was led away from school with blood on my uniform, is the tacks. The tacks were the last straw.

It happened during English class. I was out of Miss Danny's favour and Tomoya knew it. She'd hugged me that once, in private, and gone right back to her cool treatment of me. One of the quiet boys in class asked me a question about the homework as I walked to my chair, so instead of looking down, I looked at him as I took my seat.

The pain was sharp, like bees; it robbed me of breath. I lifted my butt off the chair to relieve the pressure as tears welled in my eyes. Laughter exploded behind me. I rose mechanically. *Get out. Get out. Get out.*

Miss Danny, who was writing at the board, turned. She took in my face. Then she saw the back of my skirt, where the tacks still hung. One fell onto the floor. I can still hear the sound of it clicking across the tile.

I managed to hold back my tears until I reached the hallway. I heard Miss Danny say, 'Girls, go help her.'

In the bathroom, I lifted my skirt and pulled at my mint-green cotton underwear, which was spotted with blood. I looked in the mirror: the tacks had been arranged in a smiley face on the chair; pressed into my backside, they drew a frown. I gagged, coughed, and spit into the sink. I wanted my mom to swim into the room. I wanted Miss Danny to scream. I wanted to hurt Tomoya.

Ikemi, the suck-up singer, and another girl, Mimi, came into the bathroom. Ikemi pulled a paper towel from the dispenser and handed it to me, then thought twice and wet it. The other girl stood behind her, staring at my bloodied underwear and the pile of tacks on the metal ledge above the sink.

'Why did they do this?' I asked. 'Why did they do this?'

'Those boys are jerks,' Ikemi said. 'Right, Mimi?'

Mimi nodded, staring.

'It looks like you got your period,' Ikemi said, giggling.

I had, in fact, gotten my first period a few months before. Early like me, my mom said. I'd been proud for a couple of days, and went so far as to 'accidentally' drop a maxi pad on the floor, but when I realised no one in my grade had gotten it yet, it became another shameful side effect of being *hafu*. Ikemi's comment further humiliated me. I told her I was fine, to go back to class.

'Are you sure?'

I hated the concern on her face. 'Just leave me *alone*.' I shouted the last word, and her perfect face looked scared and I felt a tiny bit better.

'Let's go,' she said. Mimi followed her out of the bathroom, glancing back for one last look before she pushed the door open.

I waited until the bell rang, fighting tears so that I would appear strong for whoever came in next. But Miss Danny never came.

Shōsan-ji is at the summit of a mountain erupting with vegetation. It affords a view of lower peaks covered in mist like pulled-apart cotton. Cedars tower above us. I understand why Danny was reluctant to get a ride: this beauty is too sweet to come unearned. I can only imagine how breathtaking it must be after a six-hour climb.

I track Danny's gestures, her expressions, and try to piece things together. Why had sending the bow to me been a secret? Danny was upset about it after reading the letter. Said she'd expected him to have burned it.

A pond dotted with water hyacinth hooks around one side of the temple's vermilion walls like a half moat. Purple-blue hydrangea bloom along the water's edge. A squirrel bounds down the temple's front steps, pauses to take us in, and scampers under a bush. If not for the menacing clouds gathering, we could be in an anime. Surely there are big-eyed dust bunnies – Lily's favourite thing to draw after first watching *My Neighbour Totoro* – zipping around inside this place.

Danny doesn't know I'm studying her. She tells us about Shōsan-ji's infamous resident priest while I re-evaluate everything I thought I knew. Could it be true that her feelings for Hiro have kept her single all this time? Could one 'tiny affair' be enough to corrupt her for life? If it was with him, maybe. His presence did things to people.

The priest, she tells us, is known to tickle his guests awake, sunbathe nude in the garden, and fuel raucous sing-alongs with blessed sake. He dug the pond himself and filled it with the countryside's eighty-eight fattest koi, which he carried up the mountain in plastic sacks over a period of weeks. He hula-hoops for meditation.

One of the made-up childhood friends I've told Sal about was a hula-hooper. Inez, I named her. She was half-Brazilian, the daughter of a couple who owned a teppanyaki restaurant where you could put black-eyed peas in your stir-fry. Inez could dance and hula-hoop at the same time. She used to hula-hoop on her roof and all the neighbourhood boys would gather around to watch. The story's so old I don't remember when I first told it. I've repeated it, imagined Inez with her dark skin and amber eyes, so many times that part of me doesn't recognise the story as false.

And there's the priest – a small man in yellow robes standing to the right of the temple, looking up at the eaves.

He throws his hands up when he sees us. 'What's this? They've been telling pilgrims to either backtrack and stay in Tokushima City, or head to Kamiyama Town, where a shelter's been set up.'

'Oh dear! We hadn't heard that,' Danny says. She's a good liar.

The priest bows – more a bow of resignation than respect. His head has been shaved in the traditional manner, but it's growing in so that his scalp looks dirty. 'Then, unfortunately for us all, you must stay here. The storm will only get worse; it grew stronger over the ocean last night. Oh, how ridiculous! Don't you people have cell phones? Well. My own room is only three mats, too small for more than one person. But' – he sighs dramatically – 'there is the chicken shed.'

'As long as it stays dry, it'll be fine,' I say.

'Are there truly' – Danny's voice squeaks – 'chickens in it?'

'One chicken,' the priest says. 'She is a sacred object, so the shed was built well. I shored it up myself last summer.'

'Is the bird loose?' Danny asks.

'Typically. But for the storm I've caged her. You look worried – adorable.' He squints up at the roof. 'But about the accommodation – you will be bored. I'd lend you my karaoke machine, but I have to save my batteries for the flashlight. Also, it is very simple, only one room.'

'I'll make a friend with this sacred fowl,' Shinobu says. 'She can aid my exam result.'

The shed is a corrugated tin rectangle pressed against the back of the temple. Inside, it smells like the straw covering its concrete floor. The priest leaves us and returns a minute later, steering a wheelbarrow stacked with blankets, two sleeping pads, an electric lantern, and a single futon. We help him unload. The lantern puts out a pure golden light and more of it than you'd guess – plenty to read by.

'Young man, would you mind helping me move some bags of mulch inside? I can't have them floating away on me.'

'Of course, sir.'

Shinobu goes outside with the priest, who waves to Danny and me. 'Good luck, new acquaintances and resident lunatics.' He closes the door.

Danny's staring at the back of the shed, where the chicken clucks agitatedly in its large wire crate. She crosses her arms. 'This is going to be a terrible night.'

She's right. But it won't be terrible for the reasons she thinks.

There's a *ping* on the metal roof, and another, like someone throwing rocks. Danny starts to say something, but she's drowned out by the sound of a thousand fat raindrops hitting the roof at once. We're inside a drum. I crack the door. Small trees and bushes bend under the downpour. Hail bounces in the grass. The small pond bubbles and froths.

'The driver was right!' I shout over the rain.

Danny looks miserable as she sets her pack near the door, as far from the chicken as possible.

I lean my things against the wall across from Danny. We spread towels and blankets over the straw. Danny fusses with her arsenal of books, baggies, and stones. Her obsession with these things is pathetic. They're probably mementoes of him. I feel powerful. She thought she could keep a secret from me? She was wrong. So, so wrong.

The black organ has detached from my heart and is striding around, kicking my other parts. It's hard to breathe. I take out my father's letter and flick it open so she can see the writing.

The chicken paces in its cage. It lets out a small squawk that makes Danny jump. After a second she registers the letter in my hands and sits up, holding the blanket to her chest as if it will protect her.

'"*I assume Danny has told you everything. Please be kind to her.*" Have you? Have you told me everything?'

'You show up expecting answers. Like a little visit will solve everything.'

'You had an affair with him.'

She drops the blanket. 'Is that what you really want to know? About something that happened ages ago?'

I realise why she didn't tell me. 'Oh my god. It happened when I was your student, didn't it? Right before—'

'Oh, for god's sake. How do you think we met?'

It's like I've sat on the tacks again. I feel them all over my body, a million punctures draining me. 'And you've been obsessed with him ever since. He paid attention to you for what, a month or two?'

'People have affairs all the time. We didn't invent the undertaking.'

'I was a kid going through a terrible time. And out of the blue, you treated me like I was invisible.'

'I stopped giving you preferential treatment.'

'You stopped protecting me.'

'I was a teacher! I was doing my job and that job did not include parenting you. Being seen as my special pet only would have made things worse for you.'

'How could it have been any worse? Knowing what happened?'

'No one could have predicted what would happen. I thought I was doing right.'

'By ignoring me.'

'By distancing myself. I was young, sheltered. I knew better and should have acted better, but we all make mistakes when we're young. It was a difficult time for me.' She twists her bracelets and sighs. 'It's been one difficult time after another.'

Her self-pity makes me want to scream. 'News flash! Life is hard. You know what most of us do? We move on. I do feel sorry for you. Because you never did.' I point at her circle of junk. 'And this shit. Are these tokens of your little crush?' My hand swipes at the rocks and shells, sending them flying against the tin wall.

Danny looks scared. Good. She's right to be afraid of me. My heart is pounding and the black organ pounds with it. Who does she think she is, claiming suffering? Difficulty?

'My mom had *just died*,' I say. 'And you scooted right in.'

'No,' Danny says, cowering in her corner. 'She was still alive when we met. It wasn't like that.' My vision blurs and what she says next seems to arrive from very far away. 'I'm sorry you lost your mother. But no. That can't be my fault. It – it was her choice. No one made her do it.'

I lunge forward and slap Danny. The butt of my palm hits her jaw and her head slams into the wall behind her with a satisfying thud. I want to silence her, to knock the cute little accent from her throat. She cries out and clutches her jaw, shields her face with her other arm. From behind her bent elbow she whispers, 'My god.' Her terror pleases the black organ. I am hot, electrified. I turn and see Shinobu standing in the doorway. His expression is a mix of shock, horror, and revulsion. On his face, I see what I've done.

It feels like a long time before anyone speaks. Both Shinobu and Danny stare at me. 'This is what it's come to,' Danny murmurs, still holding her jaw. My throat feels like it's full of glue. I try to swallow but can't.

Danny says, 'There's something else you should know.' She sits up meekly. 'Hiro left a key. I was meant to give it to you. It's in my pack.' She looks at me, asking for permission to move. I nod. She unzips an interior pocket in her pack and holds out a key tied to a length of green ribbon. 'It's a house key. To the house where you grew up.'

The copper key is old, large, and tarnished. Its weight and size are familiar in my fingers. But Hiro sold the old place. Didn't he? After my mom died and I was gone, what use would he have had for it? He'd only bought the house because of my mom.

'Why do you have this?'

'He didn't want it mailed. He asked me to give it to you, but only if you came to Japan.'

Danny stands, touches the back of her head as if to check for blood or a bump. Surely I didn't hit her that hard. Did I?

'Danny, I don't know what happened. I'm not normally like that.' I step toward her and she holds out a palm.

'Stay away. Don't touch me.' She gathers her futon and pillow.

'Where are you going?' Shinobu asks.

'The temple. I'll sleep in the *hondo*.'

'Let me go,' I say as Danny moves past me. 'You'll get wet out there.'

She tries to slam the door, but the latch has turned, so it bounces back. She stalks into the darkness beyond the pond. Shinobu gathers his bedding. 'I will go, too. You stay here tonight.' His face is a wall of disappointment and his eyes are trained on the ground.

Once he's gone, I draw my knees to my chest. Mud streaks my shins and slides from the tops of my feet like fat black tears. I try to imagine Danny with my father. It's impossible. I picture her at school, swaying in one of her pastel suits, saying '*rye-yu*' instead of '*ryu*' and crunching the R's in words she'd heard a million times, like '*arigatō*'. It's hard to believe that a music lover had such a bad ear, harder still to think my father would have tolerated it.

The weird, alien message my brain keeps repeating is true: *I hit her*. What is wrong with me? I'm a nurse. A rational adult. I slapped a fifty-five-year-old woman, a cancer survivor, a woman who is scared of a chicken, and she wasn't even threatening me. Is this who I am?

The chicken is strangely silent, lulled to sleep by the rain, or perhaps simply unwilling to speak up.

10

WHEN I WAKE IN THE MORNING, my tongue feels fat and my head is stuffed with rocks. I put two ibuprofen on my tongue, peel them off. I have no saliva with which to swallow. My water pouch is empty.

Danny's trinkets remain scattered. I gather them into a pile. The chicken stands erect in its cage, still except for its darting obsidian eyes. Light outlines the door. I grab the water pouch, slip my shoes on without tying the laces, and flip the door latch.

My feet sink with an audible squish. Overhead, ragged clouds travel quickly, like soldiers off to battle. As I watch, one cloud tears open to reveal a small patch of brilliant blue. Storm's over. I walk to the *hondo*. Shinobu's asleep under the bell. I don't see Danny. Drool trickles from the corner of Shinobu's mouth. His lips are bright red. I whisper to him, but he doesn't stir. I poke his side and he finally opens his eyes.

'Get up before the priest sees you,' I say. 'Where's Danny?'

'There,' he says without lifting his head. He points to a space at the back of the *hondo* between a Buddha statue and a lacquered demon figurine.

All I see is a folded futon with a pillow atop it. 'No, she's not.'

He sits up. 'Did she leave?'

I pick up Danny's bedding and Shinobu packs up his. We circle the temple, looking for any sign of her, but find nothing. There's a spigot on the side of the building. I set down the futon and stick my mouth underneath the spigot, gulping the sweet, cold water and letting it splash my face.

'How did you and your – ahem – *family* manage?'

It takes me a moment to recognise the priest in his yellow slicker, matching rubber pants, and camouflage-patterned galoshes. I wipe my face with my sleeve and try to make it seem like two of our party did not snooze among the temple's venerable artefacts. 'We stayed warm and dry, thank you. We'll be out of your way in a little while.'

He laughs so hard, and with so much joy, that I begin to worry. Finally he manages, 'You'll need those beds one more night. This is only the eye of the storm!'

'It is?'

'Yes. To Dainichi-ji, the next temple, is five-point-two kilometres. To go now would be asinine.'

How long would it take Danny to hike five kilometres? I don't know how long ago she left. The Chizuru in me wants to forget about her. But the nurse and mother in me can't help but wonder at what happened to her. 'Is there anywhere to stop along the way?'

'I'm beginning to think you're mentally challenged,' he says. 'I find that with many foreigners, actually. Now, how shall I put it? You. Stay. Here. Today. Enjoy the company of a good chicken.'

Shinobu and I bow. I say, 'We'll do as you suggest.'

In the shed, I turn on my cell phone. Maybe Danny's left a message. But the animated gremlin on the screen frowns and shakes its head, conveying bad news the Japanese way – adorably.

Shinobu pulls on a thin plastic poncho and flips up the hood. 'I should have watched her and followed. The trail from here is dangerous.'

'You can't go now. The storm's due to start again.'

'She could be injured.' His palm rests on the door handle. He looks away. 'And I'm not sure I should stay with you.'

'I'm sorry about last night. You must think I do that kind of thing all the time, but I don't. I'm not a violent person.' This boy, who hailed me as a hero yesterday, now looks at me with pity. Shame covers me like a veil. 'Please stay. We'll find Danny as soon as the storm's over,' I promise. The chicken squawks as if in agreement. Its head pops up, down, up, down. 'If you leave now, you might get in trouble yourself. And then you wouldn't be helping me or Danny.'

Shinobu looks from the chicken to me with reluctance. He's feeling real pain over this decision. 'Maybe this is an omen,' he says uncertainly. 'I should study more. Already, I must return to Tokushima for the exam in four days' time.'

The storm rages all morning and afternoon. Twice, heavy objects – tree branches? – slam into the shed's metal siding. But inside, we are dry and safe. Safe not just from the elements but from life: there are no obligations in this shed. The battery-operated lantern glows like warm, mellow twilight all day. Shinobu lends me *On the Road*, which I read while he studies. He mumbles as he goes. Occasionally he translates a question out of his test prep book, makes me repeat it, then tries to answer it in English. He theorises that studying in two languages will 'more completely activate' his brain, leading to better retention.

'How may a company implement a reverse triangular merger in order to transfer the licences and permits of the target company to the surviving subsidiary without running afoul of the Companies Act?'

He rattles off an answer.

'You pass,' I say.

He skims the guide, shaking his head. 'I always forget about the foreign-subsidiary pending-patent exception clause.'

The low light does funny things to my sense of time. At eleven, I swear it's evening; by sundown, I put the time at early afternoon. Shinobu asks me to read aloud from *On the Road*, the chapter in which the guys drive to Mexico. They get so stoned they can't talk, and they party with teenage prostitutes and later go to sleep in jungle so deep they wake the next morning covered with their own mosquito-drunk blood, full of joy.

Finally, real night falls. The storm quiets. I step outside and pee in the bushes. A sliver of moon shines beyond the branches overhead. A frog gives a tentative croak, and all at once a thousand frog-voices respond from the darkness and bring the night to life.

I doze while Shinobu opens and closes his test-prep book. He listens to music on his phone through the single earbud.

'What are you listening to?'

'Now, it is Bob Dylan. I am also a fan of Michael Jackson and was very encouraged by his songs to start learning better English.

And I love Dragon Ash, Red Hot Chili Peppers ... Recently, I became into Sloth Love Chunks. Would you like to hear?'

I stick the earbuds in, pull them right back out. 'It sounds like a garbage disposal.'

'You are like my mother,' he replies. His phone dings and he scrambles to look at it. 'I had some signal for a moment, but now it's disappeared.' He frowns, reading something. His face slackens and his shoulders slump.

'What's wrong?'

It appears to take all his energy to get the words out. 'I receive e-mail from Linda.'

His voice has no force behind it. My heart twists for him. I know what's coming.

'"Moving on," she wrote. I know this meaning. It is finished.' He makes to hurl his phone, but stops short of doing it. He crouches down and, in Japanese, counts to ten over and over.

His heartache is so pure, so bare, I feel it, too. 'I'm sorry. Long-distance relationships are hard, but what she did was unfair. She should have at least called you.'

He puts the phone away. An eerie calmness has overtaken him. 'I will not say badly about her. These things cannot be helped,' he says mechanically. He gets into his futon fully dressed.

'Don't you want to get ready for bed first?' For a second I feel like I'm talking to Lily.

'*Hottoite kudasai,*' he whispers. Then, remembering himself, adds in English, 'Leave me alone, please.'

We head out at first light. The priest isn't up yet, so we leave him a note and a small cash offering after folding our bedding and sweeping out the shed. When we're ready to go, Shinobu looks at the sky over the temple. 'It feels so strange today. Like wanting to sneeze, but I cannot.'

He's right. There is no breeze; even the birds are silent. No *uguisu* here. We could be indoors for the lack of movement; the forest is like a museum, with each drop of moisture placed just so, every layer of moss expertly applied. Shinobu doesn't mention last night or Linda's e-mail. His *tatemae* is up; I have a feeling he is suppressing *honne* even within himself. His resolve is admirable. I've begun to feel protective of him.

We backtrack. The trail has become soupy mud threaded with hidden roots, but the trails through the mountains will be worse, Shinobu says, completely washed out and likely impassable. The dangers in this area are real: steep riverside drop-offs; sharp, unforgiving rocks; animals. We follow the narrow gravel road back toward the highway, where we'll hitch a ride to the next temple and see if we can find Danny or someone who's seen her.

When we reach the highway, my legs are spattered with mud and I'm dripping – the humidity is even worse after the storm. I can taste sweat on my upper lip.

It seems the human population has fled along with the birds. We walk down the middle of the road. The sea is flat and the surf, what little there is, makes no sound. It feels wrong to speak, as if the words might collapse something. The chime from my phone jolts me like a shock. It's a local number.

'I'm calling from Nakatani Hospital in Kamiyama,' says the sing-song voice on the other end. 'We have checked in a' – she pronounces each syllable separately – 'Da-nee-maku-fa-rain.'

'Hospital?' I repeat dumbly.

'Da-nee-maku-fa-rain-san is here and yours is the last number called from her cell phone,' the woman says. 'Are you a family member?'

'A friend. What's her condition? Hello?'

I hold out the phone: the screen shows a distraught gremlin.

'Danny is in the hospital? I should have followed! I will find the location and we will go. Where is a taxi? Look for a car, please.' His eyes flick back and forth over his screen.

The hospital? What the hell happened to her? I imagine gruesome scenes: compound fracture in the tibia from a fall, boar attack, injuries due to a robbery by glue-sniffing teenagers. My phone beeps: two texts from Sal. He heard about the typhoon – am I all right? I try to call him, but only get dead air.

Shinobu's nubby fingernails tap his plastic screen frantically. Whatever cell service he has, it's better than mine. 'Past the park, turn right. About one kilometre from here. We can walk if there are no cars.' A bird cries overhead – the first we've seen all day. It's large – a vulture, maybe, looking for a meal among the coastal debris. It can probably see all the way to the city. Does it notice us?

Shinobu's eyes are glued to the screen. His jaw works unconsciously.

'Don't read it again,' I tell him. 'You're torturing yourself.'

He looks up, his eyes glistening. 'I can't help. This was my dream.'

'You can still visit America. Focus on that.'

'You don't understand. If I go, every man I see – I will hate him. I will look at his face and if he smiles I will think, You *motherfucker*, you *asshole*. Because I know it will be one of them. Because I didn't arrive on time.' He looks up at the bird. 'The bird is lucky. He is free. His job is only to hunt and eat.

I want to be a hawk like this. I would wear an iPod and fly where I want to go.'

We continue walking, faster now. My pack bounces on my shoulders, its contents jangling as we make our way past grey smears of concrete holding up the hillsides. I slip the bag off and cradle it against my chest.

I don't know what to say to Shinobu. His anger is surprising. If it were Lily with a broken heart, I could talk her through it, but Shinobu's a young man. Is this how it'll be when Lily's a teenager? A new blister is forming on my right instep, probably due to my favouring the first blister that ravaged my big toe. Let one area heal, another is stressed, and so on, and we can only hope that once we make it back to the original place of pain, we are fresh enough to endure more.

11

OUTSIDE THE ENTRANCE to Nakatani Hospital, an empty potato chip bag – squid-flavour – floats beneath an overhang, buoyed by airflow from an out-of-sight vent. The glass doors split as we approach them. The rush of dry indoor air smells like St Mary's, like every hospital in the world: bleach and new plastic and underneath that, impossible to hide, the odour of illness.

The waiting room is carpeted with shabby pile the colour of dried-out limes. Three rows of padded chairs face a TV mounted high in the corner of the room. The Mariners game is on. Under the television, a vending machine offers bouquets of roses and sunflowers and beside that is a pair of coin-operated massage chairs.

I was ten the last time I was in a local Japanese hospital like this. Back then, my mom helped out in a woodworking shop that specialised in sliding shoji doors. Something happened – she slipped or wasn't paying attention, we never really found out – and she wound up with a five-inch gash along her forearm. She stayed overnight and I was allowed to sleep in her room, on a futon one of the nurses set up on the floor. Though I'd been to hospitals before, I'd never stayed overnight. With the lights out, the place went from a bustling clinic to a shadowy lair full of strange equipment. I was frightened and fascinated.

Shinobu and I approach the glass-shielded reception desk, where a nurse in a white hat shuffles papers. She speaks without looking up, her formal Japanese like a recording as it comes through a small speaker installed in the glass. 'Please fill these out in triplicate, stating the nature of your illness.' She pushes a stack of papers at us through a slot.

'We're here to see a patient.'

She looks up, sees our *hakui*, and hiccups in recognition. 'I know who you're here to see.' She presses a button and speaks into the intercom.

A door swings open near the vending machines. 'Right this way,' calls a nurse. She's taller than Shinobu by a few inches. A frog sticker clings beside the name on her badge: KANAKO.

Despite the apparent lack of emergencies, Kanako and the other nurses – all young women – are out of breath, with spots of colour high on their cheeks. I glance inside the rooms we pass. No one looks particularly sick. Japan is different from the United States; everyone has health care through the national system and it's normal to go to the local *byouin* for anything from the common cold to major surgery, or even to try out one of the new gadgets. Japanese hospitals, I read recently, performed the highest number of MRI scans in the world. 'The citizenry of Japan,' the article declared, 'takes great joy in being analysed by machine.'

The corridor widens and the smell of the air grows lighter, powdery. I know that hopeful smell. 'What's the problem?' Shinobu asks. 'Is it serious?'

We pass the long window that gives a view into the nursery. Kanako doesn't answer his question directly. Instead she jokes, 'She's in the maternity ward, but don't worry, she's not pregnant. We are just a little bit full now.' Her speech has a cute regional twang.

On the other side of the glass, four pink-skinned newborns lie asleep. One baby twitches awake, his arms and legs lolling, a patch of black hair matted to his scalp like leaves on a tomato. Lily was born completely bald and remained that way until she started crawling. Then her hair was unstoppable. Mobility activated her follicles with the message *If we're on the move, we gotta look good*. By two, her hair reached her waist. She rarely allowed me to touch it; cutting it was out of the question. She saw me cut myself with cuticle scissors once and avoided scissors of any kind, so one day I held a pair to my hair and snipped a piece to show her it didn't hurt. She cried for twenty minutes. I resorted to trimming her hair while she slept, a little bit at a time so she didn't notice anything had changed. 'Like cooking a lobster alive,' Sal said, 'but not as mean.'

We follow Kanako into the first room past the newborns. 'It is the only available bed,' she says. 'There's a cold virus going around. Happens after a typhoon.'

There is barely enough space in the room for a single bed and a metal stand. On the stand sits a stack of clean, folded clothes. Sunlight pours through the room's corner window and glares off the tile floor. I squint to get a better look at Danny.

Her ankle is bandaged and elevated; her face pallid. Violet and yellow clips hold her hair off her face. I recognise the gleam in her eyes: they've got her on some kind of opiate. Her eyes land on us and she says, 'They decide to turn up! Maybe they stopped at the hot springs on the way, had a hot dinner...'

Kanako lays a palm on Danny's forehead. 'Medication,' she whispers. 'It makes them talkative.'

'It's not the medication,' I say.

Kanako grins, revealing large buckteeth.

'What happened?' Shinobu asks.

Kanako looks at Danny and hesitates. 'She twisted her ankle pretty badly. And she has an infection. We can't get her fever down.'

'Giardia,' Danny says in English. 'Pneumonia of the colon. The mud was knee-deep. Sucked a shoe right off. Then I caught my toe on a root and had to crawl to the road. A lovely couple picked me up and brought me here. Head to toe in mud! Absolutely spoilt their upholstery.' In Japanese she adds, 'Buggers told me I looked like a demon.'

Kanako fluffs the pillow around Danny's pale face. 'Well, you sure look pretty today.'

'And you know what they found when they took off my clothes, after all that scooting through muck? Leeches. Leeches everywhere!' Danny holds her thumb and forefinger apart to show their size. 'Gluttons.'

Even if Kanako doesn't understand Danny's English, she sees what she's talking about. 'A very brave *henro*,' she tells Danny in Japanese. To Shinobu and me she says, 'She has pneumonia. We are keeping a careful watch.'

Shinobu gasps. 'That's very serious.'

I can see on Kanako's face that there's something else, too. Something worse. The room feels creepily small, as if there are hands in the walls that might reach out and choke me. My shoulders and neck are tense from being around Danny.

Kanako, thankfully, fills the awkward silence. 'I see you are also pilgrims. I've always wanted to walk the path myself. But I'm always working.'

'Teaching has that advantage, at least,' Danny says. 'Goddess bless summer vacation.'

'Teachers deserve the time off,' Kanako says. 'And what do you do?' she asks, looking politely at Shinobu and me, though her glance lingers on Shinobu.

'He'll be a lawyer soon,' I say.

'A lawyer!'

'No, no, I haven't passed the exam.' Shinobu puts up his hands as if to block her enthusiasm. 'Yet,' he adds.

Kanako claps in a prayer-like gesture. She points her fingertips toward him. 'You will pass. I know it by looking at you.'

'*Hara no mushi?*' I ask, raising my eyebrows at Shinobu.

Kanako pats her stomach and nods. 'Exactly.'

Shinobu is embarrassed – and pleased. He thanks her profusely, and I can't help but hear the literal translation of what he says in my mind: *Your stomach worms bestow unworthy respect upon me.*

Kanako glances at Danny. 'May I speak to you both outside?'

We step into the hall and my shoulders relax. 'Summer vacation, summer loooove, sum-sum-summertime!' Danny sings in English to the empty room behind us.

'Your friend – well, it's lucky she was awake when you arrived. She's been unconscious since yesterday. We gave her morphine half an hour ago when she woke up complaining of pain, so she'll be manic like this for another hour.'

'Unconscious? Because of a fever?' Shinobu asks.

'The fever is only a symptom. There are tumours. The one around her small intestine is the main culprit. But there are several, on the liver and stomach as well.'

'Does she know?' Shinobu and I ask together.

'I thought you would be able to tell me. Doctor Yamagata has not shared his findings with Daniela. She would likely have had some pain, but if she had not been X-rayed, she may not have understood what was causing it.'

She knows. Of course she knows. She even said it: I'd rather die than go through more chemo. That's what her pills are for. I should have known what was happening.

I close my eyes. 'I'm a nurse. How did I not see what was going on?'

Shinobu waves his hands emphatically, as if to erase my words. '*Shō ga nai, shō ga nai,*' he says. The most Japanese utterance there is. It means 'It can't be helped.'

He continues in Japanese, 'Don't look at it like that. You weren't here in the context of your profession. You were focused on personal matters. There was nothing you could have done. Besides, it was Danny's wish to spend her days in this fashion. We should be honoured she chose to share her pilgrimage experience with us.'

I am touched by his words, and surprised at his eloquence and the grace with which he speaks. His regional accent is hardly noticeable; he sounds like a Tokyo newscaster. Other than the time he read my father's letter, I've only known him in English. But in Japanese, he's, well – fluent.

'How much longer?' I ask Kanako.

'We could send her somewhere for treatments, but ...' She trails off, her voice weak. 'The pneumonia makes that difficult. And the doctor says it's a matter of months before the tumours incapacitate her completely. In this case, pain management is all that's left.'

Shinobu says he's going for a walk. His voice suggests that he's distressed by Danny's news and needs time to process it, but I see him pull out his phone before he turns the corner of the hallway. I head back to Danny's room, nervous, ashamed. I keep forgetting who I am while I'm in Japan. It's as if I'm being tugged between two universes, and the borders are dissolving. I let in that old self, the dark one powered by the black organ. I let in Chizuru and she turned me into Rio Silvestri, the nurse who slapped a woman dying of cancer.

'Nice girl. Energetic,' Danny says when I enter. 'And those teeth – adorable. Oh, crack the window, won't you? They keep you shuttered like an invalid. I'm suffocating.'

The window bolt is hot to the touch. I flip it up and slide the panel in its track. White flecks crumble as it moves – salt from the sea air. 'You should have told me.'

'You wouldn't have understood. He and I—'

'Not my father. You're *dying*.'

'Oh. That.' She stares at me stubbornly.

'If you didn't want chemo, fine. But why put yourself through this pilgrimage? Why take on Shinobu and me?'

'I don't know if you've noticed, but I am bad at saying no. I'm also bad at dying. There are no five bloody stages when it's you that's on the way out. I'm in the fuck-you stage and that won't change. I didn't want to see you. I didn't want to think about those days. But there you were. I helped you because of Hiro. Because he asked me in the end to make sure you were well. I promised. It was the last thing he said to me. Not "thank you" or even "I cared for you, a little bit, at one point."' She slaps the bed. 'Goddammit, you look so much like him.'

I run two fingers over my lips. There was a time when these words – that I looked like my father – would have thrilled me.

As a child, I often heard how much I resembled my mom. To me this meant that I looked like someone who didn't belong. But my hair is dark, like my dad's, I would point out. And my mom has blue eyes but mine are brown. My skin isn't as pink underneath. I would get so angry. As if by saying I didn't look like my dad, they were saying I didn't deserve positive attention like he received, either. I hadn't inherited enough of his face – only our thin-lipped mouths were identical, and the webbing between our first and second toes on both feet – and I certainly hadn't inherited his genius. I learnt that when it came to family resemblance, certain qualities counted more than others.

It doesn't matter, though. Danny sees him in me because she misses him. I wish she didn't. I wish she'd acted like an adult and stayed away from my father.

I force myself to say, 'I'm sorry about what I did in the shed.'

'What you did.'

'I …' It's hard to speak it. I whisper, 'I hit you.'

'And it hurt. Is that what you wanted? To hurt me?'

I think of my mom in her hospital bed, her arm bandaged from wrist to elbow, and the cut I had seen the doctor dressing from my hiding place in the closet. The cut was deep and long. You could see the slippery white fat under the skin. I had wanted to go to her, to touch her, to hold her together. But there was another idea, too, one that I tried unsuccessfully to push away: I could pull her apart. I could wait till she was sleeping, remove the bandages, and spread the flesh of her arm like a gutted fish, a piece of fatty *toro*. In my imagination, I would pinch the skin on either side of the cut and pull, like doing *ayatori*, the string game, and inside my mother there would be no blood or viscera. Inside my mother, it would be revealed for the world to see, there was nothing at all.

'Maybe. Yes. It was hard, hearing the truth all at once. Being lied to like that, for so long. You were prepared to take this to your grave.'

Danny raises her hands; she loves to move them as she speaks but it's bad for her IV. I adjust it automatically as she talks. 'It's good you found out,' she says as I pull the pole closer to her waist. 'Because I don't care about any of it any more. You know what I want now? All I want is to *not die* in a hospital. I want to be outdoors. That's how I pictured it and that's how it'll be.' She rolls her eyes at the IV. 'If a needle in my vein is all that's keeping me going, it's time for my graceful exit.'

'I wish I hadn't shown Shinobu the letter.'

She goes on as if I haven't spoken. 'I have enough pills. Take me someplace pretty. Afterwards, call my boss at the uni – Nakagawa's his name. He's got my brother's e-mail. Cremate me and scatter me here, on the island where he was born. At Kirihata-ji. I'm the girl who served. Who gave of her cloth freely.'

She is 100 per cent serious. I've seen the look before. 'I am not smuggling you out of here,' I say.

My mom had hated her time in the hospital. She didn't like that they forced her to stay a second day. 'It's not like I'm going to rip the stitches out purposely,' she griped. She complained about the food, about the unfeeling nurses, about how cold the rooms were kept. That morning after she was told they needed to keep her under surveillance, she started yelling; the incident ended with pale green melon-flavoured gelatin splattered on the wall. I sat on a chair beside her bed wondering when I'd get my mom back. In that hospital bed, she looked and acted like a child.

Danny continues, 'I'll check myself out. They can't keep me. All that's left is for me to tell you what I need to tell you,' she says. 'Then I'll be ready.'

It feels like my blood's stopped flowing. 'What do you need to tell me?'

'And then, you'll help me do it. Make sure it takes. I get one shot. If I screw it up, some do-gooder like Kanako will lock me down.'

'What do you need to tell me?' I repeat.

'The whole story. Don't you want to know the whole story?'

My blood begins to flow again, unsurely, thickly. It wants to know.

'Good,' Danny says. 'It will be a trade. You get closure, I get closure. Literally. Ha.'

I hate the word 'closure'. As if our problems are little sacks with string around the opening that we can cinch shut and forget. I've watched families witness the long, slow descent of a loved one. There is rarely a feeling of satisfaction when death finally arrives. Relief, sometimes. But closure implies a binary; if something is not closed, it is open. This is not how our feelings work.

'Closure's a joke,' I say.

'Give it some thought,' Danny says. 'Who knows, after all that's happened between us, you might enjoy it.' She cracks a smile.

It's common knowledge at our hospital that doctors help patients who ask for a 'smooth exit' all the time. I've witnessed this, but I've never participated, myself. If I do this, what kind of nurse am I? What kind of person? What if I don't do it?

What if I *want* to?

The air is still. In the parking lot below, a car engine stutters and fails, stutters and fails again. In the interim I can make out the sound of waves, though I cannot see the water.

I find Shinobu sitting on a shaded bench in front of the hospital. He's sweating. Everything about him – his relaxed posture, his size, his ill-fitting T-shirt – looks so out of place. I want badly for him to be happy.

I tell him what Danny's asked me to do.

'It's wrong,' he says immediately.

'Is it?'

He grimaces. 'The law says it is wrong.'

'What do you think?'

He leans forward, runs his hands through his puffy hair. 'I don't know. In her position, maybe I would think the same. It is difficult.'

We sit in silence. An ambulance with its lights off pulls up. Two uniformed men and a tiny beige dog get out of the front. The men are laughing. The dog circles their feet, its tail vibrating with joyful energy.

'I'm going to do it,' I say.

The dog runs to Shinobu and licks his hand. He startles badly, squeezes his eyes shut. 'I don't like dogs,' he says quietly. I shoo the thing away.

'What do you think of that? Of me doing it?'

'Does she have a family? Friends?'

'Just a brother she doesn't talk to, in New Zealand. She didn't mention anyone else. Her boss? Her herbalist? My dead father.'

'I know nothing any more about what is right,' he says. 'I want to give up.'

'Listen. It happens often—'

He shoves his study guide under his arm. '*Sono koto o kikitakunai,*' he says. *I don't want to hear such things.* The authority in his voice is startling. He switches coolly back to

English. 'My train departs in one hour from now. When you leave here, you must come to my family home in Tokushima City. There will be no hotels available due to the Obon holiday.' He runs his hands over his face, then writes his number, a train station, and an address on a piece of paper. I want to argue him over to my side, to get his approval, but it's evident that this conversation is closed.

We go to Danny's room. Shinobu places both hands on Danny's cheeks, leans down, and kisses her forehead. 'You improved my life.'

When he pulls away, his eyes are wet. 'I'll finish the exam in the afternoon of Tuesday. Then, Obon. The holiday will be either my celebration or my death.' He catches himself on the word 'death', hesitates, and continues, 'If I fail this time, I won't try again. I will enter the monastery.' He sticks out his chin on the word 'monastery'.

In the doorway, he bows so low his pack slips up onto his neck and he has a hard time righting himself. 'Goodbye, Danny-san.' And then he's gone. His shoes make sticking sounds that grow more and more distant until they disappear under the wail of a newborn.

For a long time the only sound in the hot, still air is Danny's breathing, quick intakes followed by long exhales, like someone alternately shocked and relieved. She's crying. Or trying to; there are no tears because morphine is drying her mouth, eyes, and everything else. There are eyedrops on the table. I squeeze the saline into her eyes and she blinks the false tears out.

'I didn't mean to fall for him,' she whispers. 'I wasn't an adventure seeker. Certainly not the "other woman" type. I was twenty-six, planning to be a primary school teacher. Everyone said I should travel before settling down. I didn't know anything about Japan, but a friend of mine had made enough money there to pay off her student debt, so I gave it a shot.'

I sit in the plastic chair beside her bed. It tips forward unevenly.

'He came in to talk about your problems at school. Your mum had been in but the meeting didn't go well. He was angry and full of life. Utterly wild. I'd never met anyone like him. I promised I'd look out for you, and I did. He invited me for a drink. Said he liked my accent.'

This is the first I've heard of him going to school about me. He must have hidden it from my mom and me.

'I was flattered. Thought, Why not? This might be the most exciting thing that ever happens to me. And then – it was like getting hit by a truck. I'd only had one boyfriend in my *life* before this. I was practically a virgin.

'It was – it was simply heaven – for three weeks. Twenty days. But he grew tired of me. I wasn't unique. I was one of an endless series. The switch flipped off and there was no flipping it back on. Yet he was all I could think of. It was like someone dipped me in hot wax and stamped me with him and I dried and that was it. Maybe I could have gotten over it, with time, if I refused to see him after that first night. But how could I have known?

'The school principal – what was his name, the bloke with the funny eyes? – found out. He never said so directly, but I could tell he knew. He called me in and told me that it was important, as a foreign teacher, that I set a good example of adult behaviour for the pupils. And that I should be sure not to play favourites.'

I rock in the chair. 'With me.'

'So I held back. I didn't want to ruin what I had with Hiro. I was powerless, possessed. It sounds romantic, and it felt that way, but looking back, the relationship was full of darkness. I spent ninety-nine per cent of my time suffering but that one per cent made up for it. When you stabbed Tomoya Yu, he changed. Went to Europe and didn't even tell me he'd left. He stayed away for months. I felt like my heart had cracked open like an egg and slid out of my chest. I flew back to Auckland and tried to start over, but it was useless. I got depressed. I took a volunteer teaching job in Ghana to clear my mind. But I couldn't erase him. I wrote him letter after letter. One day I got a letter back. He'd had a stroke and was taking a break from performing. He needed help and he'd asked *me*. I flew to Japan and began helping him out, buying groceries, shopping, cleaning – playing wife. I told myself that my faith had paid off, that I always knew I'd see him again. Told myself not to expect anything, that love was not selfish, but … he wasn't interested in me romantically any more at all. I was crushed.'

'Who was he interested in?'

'I don't know that there was anyone in particular after the stroke. He'd go to these parties – sex parties, orgies, I don't know – and come back smelling like ten different people. A tabloid reported that he liked men. My theory is that he liked everyone and no one. Sex and attachment didn't work for him the way they do for the rest of us.'

While I was at Kawano, growing up without a family, *this* is what was happening? This is the reason for all that wondering and heartache? 'And that's why you never visited,' I say.

'When I came back it was clear that you were not to be mentioned. Like he'd erased you and your mom from his memory and expected me to do the same. You can't imagine how bitter he was after that first stroke. Even after he recovered, he complained that things felt different. It killed him that he was no longer the best. Even though he continued to play the top halls, he said it was only a matter of time before someone younger was offered this or that solo, the performance in Vienna or New York. I told him that would happen anyway, everyone ages, but you know how he was.

'I looked for you online at CU-Boulder – Hiro knew you'd gone there, from the court – and found your college running-group photo and some race times in the newspaper. There weren't many other Akitanis in the area.'

I stand, go to the window. A group of three nurses in hydrangea-blue scrubs gets into an old hatchback. They're all smiling. 'There was only one other Japanese person on the whole campus.'

'I realised you'd changed your first name. And there was your wedding announcement. Silvestri. It was easy to find you. A website sold me your address for a few dollars. I didn't dare tell him, of course. I was tempted to get in touch. I even went so far as to call a travel agency about tickets to Colorado, but I would always get scared and tell myself the idea was stupid. But after the second stroke, which was more serious, he developed a soft side. He would hold my hand, which he'd always refused to do. He asked me to find you and I showed him the stuff I found online. He never said a word about it, just looked and looked. He looked at those pictures every day when I was out running errands – I checked his search history.'

I feel numb. Everything she's saying makes sense on one level, but I can't incorporate it into the story of what I thought was my life.

'Was it worth it?' I ask.

'No,' she says. 'I should have left. I could have had a life.'

'This is my third week,' Kanako says. 'With the exception of emergencies, she'll be my first patient to … pass away.'

Kanako's face is so sincere, I feel like she can accept anything. There's a tenderness to her, but underneath there's a toughness, too. I tell her about Danny's wishes and her mouth drops. 'You'd never do such a thing. It's unethical.'

'Some people think forcing a person to live is unethical,' I say.

She clutches a patient's chart to her chest. 'That is not what we *do*,' she says. 'We are nurses.'

I leave her and walk outside, through the parking lot to the shore, where tiny waves lap against concrete blocks set there to maintain the coastline. I'm disappointed in Kanako. She doesn't understand how complicated her profession is yet. A low-tide beach spreads out in front of the blocks. I hop onto the sand and pass a gull lying in a bed of emerald seaweed. One eye is open, fixing me with an orange iris.

The sand is wet, but I sit anyway. Cold dampness seeps through my shorts and that seems right: my life is uncomfortable and messy.

As I reach for my phone, it rings. Sal.

'I miss you,' I answer. 'I haven't had reception in forever.'

'Hey. The typhoon was that bad? The weather channel said it weakened before it hit land.'

That had been the weak version of the storm? 'We were stuck in a chicken shed for two days.' I push the thoughts of what happened in the shed away. I tell him about Danny. 'She had stage four cancer and I had no idea.'

'I'm guessing you've had other things on your mind.' His voice sounds odd. Emotional.

'She's got no options. She was planning to do this pilgrimage alone, hopped up on pain pills so she could hike, then OD when she couldn't go any further. Now that she's stuck in a hospital she wants me to help her.'

'Are you going to?'

'It'll be months of suffering for her if not.'

Sal doesn't say anything for a while. 'Nonna Emilia was like that. We're pretty sure she willed herself into that coma at the end.'

It's a relief to hear the sympathy in his voice, the lack of judgement. 'I'm so tired. I want to be there with you. I want to watch *The Office* reruns and make popcorn on the stove and fly kites with Lily on Frenchman's Hill and sleep in a real bed.' And because I crave his warmth, I add, 'Work on making Silvestri number four.'

He laughs this off. 'Hey, this isn't the best time to ask about this, but … I got curious about your dad, so I Googled him.' His voice is controlled, quiet, too even, like a doctor delivering bad news. 'You didn't tell me he was famous. Like, *famous* famous.'

I stare at the dead bird. I can't unlock my eyes from it. 'When he was younger, he was … well-known.'

'He had a state-sponsored funeral at the capitol?' I can hear the clacking of keys: he's on the computer. 'He was a Japanese National Treasure?'

The gull's wings are white, silky, like a dove's. Where did it come from? How far did it fly before giving up?

'And there's something else.' His pause is a pit with no bottom. I fall and fall while I wait for what's coming. 'Did you have a sister? Someone named … Chizuru?'

12

I PACE between the window and the door: four steps there, four steps back. 'He read some articles about my father online. It's not like they're hard to find. Shinobu did pretty much the same thing. Did you know I have a fan club? I hate the Internet. When he asked about Chizuru, I panicked. I hung up and turned my phone off. I'm afraid to turn it back on.'

Danny speaks slowly. 'Why not just tell him?'

I miss Lily. Our house. Dry air. I want to take back everything, rewind to the day that box arrived and hurl it unopened into the back of a garbage truck along with my birth control pills. 'I can make something up. I can tell him I had a sister that I was too embarrassed to talk about.'

'The universe is handing you an opportunity to tell the truth.'

My legs are rubbery, but I don't want to sit. 'What if he can't take it? Who'd want a murderer for a wife?'

'You were a child.'

'What if he leaves? Takes Lily?'

'The worst-case scenario.'

'She's my *daughter*.' I imagine Sal at his computer, reading online accounts of what Chizuru is rumoured to have done, his desk covered with stacks of jigsaw mock-ups or receipts from calculating our year-to-date gas mileage. 'He'll never get over this.'

'These things eat at you. You know they do,' Danny whispers. 'That's why you came here.' Her cheekbones have begun to show, like the sprouting of small wings. I sit on the edge of her bed and cry. My life is disintegrating. It's not fair – I put so much work into creating it.

She coughs twice, shallowly, and winces. 'I'm ready now.'

'What?'

'Have you forgiven me?'

Another shitty word. Why are people so obsessed with forgiveness? Closure and forgiveness, closure and forgiveness. Maybe it's a Western thing. I've been hearing these words from therapists, on TV, in songs, since coming to the United States. If you've been wronged but haven't forgiven, you're only hurting yourself. Forgiveness is a choice, goes the wisdom. It's not easy; it takes work. This is a country that believes in hard work. Not forgiving means you are lazy.

I'm a fan of unforgiveness. Choosing not to forgive is a fine choice for some of us. Unforgiveness is its own power. To resist the forgiveness bullies is to be strong.

'You tell me you had an affair with my father, spent your life obsessed with him, abandoned me for him. You planned to keep it a secret forever. My mom might still be here …' I wonder what my current life would be like with my mom in it. She'd have been sixty-five. Maybe she'd live near us; I could see her in Boulder or Fort Collins, maybe even the artsy side of Colorado Springs. No doubt she'd have kept her hair long, and it would've hung down her back like a grand cape, opalescent and white. She'd encourage Lily to question authority, especially her parents', which would delight Lily and frustrate me. Even though I know, in theory, that my mom's death led me to Sal, and therefore Lily, for a moment I let myself believe I can have it all. Keep my family and block out Danny. Danny, the traitor who's looking at me with such tired eyes. Eyes that look too tired to hold their sadness much longer.

I'm a hypocrite. My whole life is based on forgiveness and second chances.

Early in our marriage, I screwed up. It was a brief thing, two afternoons in a backseat, and an overpriced Sri Lankan lunch buffet. This was not long after Lily was born and I was back to work from maternity leave and feeling like I'd been strapped to a rocket with no way off. He was a medical resident – just a kid. Tilted green eyes and sideburns. We didn't even have sex. It was cute for a week, something even more unreal than motherhood, and I'd already lost interest when Sal found a note in my purse – MISSING YOU'RE GUMDROP LIPS.

After I'd confessed, Sal said, 'Not even a real doctor?'

'Is that supposed to be a joke?'

He just looked at me like I was a stranger.

'I'm all over the place,' I told him as I nursed Lily. 'I wanted to be absurd. Being a mother is absurd.'

We saw a couples counsellor for two months. I was good at therapy; I said the right things. I recommitted myself to Sal, and he let me. The term 'postpartum depression' was mentioned. Hormones were discussed in detail. The fact that I couldn't run as I normally did, and how running was what made me feel like *me*. The whole thing was so out of character – even I agreed that this was so – that, bewildered, Sal let it go. We haven't spoken of it for years, and on the rare occasions I'm reminded of that time, it's like it happened to a different person. But now I wonder if Sal's forgotten my breach of trust as easily, as eagerly, as I have. What he would think about the birth control pills hidden in the tampon box. Cold regret pools in my gut.

Danny says, 'When a dead lady asks for mercy, you ought to give it. It's only polite. I'd change what happened if I could. It's too late, but my regret ought to count for something.'

'It does,' I say. And I believe it.

Kanako knocks, enters the room. 'How are you doing?' she asks Danny.

'All better,' Danny replies with a sly smile. 'Ready to check out.'

She begins to object but Danny interrupts her. 'You can't keep me. I'm ready to go.' She looks to me. 'Shall we?'

'I don't want anything to do with it,' Kanako says when we check out. Danny's still in a hospital wheelchair.

'Can we borrow the chair?' I ask.

She looks at me, looks at Danny. 'Maybe this is not the profession for me.' She kisses Danny's cheek and bows to me before rushing back through the swinging doors.

I push Danny around the back of the building and along a path that leads to a small hill dotted with saplings. There's a picnic table in the clearing. One of the other nurses told us that she liked to eat lunch out here sometimes, and that the trees were planted in honour of patients who'd passed away.

The light is warm. It illuminates sweetly and fully, as if from a sun that would never allow itself to burn you. Light like honey.

And you can see the ocean. The water's blazing, so turquoise it appears lit from the bottom.

Lily will be seeing the ocean for the first time on this trip to California. I wonder what she's doing right now. What would she think of what *I'm* doing? She's no longer the child who accepts what her mom does unconditionally. She asked me last month why I didn't do a 'real sport' instead of running. The only one who can comfort me is Sal. It's hard to believe that I'm here, doing this, and not at home with him. Explaining myself, explaining Chizuru. I can't handle not knowing what he's thinking.

'Who made it a rule that there should be dignity in dying?' Danny says. 'It's the least dignified thing a person can do.' She holds out her hand. In her palm are a syringe and three vials. Morphine. 'Pill me first. Then do the injections.'

How does anyone decide what's right or wrong when there are so many places in between? Duty is no judge; duty tugs from both sides. No god speaks to me. All I have is my own brand of imperfect morality, like anyone else. I open the canister.

Danny is weak and the pills are difficult for her to swallow. I have to massage her throat to get the last few down. I give her a sip of water through a straw and push the first needle into a vein in her arm.

The cicadas pulse. One bird calls and another responds. Danny closes her eyes. 'I rehearsed some wonderful last words and now they're gone. Oh well.' She sighs deeply. 'Did he ever tell you about the fairies dancing on his chest?'

'He did.' I inject the second vial into her other arm. The pills will take a few minutes to hit her bloodstream and when they do the morphine will be there, waiting. She mumbles a string of unintelligible words in Japanese and English. I feel compassion for her, for our shared history, and then it passes. Her hair is greasy. Looking at her is like looking at my mom's ashes in an urn. There is already something operating outside of us, occupying the space between experience and memory.

The wind sizzles through the trees. 'Danny?' I ask. Two may be enough. Too much and she could have a seizure.

I watch her for – minutes? Hours? Her skin is dusky. Dark moons hang beneath her closed eyes. I pick up her hand; her fingertips are cool. The short, square nails sit in bluish beds. I watch and wait. The sun is low enough now that we're in shadow. The cicadas stop their hum. I press two fingers to Danny's wrist. She's gone.

People die at St Mary's every day. They die everywhere. This has never bothered me. When someone dies in a hospital, there's always someone else, alive, who needs you. Life sweeps in and fills the gap. But out here, there's nothing. Just the trees being trees, birds flitting around, plants flourishing. Flowers bouncing on thin stems in the breeze, ambivalent to our presence.

I roll Danny back toward the hospital. The weight of a dead person is different from the weight of one who's alive. Not any lighter or heavier, but less dense.

'She slipped off to sleep while we were taking a walk,' I tell the nurse at the front desk. 'It was peaceful.'

I find Kanako at the nurses' station with a few other women. She can see the truth on my face. 'Thank you for all you've done, Kanako,' I tell her. 'All the extras – Danny's laundry, the gifts. Your friendship.'

'*Osettai*,' she says. She turns away and begins to stack a cart with food trays. She's crying.

'It's best this way,' I say.

She excuses herself from the other nurses. In a low voice, she tells me, 'My mother is gone. It happened eight months ago, ovarian cancer. Daniela was a lot like her. Feisty. When I'm home, it's only my father and me. My good friends have all moved to Osaka or Tokyo. My patients cannot be strangers to me. I have to care about them. I don't mind if it makes my job harder.'

She agrees to take Danny's remains to the Temple of Cut Cloth. In Danny's room, I paw through the bag of her things. Inside the silk bag of stones and shells, I find the creased ten-thousand-yen note. I leave it in the bag.

'Daniela slept with this bag under her pillow,' Kanako said. 'She can take them with her in cremation. Last week, a grandpa brought his entire comic book collection to the other side of the Milky Way.'

It takes me a second to connect that Japanese phrase – literally, 'the heavenly river' – with the white band of stars visible on a clear night.

'I can't remember. Is the Milky Way the river in the Obon legend?' I ask.

Kanako shakes her head. 'That's the Sanzu, the River of Three Crossings. But you make an interesting point. We Japanese have a lot of water in our sky, don't we?'

When we visited Ojīsan in Ehime Prefecture, my mother loved to take side trips to Shimantogawa, the only undammed river in Japan. It was ferocious and alive, she said. Even the bridges built over it were built to sink: they had no parapets so they wouldn't get washed away when the water rose. The Shimanto was beset by gorges and there were sections you could cross on old vine bridges. The darkness at night was so total, you could see the Milky Way mirrored in the river. The stars were bright as lanterns on the water.

At 7:25 the next morning, a single-car train chugs to a stop in front of me. I take a green upholstered seat as the rhythmic clack of wheels on rails begins, and ratchet open my window. The sun is low in the sky. A patchwork of rice paddies blankets the countryside. Wooden buildings stand in the distance, and beyond that, mountains. Out here, nothing happens quickly. The view has probably looked like this for a hundred years. Rice grows, and every year during the same week, the frogs arrive, filling the humid air with their morning song, swelling and diminishing like a symphony.

I have not found the courage to turn my phone on. If I do, I can call the airline and arrange for a flight home. But Sal will have left messages, wondering why I hung up at such a crucial moment. Or worse. Maybe he's already put the pieces together. A real-life jigsaw. It's possible he's already sprung into action, the way, when a bulb burns out, he's back with a replacement before the original one has cooled off.

What if he moves himself and Lily into Tuscany Terrace and I return home to a stranger on my own front step, the living room full of someone else's furniture, a cement slab over the garden? I love our house: its hardy brick, the pine banister Sal carved, the freak peach tree that shouldn't have lived through all these winters, yet still produces a bushel of fruit each summer.

The train clicks onward toward the lights of Tokushima. The sun hangs above the mountains, casting orange light over the rice fields. I finger the ribbon around my neck. The house key is heavy against my breastbone. I will go to Shinobu's house,

use his computer and book a flight home. I'll stop by the old house on my way to the airport. Once I'm back in Boulder, I'll throw out my pills for real. Once I'm back, everything will be fine. I know it will. It has to be.

I turn automatically to a companion for consolation, distraction, whatever; it takes a moment to register Danny's absence. A cold emptiness surrounds my heart. I can't ask her advice. I can't call or e-mail. Danny's death is a real, permanent event. It has left a dark cave in me. She was the connection to the old life. She held a piece of the memory. Now that she's gone, I have to hold it all.

13

SHINOBU GREETS ME at the station. Out of his trail clothes, he's a different person. Instead of the T-shirted free spirit, before me stands a preppy young man in khaki pants and a black polo shirt a size too big. He's gotten a haircut, which I compliment.

'Too short,' he says, running a finger along the top. 'If I fail, I'll shave them all.'

'The exam! How'd it go?'

He turns up the street. 'Like all the others. The truth will reveal very soon. Since many less people take the old exam this year, we can learn the result quickly. Those who fail can meet the law schooling deadline.'

'Your parents must be anxious.'

'All day, my mother vacuums. My father looks at me in a strict way if I am too relaxed. If he is tense, I must be tense, too.'

It's dark, but I'm perspiring anyway. City heat feels different than country heat. Warmth clings more in the city. The streets of this place are at once familiar and alien. All the elements of my childhood years are here, but arranged differently, a change I can't put my finger on, like when a friend takes off a few pounds. The neighbourhood has lost weight.

Futons loll over railings like tongues. Concrete apartment cubes rise between wooden houses; in some cases it seems the new building is the only thing keeping the old one from falling over. Such a variety of doors: half doors cut into wood that only children and the permanently stooped can use comfortably. Sliding doors. Metal doors that yawn and slam. And every so often, a panelled door out of Bedford, Ohio, like the one we stand before now. Shinobu's house is two storeys, in a Western style, with a square of grass out front protected by wrought iron. He pushes open the gate and says, 'Honey, I'm home.'

The door is painted red – 'Mother painted to attract good fortune' – and instead of pushing it open or using a key, Shinobu rings the bell. A familiar melody is audible through the door: Rimsky-Korsakov's 'Flight of the Bumblebee'. Hiro played it while walking barefoot around the house Sunday mornings, that rare window during the week when he didn't have anywhere to be. My mom complained the tune gave her a headache. 'All that movement,' she said. 'I like it better when the notes stick around.' But I adored it. I'd jump around like an out-of-control aerobics teacher, relieved to dance in front of my father the way I did when my mom played her tapes. Seventy-four seconds. Seventy-two. The world record was sixty-seven. One day he clocked in at sixty-six. After that, he never played it again, no matter how many times I asked.

'This is for show,' Shinobu says, pointing to a gold knocker in the shape of a lion. Something crunches under my right foot; a handful of pink beans are scattered on the step.

The door opens to reveal a regal woman in purple lipstick. Mrs Oeda is half the size of her son but identical in her features. The familiar cowlick at her temple makes me laugh out loud.

'Welcome!' she cries, and beckons us into the cool, dim entrance hall. The house smells of lilies, though no flowers are visible. Mrs Oeda's gaze falls onto my filthy backpack. 'Just a second, let me find a place for your … luggage.' She slippers around the corner and emerges a second later with a fluffy towel. I set my pack on it, careful to avoid letting even a strap touch the glossy wooden floor.

'Mr Oeda is out golfing,' she says, and uses her fingertip to nudge my pack away from the burgundy-papered wall. In a confidential tone, she says, 'It is always a pleasure to have my house and guests to myself.'

In English, Shinobu says, 'Ever since my father retired, Mother has been going crazy.'

Mrs Oeda asks him to repeat himself. She mouths the words after him – *ever since … Mother's been going crazy* – and shakes her head. 'I – study – English,' she says to me. 'But, I am poor.' She switches back to her elegant Japanese: 'My firstborn refuses to practise with me.'

I translate what Shinobu said, ignoring his dirty look.

'It's true,' Mrs Oeda says, leading me through the dining room. A huge mahogany table occupies the space. 'I'm used to being home all day. I stay busy. But he needs a hobby. Unfortunately, his golf skills are awful.'

Mrs Oeda slides open a door and we step into the next room. The wood flooring gives way to the smooth weave of tatami. The room is typical, small and spare, little more than a people-container. Unenthusiastic yellow light shines from an overhead bulb. An ornate pink vase filled with dandelions has been placed in the centre of a low, square table.

I inhale the baked-grass scent of the tatami and look around for a computer. 'I love that smell. It's so homey.'

'I'm sorry the room is so plain,' Mrs Oeda says. 'Please, make it your home for as long as you like.' She slides the vase over a few inches and squares her shoulders. 'I'm off to the market. Can you eat pork? Shrimp?'

'Please, there's no need to cook. I can just grab an *onigiri* from the convenience store,' I say.

'Nonsense. You're a pilgrim and you took care of Shin-kun on the trail. I'll whip up something simple. Son, take care of your guest.'

After she leaves, Shinobu says, 'In the past, she always follows my father. Because it is her duty. But these days, things are changing. She wants more freedom. I am her son and she always told me, "Study hard, become a great lawyer." Now, I think she doesn't care what I'm doing.'

'Isn't that a good thing?' I ask. 'You said you might not want to be a lawyer anyway.'

'She is not cheering me any more. She knows my test result will arrive anytime and she says nothing.'

'How will the news come?'

'The results arrive in registered mail.' He opens a drawer and removes a manila folder. Inside are five identical letters, government seals at the top. The only difference is the year stamped in the top left-hand corner. The first and second look as if they've been handled a lot; the paper is wrinkled and corners are creased. The top three are crisp, like they went directly from their original envelope to the folder.

'This year, she even forgets to throw beans,' Shinobu says. 'My father threw.'

'Those beans out front?' I ask.

'Yes, for luck. But my father doesn't know anything, so he threw the wrong type and in the wrong month. Soybeans are the lucky ones.'

Though Setsubun shows up on calendars, it's more superstition than holiday. It has something to do with the changing of the seasons. The idea is to ward off bad luck by throwing soybeans from your stoop while shouting, 'Demons out, good fortune in!' My parents never bothered with it, but at school I pretended I'd eaten roasted soybeans for breakfast just like everyone else. One year I stopped at a convenience store before school and bought a bag so I could eat them in front of my classmates.

'Is there a computer I can use? I need to book a flight.'

Shinobu looks alarmed. 'Why?'

'Yesterday, Sal asked me about Chizuru. He knows.'

'Oh my god!'

'Not everything. At least, I don't think. I have to go home and explain it to him properly. It's not something I can do over the phone.'

Shinobu considers this. He leaves the room and returns with a laptop. 'It might be a little difficult to find a flight during Obon week.'

Of course, in Japanese 'a little difficult' is code for 'damn near impossible'. Airfares are ridiculous. Obon is the busiest travel week of the year, and there are few seats available in or out of Osaka. One of the cheaper itineraries to Colorado that pops up will take over seventy hours with five stops – Osaka to Tokyo to Shanghai to Paris to New York to Denver. And will run me ... $3,940. Plus a change fee of $150.

I start to laugh, though nothing is funny. I'm laughing because I need physical release and crying is not an option; if I start to cry, it's over. I'll come apart.

I have to get home. If Sal is going to find everything out, it's better if I tell him. But – maybe he won't find out. I'm still laughing. Maybe I'm overthinking it. No, that's not possible because I can't think. I can't think at all. Before calling Sal, before I do anything, I *need* to run.

I try to focus on the motion. The world is closing in its usual style – all at once. The blisters on both my feet scream, but the pain is nothing compared with what's going on in my head. Count your steps. One thousand five hundred and thirty-three. 1-5-3-3. I go around the block again, running now, forcing myself to keep count. One thousand four hundred and seventy-one. 1-4-7-1. I play with the numbers: fifteen, thirty-three, fourteen seventy-one. Sal found Chizuru. One plus five plus three plus three. Twelve. It is the twelfth of August. Run. Run. Run.

The memory of the murder came back to me fully about eight months after I arrived at Kawano. I went into a closet to pick up cleaning supplies and was overwhelmed by a familiar smell. KLEEN. The harsh imitation-floral odour made it hard to breathe. Something familiar swirled in my stomach. The body remembers – Dr K had repeated this. *Your mind will close the door to memory and push the universe in front of it. But the body remembers. Until you drag away the blockade and open that door, you will be less than whole.*

I'll always be less than whole, I responded. It doesn't matter what I do – I'll always be *hafu*.

My throat closed. I gagged, fell to my knees. Between gasps and hacks came a feeling of shaking loose, each retch an exertion and a relief, a primal drive, like swimming to the surface during a lightning storm: what lay above might kill me, but if I stayed under, I stood no chance at all.

The tacks on my chair – that had happened in the morning, the period before lunch. When the bell rang, I was still in the bathroom. I couldn't sit without crying. It wasn't just the little punctures in my skin; they would heal. But the burn of embarrassment would return full force each time I thought of that moment. *Why did you do this?* I asked aloud. The words hit the concrete wall and died and I repeated them until I heard their echo, until the sound turned in on itself and it seemed I wasn't the one speaking at all; the walls were asking me.

Seven of the tacks had poked through my wool skirt and pierced my skin. The spots on my green underwear had turned brown, like the freckles across my nose. I looked at my face in the mirror, and craned to see my gross *mochi*-cake backside. I had never felt so humiliated.

But I wouldn't let it show. I couldn't. I would get the sandwich from my desk in Miss Danny's room and hold my head up high the way my mother had instructed. 'Never let them see you cry,' she always said. 'Never give them the satisfaction.'

The bell rang. I smoothed my skirt, the wool of which was thick enough to hide the holes the tacks had made. I grinned at my reflection. I couldn't do anything about the gossip that had spread through school already about Tomoya's prank, but I could control what people saw when they looked at me. Chin up, I strode to the bathroom door and pushed it open.

Miss Danny patrolled the first-floor bathrooms during cleaning period, so I knew I could continue rehearsing my confidence in the privacy of her empty classroom. I stepped in, feeling the strength gathering within me. But the room was not empty.

Tomoya stood near my desk at the front of the room, mop in hand, picking his nose. The smell of KLEEN was strong. His eyes lit up like those of a hunter who's just seen a twelve-point buck stride into a clearing.

'You waddled in just in time to do the floor. It's your fault I have to do it anyway.' He spat onto my desk and held the mop toward me.

Startled out of my thoughts, I could say nothing. I kept moving, my instinct to run from Tomoya battling my plan to retrieve my lunch.

He gestured with the mop. 'Didn't any fat drain out after you sat on those tacks? We thought your ass cheeks might pop like balloons!'

I had reached my desk, which stood across from Miss Danny's. Tomoya leaned his weight on the top so I could not open it. He pushed the mop at me. The handle hit my shoulder and clattered to the floor. 'What a cow,' he said, and clutched the roll of fat at my waist. 'I bet you give milk like one.' He raised his fingers to my nipple and pinched. I cried out in surprise and pain. The pain wasn't limited to my breast, however. That subsided right away. There was a far greater ache in my chest; it felt like a twisting blade. The black organ.

I jerked away, my hip slamming into Miss Danny's desk. My eyes fell on a letter opener gleaming in its blue velvet bed. My hand travelled toward it. I perceived every detail: the way the top of the opener curled like the head of a fern, the pearl that dangled beneath it. The opener's other end was flat and came to a sharp point. As I raised it I caught sight of my distorted reflection in the narrow blade.

I stuck the point into Tomoya's neck. It went in deep, up to the fern. He made a pathetic sound and fell to his knees. I pulled the letter opener out and blood shot from the hole. I wanted to fill him with holes: one, two, three-four-five. Like the children's chant: *Ichi, ni, san-shi-go*. Go, I thought. Go away. But I stood frozen at the sight of his blood. It seemed impossibly red, like the glowing pit where my heart had been.

Tomoya lay on the floor. His eyes were still open. Blood spurted from the hole for a while and then settled into a smooth, rushing stream that formed a lake on the floor. When the edge of the lake touched my shoes, I ran.

A horn blares to my right. Proximity, the colour of the car – none of it registers. Is there sidewalk beneath my feet? Yes. Hot. The earth is full of energy, pushing at my feet, urging me to move. I'm dripping in sweat. My lungs ache. This is better.

I take in my surroundings. I've made it to the old neighbourhood. There's Ame-Ame, the candy shop. My childhood sanctuary. I go inside.

Converted from a family home, the shop has no aisles, just three walls hung floor-to-ceiling with wicker baskets. Plastic buckets of one-yen treats line the dusty floor's perimeter. The containers are brimming; you get the feeling that if you don't grab a piece or two from each, they might overflow. In the middle of the floor, hunks of home-made chocolate wrapped in plastic are stacked into a haphazard mountain taller than I am. The pieces range from bite-sized nuggets to slabs big enough to crack a skull, if you swung hard enough. Sawdust powders the creaky floorboards, which, I can't help but think, have been worn smooth by the feet of children like Tomoya and me. I pick up a small basket from the stack near the entrance. The man behind the wooden front counter greets me.

It's Mr Nigata, the same man who ran the place when I was a kid. He looks, as he did then, a little too rugged to own a candy shop.

'Nigata-san?'

He looks up sharply, the way he always did, but there is softness around his eyes. He used to set the scale a little low, making a show of adjusting it so you would know he was giving you special treatment. The adjustment was probably only equivalent to a few gumdrops, but it made you feel good, like you were in on something.

'I've been called worse.'

Of course it's not the same man. This is Mr Nigata's son. I remember him from Motomachi Elementary. He's a year or two older than me.

'Grew up here, didn't you?' he says, leaning on the counter so it groans.

'Yes. I killed that boy. Tomoya Yu. Stabbed him in our classroom. He wanted me to mop the floor and when I said no he grabbed my breast. Then I stabbed him in the neck.' I've never said it out loud before. I feel wild and joyous.

Nigata stares. He lets out a breath and grins. 'You had me goin' for a second. But I said to myself, she doesn't look anything like that girl. You're that singer, right?' He gives the name of a girl the year above me whose father was Canadian. 'I had a crush on you in fifth grade.'

'No – I am that girl! I stabbed him with a letter opener with a fiddlehead on the end. A Morimoto.' I grab the plastic handle of a samurai sword lollipop and brandish it at him.

He holds up two meaty palms in mock self-defence. 'Okay, okay! Should I be scared? You don't *look* dangerous.'

The phone rings and he answers it, immediately raising his voice. 'We agreed on the price of those last month! I don't care what oil costs per barrel. You shoulda shipped them when I put in the order. I'm not charging a kid two hundred yen for a gummy panda.'

I fill my basket with the candies I loved as a kid: sesame sticks, caramel frogs, tubes of sugar decorated with astrological signs. I choose tiger for me and dragon for Lily. I don't know Sal's sign in the Chinese zodiac and have to scour the tiny print along the tube. Nineteen seventy-three: ox. Steady and solid, plodding and methodical. More accurate than his other sign, dreamy and creative Pisces, like my mom, though he once protested he was more Piscean than I gave him credit for.

Nigata slams down the phone. 'You still in the murdering business? I've got a distributor with a lesson to learn.'

He doesn't believe me. He can't shake the notion that I am a normal person standing in his candy shop holding a basket of caramel frogs. Look how sane I am! How Canadian. The image of Tomoya on the floor, blood pouring from his neck, overpowers my thoughts. My discomfort must show because Nigata, who's lost his smile, tries to change the subject.

'You here visiting family?'

'I came for my father's funeral.' I reach into the nearest basket and study the wrapper of a gumball. From the looks of the packaging, the gumball is supposed to last through all four seasons.

A funny look comes over Nigata's face. 'Akitani, right? I remember. Damn – you really are that girl. Chizuru.'

I look up at the sound of my name.

'Sorry, but it's like you're a different person, ya know? It's messing with my head. I've seen a lot of old classmates since taking over the shop. You'd be amazed how many look exactly the same, how many folks never left town.' He rests his hands on top of his head. 'I bet it wasn't easy coming back. People can change, ya know; I'm not a man who thinks they can't.' He laughs loudly. 'I have to say, with all due respect and whatnot, your old man stayed an oddball till the end.'

'You knew him?'

'Nah. Hardly came to town and then all he ever did was play his violin or keep up that house. You'd see him sweeping the sidewalk out front like a grandmother. Or hear him till all hours, sawing away at that hyper song. Didn't say hello or even go out for groceries. Shimamoto owns the market down the block—'

'What song? "Flight of the Bumblebee"?'

'Weird guy. But anyway, what do I know.' He drums his fingers on the warped wood. 'I'm just a simple guy who runs a candy store. If you're that girl, his daughter, you ought to know better than me.' He takes two backward steps. 'Have you been pulling my leg?'

'I killed him,' I say, and lift my basket. 'I promise.'

'Whatever you say,' he mutters, shaking his head. He zeros the scale – it's the same one from years before – but does not shave off any weight.

'Very good to have seen you again after all these years,' I say, using the formal Japanese goodbye. My mind is already out the door, on the way to the blue house.

I jog past unfamiliar storefronts. The old movie theatre is now a skate shop. Teenage boys in helmets break-dance out front. A woman in a banana-coloured skirt and matching high heels wobbles toward me, the head of a tiny white dog poking from the Louis Vuitton purse slung over her shoulder. She moves out of my way.

Wasn't Tomoya's house down one of these tiny side streets? I knew where he lived because it was necessary to avoid him as much as possible. His house was near Ame-Ame, though, which made it hard. That's right – it was on the shortcut road to the shop from my house. I always took the long way around. Might his parents still live there? Had they had other children after Tomoya's death? Whenever I worry about Lily getting hurt or imagine life suddenly without her, I think of his parents and wonder how they managed. How does a parent survive the death of a child?

Electrical wires reach from poles and rooftops, webbing against the overcast sky like a cracked windowpane. I walk on, nearly stepping in a pile of rotting persimmons. Is it one block farther, or two? I can't shake the sense that this was not the place I knew. This place is so tangible, so unlike memory.

The day the box from Hiro's lawyer arrived, I read a study about sense of direction in one of the psych magazines lying around the hospital. Researchers dropped people in the desert and told them to walk a straight line. The hikers did well until the sun or moon went behind a cloud; then they'd veer off, sometimes at right angles to where they'd been headed. And they didn't believe it when you told them what'd happened. Even faced with a map of their spiralling route, people refused to believe they'd gone off course.

The persimmons smell like strong wine. Inhaling gives me a momentary buzz, and I feel like those people in the desert, walking in circles. It has been cloudy for a long time.

Once, the skinny two-storey house with inlaid blue tiles seemed like a tower, the dark tile reaching to heaven like a Van Gogh night. Now it looks more like the interior of an oversized shower. The grout between the tiny squares has yellowed and in some places turned grey. The place could do with some Mr Bubbles Plus. The chip in the front step has gotten worse. I recognise the way the antenna on top of Mount Bizan rises like a conductor's baton in the distance beyond the roof.

There's a construction horse in front of the house with a sign on it that I can't read. I move it aside and climb the nine stairs to the metal front door, lift the ribbon and key over my head. The lock clunks open.

The scent is musty and familiar. It's the smell of the three of us. Wood oil and rosin. Powdered laundry soap. Earl Grey.

I remove my shoes in the *genkan* without thinking about it. We don't have a no-shoes policy at home in Colorado; it's been years since I frequented a place that did. But this home and its habits have been frozen in time.

The living room walls are covered floor-to-ceiling with newspaper clippings. I examine a few. They're all about him. Every concert, every review, every article about his mysterious life. Some are cut neatly, but most are ripped, tacked haphazardly, sometimes on top of one another. Danny said that his demise was intolerable to him. Unacceptable. When you're in a room like this, it's impossible to forget your importance.

In the next room, five paper cranes made out of fifty- and hundred-yen bills perch in the tokonoma alcove. My metal box of folding paper is on the tatami floor.

He's left the house exactly the same.

In the kitchen, two boxes of Golden Curry sit unopened on the shelf. My mom made that meal all the time. I can picture her popping the hefty rectangular chunks from their plastic tray and dropping them into the copper pot that lived – still lives

– on the stovetop because it was too big to fit in the cabinet. Above the sink hangs a framed picture of Hiro and my mom – him grimacing, her sticking out her tongue. I remove it from the wall and brush a layer of dust from the glass. I can feel the electricity between them even now. I'll take the photo home for Lily. She hasn't seen any shots of her grandparents together.

In my parents' old room, the low table is covered with photo albums. Many are familiar; I've looked through them, demanding explanations about events and people from before I was born. It was usually my mom who filled me in. But my father had one story that I always liked to hear from him.

Hiro had moved to New York City to attend Juilliard. My mom was living in a crumbling SoHo loft with five other people, less than a year out of Texas and high school life and flat broke, but her charm connected her with the city's hip crowd and she had shows in garages and walk-ups and it was at one of these shows in an abandoned iron manufacturing warehouse that the child prodigy, just eighteen and still troubled by a layer of baby fat, first laid eyes on Elena Brown.

Their early courtship was shaky; she was a year older and many men – full-grown men, men of means, with cars and homes and position – took her out. But, as with his health trouble, this hurdle only made Hiro more determined to succeed. He studied Elena the way he studied the performances of concertos by virtuosos. He attended every show she had – and they were becoming more numerous, one even in a real gallery on Bleecker Street – and, once by her side, stayed until she tired of him. Then he'd stay up half the night to make up for the practice he had missed. Juilliard wasn't hard, Hiro said; it was just a lot of work.

Maybe he'd been famous in Japan, maybe he'd played with Shinji Okamoto as a first-year elementary student, but at

Juilliard child prodigies were the norm, not the exception. All the better for Hiro. The competition was like compost to a rose-bush. He reached for the world and the world reached back. Elena was part of that world.

If only I could have witnessed the dynamic of their marriage as an adult. They argued plenty, but my mom was capable of such tenderness it must have neutralised their differences. And though he didn't show it, he must have needed that tenderness.

I go to my old room. A futon's folded neatly in the open closet along with a few tubs of clothing. There's my bookcase, full of my beloved chapter books – books I can no longer read. I pull out one with a fox on the cover. A clump of lint dangles from the spine like a scarf.

I remember this story. It's about a fox who is very short, which makes him an outcast, but his stature is perfect for spying on people, and he solves all kinds of crimes in the neighbour-hood by fitting into small spaces. There's only one human who believes him, though, a girl named … ah, what was her name? I sit on the tatami and flip through the book. I can read these hiragana characters, the syllabic ones. Su – there it is. Her name is Suzume. It means sparrow. Suzume had extremely long hair and when she ran she had to be careful not to trip on it. I can still picture her school, the block where she had her adventures with Spy-fox, in my imagination. It's a block like this one, but rearranged. It lives on in my head after all these years.

On top of the bookcase are a few dust-coated candy wrap-pers – from Ame-Ame, I'm sure – including one from the same caramel frog I just bought. A crumpled, half-complete kanji worksheet where I'd written the same ten-stroke character ten times. I have no idea how to read it or what it means. I pick up a pen and fill in one of the empty blanks. The result looks awkward and lopsided next to the neat, perfect renditions before it.

I wipe sweat from my forehead. This is who I am. Neat. Messy. Imperfect. Someone willing to practise. I'm ready for whatever comes.

I take out my phone and call Sal.

'I've been up all night,' he answers. 'What took so long?'

I walk to my river window, beyond which the Yoshinogawa twists and spills into the sand-edged sea. The water seems to rush in some spots and pause in others. This river can shoot you down from the mountains into the open sea. My mom told me that Native Americans didn't name entire rivers as bodies of water; they referred to specific places along the river – Little Bend or Slow-Moving Through Trees. The concept of the water as one entity didn't serve them. I am that river. And like that river, instead of defining who Rio is, I can only name certain parts of myself: Mom. Nurse. And the part left unshared.

'Hello? What's going on?'

It takes a few seconds for the words to come. 'Sal, I'm sorry.'

'Sorry for what? Rio?'

'I'm not sure of anything any more. Who I am. Who I should be.'

'You're scaring me, babe. What are you talking about?'

Danny's gone, I want to say. The last one who knew my story. I want you to know me, now. 'Sal, the girl you asked about was me. Is me. I am Chizuru.'

14

I STARE AT THE RIVER until it becomes a blur. I listen to Sal breathing. His breath becomes the river's breath.

Finally he says, 'The girl who killed her classmate is you.'

'Yes.'

'You're fucking with me.'

'I'm not.'

'You're the one in the story.'

'I didn't tell you because—'

'Shut up. Just shut up for a second.'

The river seems to stop flowing. His voice comes from a distance. Deadened. 'You never told me.'

'I wanted a normal life. There was no point in making … in making you or Lily deal with it. It's over. I'm past it.'

'How can you say that? You're past *killing* a kid? That's horrifying.'

'I mean that it doesn't … it isn't – wasn't – who I am.' Is this true? It feels true. Or it feels like what I want to be true. 'I lost everyone at once. My mom committed suicide, and my father – he could have taken me home. But he saved face. He left me. I couldn't risk that with you.'

'So that's why you didn't have a relationship with your dad. And that's why you never wanted to visit Japan.' Sal talks faster and faster, as if my past is a ball of string he's unravelling. 'Why you didn't want Lily to go to Hasegawa School, or do the cherry blossom thing in Denver. Oh my god. How many conversations did we have where you were just managing your ignorant husband?'

A young couple passes along the sidewalk below, the girl holding a wailing infant. The baby's redness is startling against its mother's white skin. It is crying with every ounce of its energy. I wish I could express myself so easily. 'Wouldn't you have left me if I told you?'

'I have no idea. But it would've been nice to get to decide.' He pauses. 'Wait, she was twelve – you were twelve. Did you even go to high school?'

'In a juvenile detention centre.'

'What about all the stories you told? About being the worst on the volleyball team and sleepovers in your friend's closet?'

'I made them up.'

'So you didn't have two best friends, Tamiko and Eriko, you were inseparable from. And Inez the hula-hooper and Taro the cripple who was mauled by a wild boar don't exist. And you didn't take a class trip to Okinawa and watch a mongoose win a fight with a cobra.'

It's humiliating, hearing my lies repeated back. 'No.'

'Fuck.' His voice is shaking. 'Fuck fuck fuck.'

'Sal? Wait.'

He's gone. The little gremlin taps its toe and blinks at me. I have plenty of battery power. Sal hung up. I call back but it goes straight to voicemail. I leave him a message, and another, pleading him to call me.

I dial Lily's camp, half listen while a squeaky-voiced man struggles to project his authoritative self. He can only call a student out of an activity if it's an emergency. Fine, I tell him. It's an emergency. Just put my daughter on the phone. I endure a Muzak version of Toto's 'Africa' while on hold.

'Hey, Mom, what's up? They called me off the set. I'm key grip today.' Lily's voice puts a knot in my throat. I cover the receiver with my hand and inhale big so I don't cry.

'Mom?'

'Hi, sweetie,' I whisper.

'Are you still in Japan? You sound weird.'

'I – just wanted to tell you that I love you more than anything in the world. No matter what happens, that will always be true.'

'Is something wrong?'

'No, babe. Just wanted to say hi. What's a key grip?'

Someone screams in the background on Lily's end. 'Oookay. So, the cameras are on these dollies, or cranes, or sometimes in a random place like on top of a ladder, and the grips have to work with the lighting people and everyone on the set to make things perfect.'

'Sounds complicated.'

'Yeah, but super fun. Oh, there's two girls from Japan here – like actually from there. The one girl is from Tokyo and has amazing clothes but doesn't talk to anyone. The other one, Hana, is really nice. She's this amazing artist.'

'That's so cool, Lil. Did you tell them you're a quarter Japanese?'

'Nah.'

'Why not?'

'I dunno. I've never actually been to Japan, so I guess I don't feel Japanese or something.'

'You'd love it here. You can do karaoke in a private room, eat sushi for every meal, and the clothes are so cute.'

Another scream, followed by hysterical laughter. Lily cries, 'He did *not* say that!' A second later: 'OMG, get out of here! I'm talking to my mom.' To me she says, 'I have to go in a minute, my group is up next for green screen basic training. They make everything sound all army here.'

The joy in her voice reminds me of Sal talking puzzles. I try to make my voice as cheerful and light as hers is. 'I'm glad you're having a good time. I'll talk to you soon, okay? I love you.'

'Bye, Mommala! Love you.'

I hang up. Bile rises hot in my throat and I am sick on the floor. Forget shoes – vomit on tatami is a sin far worse. The mat will need to be replaced. Yes, the cholic acid will certainly degrade the rush grass fibres. It's already begun eating away at it. Poor mat. You served me well for so many years, never asking anything of me, and this is how I repay you.

What if he takes her? Sal could decide I'm unfit as a parent. I've killed a child the age of my own child. Getting her away from me seems logical. Just because I think nothing will happen doesn't mean nothing will. Hell, maybe I'm not in control of my own mind. I could be imagining this other self, this high-functioning American woman. I've tricked myself.

My head is pounding; I can feel my pulse in my right temple. I close my eyes and press the heels of my palms into them. Anything to stop the sensation of careening, like I'm in the back seat of a car going too fast on a mountain road. I should be driving, I started the engine, but I can't reach the steering wheel.

A vicious pounding is coming from somewhere. I open my eyes. It's the front door. I jump, nerves on fire. Who would be coming here?

The door whines open; I didn't lock it.

'Hey!' I shout. 'Who's there?'

'Police,' a man calls from the front. 'Show yourself.'

What the hell? I come into the living room and there they are: a stocky kid in his twenties, rough canvas vest, blue cap, and a second cop, older and tired-looking, standing beside him. The young one brandishes a red plastic flashlight like a toy sword.

I stand motionless, not daring to breathe. Once while I was driving Lily to school, a police car followed me for miles; I got so anxious I had to pull over. The officer cruised past without a glance at me.

'How did you get in here?' the older cop asks. He turns his head aside and yawns. 'This is private property.'

'This was my father's house. I have a key.' I put the key in the lock, demonstrate turning it. They look confused.

'Hiro Akitani was your father? Right, and I'm Godzilla. You're not even Japanese. Wait, are you? Show me some ID.'

'I don't have my passport with me. It's at the place where I'm staying.'

He yawns again. 'As a foreigner, you must always carry identification. It's the law.' His tone turns gentle. 'I get it. You're one of those obsessed fans, huh? Whadda they call 'em, Hiro waship-ahs?' He laughs at the English joke. 'Never saw the appeal of the guy, myself. First-class weirdo.'

The young guy doffs his hat, revealing a skull so flat I wonder if he was born wrong. With that broad face he's like a tree stump. He speaks again into his radio. 'This is government property. No one is authorised to be here, so you'll need to come with us.'

The seats in the back of the police car have doilies on them. The white paper crunches when I sit on it. I am not handcuffed, but there is a Plexiglas wall between me and the officers.

Fuck. I left my phone at the old house.

We drive past the candy shop. Nigata is outside, swiping his broom at nothing. He glances up as we pass and nods. If that stingy prick called the cops on me, I'll find him later. The black organ strains at the thought. I picture the old wooden shop going up in flames, the candy melting into pools of chocolate ooze, blackening, then finally turning to cinder and ash. That's what nosey folks get, Nigata-san.

'Where are you taking me?' I ask, unable to keep the contempt from my voice.

'Yokohama Women's Detention Centre.'

'What?'

'You are arrested.'

'Arrested? For what?'

He doesn't respond.

The tramway pulls lazy tourists up Bizan. I imagine the cable snapping, sagging, and collapsing with the lazy tourists inside. If I close my eyes and picture it strongly enough, I can make it happen. I focus on the older officer, who is driving. If I stare hard enough, he'll pull over and let me out, apologise profusely for treating me this way. Maybe I can drill my way into his ear canal with my mind. I wait for him to wince and clap his hand to his ear, for the blood to trickle out between his fingers, but nothing happens.

I know now that I have zero telekinetic ability. If I did, this city would be on fire.

For the second time in my life, I am locked in the back of a Japanese police car. I've explained that my current name is Rio Silvestri, that I'm an American citizen, that I had a right to be in that house. How else would I've had a key? But these guys are robots following a script. Logic does not apply. I look down and see my hands balled into fists, the fingernails digging into the soft skin of my palms. It hurts to uncurl them. Four pink moons appear on my palms.

I've avoided trouble for years. Now, days after coming back to this place, it's found me. This is what happens to me in Japan. This is why I was right to stay away. This place wants only to pick at me, to wear me down like a river eroding the stone that contains it.

As the landmarks passing by out the window grow less and less familiar, I realise that I have no sense of how serious my situation actually is. For having grown up in this country and committed a crime in it, I know embarrassingly little about the process that awaits me. I don't know where we're going or how I'll get in touch with Shinobu. Mrs Oeda will think I'm rude if I miss dinner without even calling to offer an excuse. My leg is jittering and I let it. The movement is soothing. I wish my leg could extend into the ground and shake the earth. Wake it up, force it to reckon with me.

I stare at the backs of the idiot officers' heads. They won't beat me this time. A broken bone never truly heals; there's always evidence of the fracture by the way the tissues around it grow and compensate. Sometimes, if you're lucky, the new setup is even stronger than the original. Like Hiro playing violin after his illness. Or that movie about the kid who broke his arm and threw ninety-mile-an-hour fastballs. I will be like that. I'll show them: not all things that snap are weak.

15

UPON ENTERING THE BUILDING, the officers – I've begun to think of them as Stump and Sleepy – are joined by a detective so tall and thin he reminds me of Gumby. He confiscates the key and the only other objects in my pockets: a hair tie, a ball of blue lint, and a card for the Boulder transit system. The intake room smells like peanuts.

A red plastic clock hangs over the doorway. I stare at the numbers. The '5' looks strange, like the manufacturer used a '2' and flipped it around.

'Can I call someone and let them know where I am?' I ask.

'No phone calls for foreigners,' Stump says.

I'm not allowed to wear my regular clothes, but the detention centre doesn't have a uniform, either. I'm led to a bathroom by a female guard. She hands me a red T-shirt with Mickey Mouse on it. Above Mickey's head it says TROUSERS MADE

OF JEAN. The back of the shirt reads TREASURE EVERY MTG FOR IT WILL NEVER RECUR. I relinquish my sweaty running clothes, socks, underwear, and bra. The guard, who's wearing plastic gloves, folds them neatly – even my gross underwear – and puts them in a plastic bag. She hands me grey paper slippers and a pair of grey sweatpants I have to roll three times to keep from tripping over the bottoms.

'But what are you arresting me *for?*' I ask over and over again.

'There is not yet a charge,' she tells me.

She fastens a broad leather belt, like the kind worn by weightlifters, around my waist. A thin rope hangs from it like a leash. She grips the rope in her fist, wraps it around her wrist twice. She avoids my eyes.

'How can I be arrested for nothing?' From the car to the building to the rooms in which I am prepared for holding, each step is more surreal, makes less sense. The paper slippers crinkle. I can't shake the sensation that I'm on a game show and at any moment someone from my regular life will jump out and cry, 'Gotcha!'

I am led down a long row of cells. Two women sit chatting on the floor of one. They stop talking as the guard opens the door, unclips the belt, and guides me in. One of my slippers has ripped mostly off.

Beverly is from Estonia. She's skinny and pockmarked and speaks English like it's full of hyphens. 'My real-name Margit, but I work as Beverly so-long it becomes me.' She'd been working as a hostess in an exclusive Pontocho club – 'our clients are rich-gentleman' – when a cop stopped in to check her visa, which was expired. 'I know my client told police about me,' she says, rubbing her swollen belly. 'I told this client I'm leaving. He didn't like that, no way José.'

'It wasn't his baby,' I say.

'Shit no!' She looks indignant. 'I never do-sex with clients. Only karaoke, cigarettes, drinking. Boring stuff.' Her hand still rests on her belly. She says proudly, 'When I found out I became-pregnant, I faked drinking. My glass had pop.'

I can't help but scan her body: skinny arms, extremely narrow hips. Chance of C-section high.

'The father is American navy-man from St Louis,' Beverly says. 'He is on-leave now, but he comes back in three months. Then, he comes for us.'

The other woman, a plump Japanese woman who Beverly tells me is called Hitomi, begins to hum. The sound is surprisingly rich, full of vibrato. She stares at us and when I catch her eye she doesn't look away.

'He will come,' Beverly repeats, looking at Hitomi. 'He told me. He wants us. We'll go to America, and you'll be here fuckin' rotting.'

Hitomi continues humming and staring.

I greet her in Japanese. 'I'm Rio.'

'Don't bother talking to her. She not right in her brain. Don't talk, see,' Beverly says. 'Tricky bitch, quiet kitty cat.'

Food – a mound of rice with burnt edges, pickles, processed meat sticks the colour of Pepto-Bismol – arrives on three plastic trays through a flap near the ground. The overweight female guard who delivered it coughs but doesn't bother to cover her mouth.

'Tofu-sensei,' Beverly says, jutting her chin at the guard. 'She got a jiggling problem. Too soft, see.' She pokes a finger into her thigh while making a suction sound.

I can't bear the thought of food in my cramped, nauseated stomach. I should be at the Oedas', gorging on my first home-cooked meal in over a week. Beverly gives me her pickle and

I make myself take a bite. The strong vinegar makes me gag. Hitomi eats everything on my tray except the meat stick, which she offers to me; when I refuse it she shakes her head. Just before the trays are collected, she shoves it in her mouth. She chews big and round, like a cow, and the sight makes me jump up and run to the toilet at the back of the cell. I throw up the bits of pickle.

Beverly pats me on the back. I breathe deeply. Beverly shows me a banana she keeps hidden in the toilet tank. She motions to her crotch and winks. I throw up again, this time only bile.

A chime sounds and all the lights flip off for a second. Beverly and Hitomi sit upright and scramble on their knees to the front of the cell.

Heavy footsteps echo down the hall. It feels as if the entire block is sucking in a collective breath. Beverly motions to me and I slide over near her as a man with a puckered mouth and hair greying at the temples strides up to face the cell next to us.

'*Tenko*,' Beverly whispers. 'Roll call.'

'Three-one-four!' the man bellows in Japanese.

'*Hai!*' comes a quick response from the cell.

'Six-four-eight!' he barks immediately. Another woman responds.

He makes his way to our cell, calling both Hitomi's and Beverly's numbers. When he steps in front of me, he pauses. He glances at the clipboard in his hand, whips around, and yells to the guard Beverly called Tofu-sensei. 'What is this?'

'Oh! I'm so sorry, Your Honour, she just came in, we didn't have time to update—'

He flicks his wrist, sending the clipboard crashing against the bars over my head. Papers slide out of the clip and flutter to the floor. 'Who are you? A Korean? Iranian terrorist? Something worse?' He bends forward. 'What's on your face?'

I stare at him. His lip curls, revealing yellow-stained teeth of all different sizes, like the runty candies at the bottom of a bag. 'Well, she's not bad-looking, at least. Exotic.'

Tofu-sensei says something quietly; he tells her to speak up.

'She's American, sir.'

'Filthy place.' The spite on his rat-like face reminds me of someone. What if fate has dealt me Tomoya Yu's father as a warden? But there are two kanji on his name badge, too long for 'Yu', and even I can read the first one, three straight lines, pronounced *Mi*. Mr Mi-something calls out numbers; each answers in an identical tone with the same word: *Hai!*

After he leaves, we are allowed out, two cells at a time, to brush our teeth over a long sink. I have no toothbrush, so I rub my teeth with my finger. A few women bring panties to wash. They scrub their underwear with a brush meant for surfaces, and clip them to the plastic line extended over the trough. We are led, one at a time, to a narrow, dimly lit closet to retrieve a rolled-up mat and a wool blanket.

This is a mistake. There's no way they're keeping me here overnight. I haven't done anything. 'When is someone going to tell me what's going on?' I ask one of the guards. She shrugs and looks past me. I want to scream.

The lights go out at nine. The place is dead quiet. I lie there in the dark, wondering what will become of me. What if I'm here forever? What if there's a glitch in the paperwork and they simply forget about me? Sleep, please come. Shut down these thoughts. I try meditation, counting sheep, and imagining my happiest days. I pretend I'm at home in Lily's bed. Nothing works. Despair is a heavy blanket. Under it, I cry myself into an exhausted, restless doze.

At seven, the lights flip on. My jaw hurts. I've been clenching it and grinding my teeth.

We go through the bedding process in reverse, folding and storing our mats and blankets in the closet. After a breakfast of cold sticky rice, soggy eggplant chunks, and more pickles, a bell clangs in the cellblock. I manage to swallow a few bites of rice and focus on eating a few more when the sound of the bell makes me jump. But Beverly and Hitomi perk up immediately.

'A visitor,' Beverly says.

Tofu comes to our door and I am patted, tied, and led out of the cellblock into a hallway. Finally. 'Goodbye and good luck,' I call to Beverly. She gives me a strange look.

Does the corridor actually smell like urine, or does the dark yellow paint just make it seem that way?

A man with a helmet of white-blond hair sits behind the glass. He stands. 'Hello, Mrs Silvestri. I'm with the American embassy.' His necktie has a bald eagle on it. 'I must say, this is a highly unusual situation you've found yourself in. You claim to be Hiro Akitani's daughter, is that correct?' The engraved badge on his breast pocket reads STAN PETROWSKI.

'I was born Chizuru Akitani. Hiro Akitani was my father, and I was given a key to his house.'

'He gave you this key?'

'His ... friend gave it to me.'

He writes on his notepad for a long time. 'That house is government property. No one was to enter without permission while Mr Akitani's possessions were being processed for inclusion in a museum exhibit.'

I almost laugh. They want to put our stuff in a museum?

'That said, if you can prove you're a family member, then yes, legally you had a right to be there. We've found the record of Rio Silvestri entering the country. An American citizen. The consulate is looking into the existence of a Chizuru Akitani of

230

your age. Even so, if what you say is true, it's going to be hard to prove you are who you say you are.'

'They have my fingerprints.'

'Yes, but they will need—'

'And they have hers, too. September third, nineteen seventy-six. My birthday.'

He writes all this down, looks at me dubiously. 'You're telling me that if we look into this, the prints will match?'

'I am telling you that.'

'I hope so, for your sake. Right now they can keep you for up to twenty-four days without a charge. It's tricky. You're not necessarily allowed the rights of a citizen, but they don't give you the rights of your home country, either. You've noticed that foreigners don't get a phone call. We'll do everything we can to nip this in the bud. But don't get your hopes up. Things take the time they take. This paperwork could be sitting on someone's desk for the next twenty days. Obon's about to start. And once a case is opened, once you're here, it's an unstoppable series of events. Like a pachinko ball. It drops into the machine and there's no going back. And you know those games are all fixed—' He's really into this analogy. I interrupt him.

'Are you saying I might have to stay here for three weeks? This is just a mistake. I didn't *do* anything.'

'Correct. But—'

'I need to talk to my family. They're going to worry about me.' At least, I hope Sal is worried.

'My advice? Wait it out. Make trouble and you're only hurting yourself. Ninety-nine and a half per cent of prosecutions get a conviction in Japan. Don't do anything to get yourself in further trouble, you hear? Once you're convicted, you're theirs. A judge trying to make an example of foreign criminals might bring the hammer down just to make himself look good.' He fiddles with his tie. The eagle's outstretched wings mock me.

I could break this glass. 'Have you ever been locked up? Washed your underwear in the sink, been allowed to bathe only once every three days? How about having to shit in front of two other people? I belong in my house with a real bed, a house with enough toilets for everyone to go at the same time. I don't belong here.'

After mentioning twice that he could lose his job for doing so, Stan takes Sal's e-mail address and promises to inform him of my arrest. A buzzer sounds.

The guard comes in, leash in hand. This is a nightmare. The feeling of missing my family is desperate, ugly, consuming. Like grief. I miss their knowledge of me, their easy acceptance of a habit like adding three-and-only-three blueberries to my cereal. I want to be with people who know things only we know, out of all the people on the planet: how Lily's eyes cross if she tries to talk while eating, the secret ingredient in Sal's meat sauce (baking soda), how the purple stain on the wall above the couch got there. And that parrot we'd briefly babysat from our dentist's office who squawked, 'Insurance provider?' and when asked a question responded, 'Gingivitis! A pain in the gums!' so that years later, when asking about something completely unrelated, one of us could respond with, 'Gingivitis! A pain in the gums!' and make the others laugh.

I miss Bagel, even though he makes me itch when he sits on my lap. Between ten and eleven in the morning, depending on the season, a rectangle of sunlight strikes the patch of carpet between the ottoman and the couch – five minutes after Bagel arranges himself on that very spot.

There are so many little things, stacked so high in my mind. Why have I been such an idiot? Why have I hidden so much of myself from my family? All these years spent distancing myself from Chizuru Akitani and now the only thing that will save me is to prove I'm her.

For those who behave, two to four is reading time. We can request the newspaper, mostly useless to me since I can't read it, though I ask for it anyway, to have something to look at. It arrives one section at a time through the doggy door. Some articles are blacked out, wet and still smelling of marker fumes. I imagine that's part of Tofu's job, hunting for reportage that might aid in our lives of crime and colouring over it with a Sharpie.

Stan, guessing correctly that the prison library wouldn't have any books in English, donated a crime novel for me called *Hunter, Hunted*. In the story, a young guitarist named Hunter is framed for the murder of his wife's brother. Whoever sets him up does a great job, planting evidence and even a couple of red herrings the police have to 'solve' so Hunter isn't the first one they suspect. Everyone in the book is witty and speaks in double entendres and the lead detective is a cat-eyed woman with a chip on her shoulder and an ass that could, inexplicably, 'stop a clock'.

Hunter, Hunted is 179 pages long. At 3:30 on my third day with the novel, I feel how little remains pinched between my fingers, and put it down. I'm on page 177. I do a hundred sit-ups, a hundred squats, and fifty push-ups. I smell awful – bath day isn't until the day after tomorrow – but the endorphins are worth it.

I have my theories about the murderer's identity: the creepy ex-boyfriend of the guitarist's wife seems a little obvious, like that's who the author wants you to suspect, or the wife herself, who's a preschool teacher with an occasional (as far as Hunter and we readers know) cocaine habit. I crave those last two pages. The solution to the mystery. But this is my only book. If I finish, I'll have nothing to do but worry and wait.

I turn to Beverly, who is doing leg lifts and staring at the wall. 'Don't you ever want to read?'

'Books? Nah.' She prefers to think about the future, she says. About her baby and her man. The future is real, unlike stuff in books. The life waiting for her in America is better than any novel.

Without reading the last two pages, I turn back to page one of *Hunter, Hunted*, and begin again.

Thursday is steak night. The meat's gristly and served with powdered mashed potatoes. I find myself getting truly excited about the prospect of potato flakes and gristle. As the smell of roasted meat makes its way through the cellblock, the atmosphere in the place lightens. Even Tofu seems happy. I eat my entire dinner, even the pickle. And then music pours from the ceiling.

'Thursday reward, fun-time,' Beverly says.

The sound is so full, so rich, that I shiver. Hearing real music after so much silence is like the first meal after a fast. An American country song about a tractor comes on, and I invent a line dance that combines a few moves I learnt at my co-worker Jory's birthday party last year.

'This is the Tush Push,' I tell Hitomi.

Hitomi copies my movements, wheeling back on her heels.

'Yeehaw!' I spin on the mat.

'YeeHAW!' Hitomi spins.

Hitomi yells 'Yeehaw!' so many times that Tofu comes by and threatens her with the solitary cell. After Tofu finishes her threat, someone down the line screams 'YEEHAW!' at the top of her lungs, causing the whole row to hoot and holler.

We laugh until tears stream down our faces, all the while dancing ridiculously. Who screamed? Is she old or young? Japanese or from somewhere else? Has she been in long? In our cells we hear one another whisper or turn over at night, but the only time we come face-to-face is during night-time washup, and if you don't focus on brushing and washing you won't finish within ninety seconds. We are each mysteries within whispering distance.

That defiant 'yeehaw!' sets something loose. A chorus of ill-pronounced emulations gallops through the block. Tofu stomps up and down the row. The laughter hurts my stomach; my eyes water. Finally – we all know it's coming – the music stops. The lights go out. Beverly bites her lip to keep from laughing. Hitomi closes her eyes and wiggles her shoulders. The beat continues to play in my head: ba-ba-BAH, jingle, jangle, *yeehaw*. Thirty strangers smirk into a shared darkness. For a moment, joy eclipses all of my other feelings.

The following morning, an air of caution hangs over the long sink like a raincloud. Tofu has not reprimanded us for the way we disrespected her orders other than turning off the music and lights, and the unspoken feeling is that someone will have to pay. What have I done? Stan Petrowski warned me not to get in any trouble.

Everyone freezes when the phone trills, and though a few continue with their washing, the rest make no movement until the guard announces a number.

'*San-ni-kyu*,' Tofu-sensei monotones. My heart drops. Beverly told me about the solitary cell where they stick the badly behaved.

Sometimes they forgot to feed you, she said, and they never turned off the buzzing lights, which made it impossible to sleep.

I hardly feel the rope; they leave off the handcuffs this time. Down the piss-hall to a door marked A6. Maybe they're going to interrogate me before locking me up. The guard opens the door and I step inside.

Sal sits there, hands clasped. He stands, the plastic chair screeching beneath him as he leans in to the glass that separates us.

'Oh my god,' I say, just as he says the same thing.

16

SAL HAS ON A BLUE BUTTON-DOWN SHIRT I've never seen and the slacks he only wears to weddings. His lips are pale and cracked. Beneath his broad frame, the plastic chair looks like it belongs in a preschool.

'I got the e-mail from Stan yesterday. Or I guess the day before yesterday … it all feels like one long day.'

I lean forward, touch the glass. I wish I could reach through it. He came. He doesn't hate me. At least, I haven't managed to ruin things between us yet. I feel so much relief in this moment, so much love for him that I am shaking. 'I'm so happy to see you,' I say. 'This thing is – I don't know. I don't know any more what it is.' He came. He came.

Sal looks at his lap. I wish he'd show some emotion. 'After I got the e-mail, I panicked and had Lily sent home immediately. The camp was nice about it. Someone gave her a ride to the airport. We got on the next flight here.'

'Lily's here?' My heart's going to burst through my skin. My eyes fill with tears. I look around, briefly certain that I have the strength to break through any walls or doors standing between my daughter and me.

'She's in the lobby with a secretary. They wouldn't let her in because she's under thirteen. I need to get right back. Oh, and I brought a copy of our marriage certificate with your maiden name on it, but I don't know if that helps since it says Rio on it, not Chizuru.'

'That was smart, thank you. Did you tell Lily about …?'

'I said there was a misunderstanding but that you were fine and would be out soon. Of course I didn't tell her *everything*.'

I can't handle his expression. It's like he's looking at a stranger. He presses his forehead to the glass. I place my hand where his head is. I try, but I can't feel his warmth through the glass.

'I'm sorry,' I say.

He looks up. The thick glass is like a time-travel lens: for a second, Sal looks old. The skin around his eyes is loose, his cheeks bristly and rough. Even the blue of his eyes seems lighter, washed-out. His eyelids are dotted with freckles. I'm seized by the fear that I've lost him.

'Please tell me it's going to be okay,' I beg.

He wipes his nose. 'I can't tell you that right now.'

The door buzzer sounds. A guard opens the door and I immediately jump up, saying no, no, that couldn't have been ten minutes. I look at Sal for some sign of his feelings, for him to fight, but all I can see is how tired he is.

Sal stands, squares his shoulders, and brushes off his dress pants. All he says by way of farewell is 'See you.' My heart cracks open. I slide to the floor, weeping.

When the phone rings the next afternoon I comb my fingers through my hair. Beverly motions for me to pinch my cheeks. 'Gives big glow. Very-nice.' I pinch hard. I don't care about looking pretty. But having something to aim for helps pass the time.

The number they call isn't mine. Beverly gives me a sympathetic smile and continues with her leg lifts. I do two hundred crunches and a hundred squats. I use my muscles until they shake, and use them some more. I'm scared of what will happen if I stop. The phone doesn't ring the rest of the day. I'm dreading the conversation I'm going to have to have with Sal, but that dread has nothing on the idea of staying here for two more weeks. It might as well be two years.

'He is busy,' Beverly says that night. 'Or they didn't-allow him. You can't know. Keith' – she places a hand on her belly – 'does not come, too. He is busy-travelling.' She backs this up with a look to Hitomi like a period.

'Next time we have pen-and-paper may I give you his name? When you go, you call-him for me. Like your country's guy do for you.'

I never get the sailor's name, and I don't read pages 178–179. The phone rings the next morning during breakfast and instead of a visitation room, I am led into the intake room. My week-old running clothes are in their plastic bag. The locker-room stench that fills the air when I remove them tells me they have not been washed. I throw the underwear in the trashcan and put on my sports bra, T-shirt, and shorts. The clothes can't possibly be wet after all this time, but they still feel damp against my skin.

A guard leads me to the end of the yellow hallway and opens a metal door, revealing a spacious, marble-floored lobby. I check his expression: Is this for real? He nods. My pulse is sky-high; my chest pounds as if I've just sprinted up Hell Hill in Betasso. I walk through the door and into freedom, marvelling at how warm the natural light is out here, how vibrant the colours.

A huge mural of a bamboo forest hangs behind my husband and daughter, dwarfing them. When Lily sees me, she shrieks and runs at me. Her hair's longer and has a crimp to it, as if she's had it in braids. She hits me hard and grabs my waist like she'll never let go. I don't want her to. 'Are you okay?' she asks, sniffling into my chest. 'Ariela, this girl at camp, said her dad was in jail in India and they put him in a cell smaller than a baby crib ...'

I'm crying. I breathe her in. She smells different. Older. 'Nothing like that, sweetie,' I say. 'They were nice. You don't have to worry. It was all a mistake. We'll laugh about it one day.'

'Oh my god, Mom, you kinda stink.'

Sal is not smiling. His red shirt stands out against the mural's muted blues and greens. He does not move to greet me. He just watches me come. Lily is squeezing my hand as if checking to make sure it's really there. The thirty steps feel interminable. A pilgrimage. My toes cramp in my running shoes, which I haven't worn for eight days. My blisters have mostly healed.

Finally I stand before Sal. 'Please hug me,' I say.

He puts his arms around me and I sink into him. I start to sob. 'I'm so sorry,' I whisper. 'I'm sorry about the—' He pulls away and I can see that he has tears in his eyes. He takes the plastic bag containing my paperwork and the things I was carrying when I was arrested. 'Not *now*,' he says. Lily stares at us, confused. She's never seen either of us cry. Her exhilaration turns to dismay.

'Why are you guys crying?' she asks. 'Are you gonna be okay, Mom?'

'I'll be fine,' I force myself to say. 'We'll all be fine.'

A taxi idles at the kerb. We get in. Lily refuses to let go of my hand. I have to wipe my face and nose on my dirty sleeve. Lily keeps asking if I'm okay, if I'll have to go back to jail. I tell her that jail is different from a detention centre but I'm at a loss as to how, or if that's even true in Japan. She wants to know what I did wrong. I tell her that there was some confusion about my name, the police made a mistake, and she relaxes a little. I try to downplay what happened, try to believe myself when I tell her that everything's all right now. That I'm no longer in trouble. I hate that I've tormented my daughter by putting her through this. I was only trying to protect you, I want to tell her. I want to say it to them both, but the words feel trite. All I can do is focus on not weeping when I look into the exhausted faces of my husband and child.

Sal stares out the window and lets me babble. He's with us but he's not with us. Not with me. When will we have time to talk? And what will I say when we do?

We stop in front of a nondescript three-storey building. A pink HOTEL TABOO sign hangs on the façade and there's no clear entrance. Sal fishes a wad of cash out of his wallet. The driver counts out his fare and hands the rest back.

'You're staying at a love hotel?' I ask.

'What's a love hotel?' Lily asks.

'The cab driver kept shaking his head when I told him we needed a place to stay. I even got this app for my phone that translates what you write and speaks it back in Japanese, so I know he understood me. But he kept saying, "All busy! All busy!" Then he brought me here. There was no front desk –

I just stuck some money in a vending machine outside the door and it let me in.'

Lily says, 'We got a kids' room. They have video games and a karaoke machine and there's mermaids on the walls.'

We climb the dim stairway. Sal moves slowly. He punches some buttons on a keypad and the door in front of us opens. The bed is shaped like a seashell.

I sit on the bed with Lily and run my fingers through her tangled hair. 'How about a French braid?' I start separating her hair into pieces. 'And you can tell me all about camp.'

She reluctantly lets me work. 'I had to leave a day early. I missed the dance on the last night and the premiere of my group's movie.'

'Sweetie, I'm so sorry. That must've been really disappointing.'

She nods, yawns, and the surliness falls from her features. She's too tired to hold a grudge, lucky for me. 'Something else happened,' she says. She glances at Sal, then puts her mouth to my ear and whispers, 'My period came.'

I drop the locks of her hair and yelp, hug her warm little body as hard as I can. I can't believe it. I knew it was due to happen soon, but – already. *Already.* 'That's big news, sweetie. I'm so sorry I wasn't there.' Please don't let her have a horror story. We raised her as best we could not to be embarrassed about her body, but there's nothing you can do about other kids.

'Marlena, one of the counsellors, gave me stuff and told me what to do. And I remembered from when we talked about it. She was nice.'

'That's good.' She starts to squirm away from me. 'We can talk about it whenever you want, all right?'

'What did you eat in jail?' Lily asks. 'Did you wear a uniform?'

I start back in on her hair. 'Well … there was a lot of rice. And pickles. One night we had steak. No uniforms. And I made a couple friends, and we even got to listen to music and dance. It was like a big sleepover.' She bites her lip. I stop working on her hair and take her face in my hands. 'I promise, you'll never have to worry about me going away like that again.' She nods. 'Good. And you know, there's a silver lining to all of this. You're in Japan! There's so much I want to show you now that you're here.'

With her near, Sal's stony expression worries me less. 'Do we have return tickets?' I ask him.

'Lily and I do. For Tuesday.' He says it like he doesn't expect me to go back with them.

'I'll try to book one on the same flight, then.' I don't want to let either of them out of my sight now that we're reunited.

A female voice coos through a speaker in the ceiling. '*Excuse me. Your rest session will conclude in fifteen minutes. Please insert additional funds if you wish to extend your rest session. Please take care not to leave any items behind. Once it is closed, the door will not reopen.*'

Lily looks around to find the source of the voice. 'What's that?'

'She said it's time to … check out.'

Lily mimics the woman's breathy voice, making up nonsense syllables that sound startlingly Japanese. I repeat what the woman said, and Lily repeats after me, a smile on her face. I give Sal a look, but his face only returns exhaustion and detachment.

Shinobu is the only one home when we arrive. He is standing in the doorway when our cab pulls up. 'You are safe!' he shouts, coming down the steps to greet us. 'I was very stressful.'

'I'm so sorry, I couldn't call you. I gave the police your address, but I don't think they believed—'

'It is okay. The police came here. We know everything. We will discuss later. Now, who is this?'

I introduce him to Sal and Lily.

'Is that SpongeBob-san?' He points at Lily's T-shirt. 'I love him! "I am ready I am ready I am ready!"'

She looks at him suspiciously. She's tired, and scared, and it's clear she doesn't feel like she can trust anyone in this country yet. Finally, she says, 'It's "*I'm* ready", not "I am ready".'

'I see! Wow. You must teach me everything you know.'

Shinobu leads us to the spare room. Lily spots the low square table and says, 'See, I knew there would be a good puzzle table.'

'Can I use the shower?' I ask.

'Of course, of course,' Shinobu says.

'And then—?' I make a you-and-me motion to Sal. He points to Lily and I take his meaning: we need to talk alone. I put my hands together against my cheek and mime sleep. If he can get Lily to nap, we'll have some privacy.

'I'll be back in ten minutes, Lil,' I say. 'Try to rest.'

In the hallway, Shinobu says, 'While you were gone, I reached my dream.'

'Your dream?'

'I am a lawyer now.' He beams. 'The letter came four days ago. I cried like I am a baby.'

'That's amazing. Congratulations!'

'I read it many times. I could not believe I accomplished.' He lowers his voice. 'My mother acts like nothing is new. But she feels relieved, I know. The house is becoming dirty again. When the police tell us about your situation, my mother insist to my father: we must help her! My mother believes I passed the bar

244

exam due to your effect. So she begged my father to help you and of course when she begs he must obey. He has many police friends. It was easy to hurry the fingerprint records. Plus, the document of your marriage made it very clear that you are a member of Akitani family.'

'Oh my god. You guys saved me. I might've been in there two more weeks. I'll be sure to thank your father.'

Shinobu looks horrified. 'No! Promise you do not say about this to him.' He buries his face in his hands. 'You must pretend nothing happened.'

In eight days I've taken two barely lukewarm baths, the first without soap. Tonight would've been my third, and I am ripe. This clean, huge, private shower with its tiled floor and matching deep tub makes me feel like a spoilt queen. I turn the water as hot as it will go and scrub the detention centre off. I breathe the steam in and push it out, imagining my insides getting clean as well.

Mrs Oeda has washed the clothes from my backpack. A clean white T-shirt and my sweatpants have been folded and set on the counter near the shower. Under the T-shirt are a pair of underwear and a bra, both folded neatly. I dress, take a deep breath, and look for my husband. My heart is pounding. I've never felt nervous around Sal before.

He's at the table with Shinobu, typing on a laptop. He's got his blue bandana on, the one he loves because it's worn and soft, the one he looks most handsome in. I come up behind him and gently place my hands on his shoulders. I want to touch his hair, gathered upward by the bandana, but I don't dare. Hands on the shoulders is already a cheap move in front of Shinobu. Sal stiffens at my touch. 'A hundred and forty-three hotels in this city and not one room available.'

'Don't think of hotels,' Shinobu says. His tone has grown fatherly now that he's passed the bar. 'If you leave, my mother's heart will break. Let her spoil you until Tuesday.'

Sal turns to me. 'Lily's asleep. She'll be out for a while. Let's go for a walk.' He turns to Shinobu. 'Will you be here in case she wakes up?'

My legs feel like lead. I can't do it out there. I can't face Sal's anger in a public place. 'Can we talk in the room? I don't want her to wake up without me there.' If we're quiet enough, we can have a conversation over Lily while she sleeps. We've done it before.

The box for a sushi-themed puzzle stands on the low table next to a mound of unsorted pieces. Of the twenty or so nigiri rolls shown in the picture, only the eel and scallop have been completed. 'Looks like she didn't get too far,' I say.

Sal sits on one side of our daughter and I sit on the other. He looks at me expectantly. The lack of compassion on his face makes my stomach turn. There is so much to say and I don't know where to start. Shinobu sneezes in the living room and I jump. My nerves feel exposed and raw.

'I have a lot to explain,' I begin. My head feels full and empty at the same time. Finally, I say, 'I never had good friends growing up. I was "half" – not Japanese like everyone else. And I was fat. *No one* was fat. My father was famous and people thought that was cool, but he travelled all the time and he wasn't there. For me or my mom. And my mom had her own stuff to deal with, being a foreigner and being married to him, being away from her family. I was lonely, I overate. Then in sixth grade, a new kid named Tomoya Yu came to school. He did things to me.'

His eyes are locked onto mine. 'What things?'

'Just hold on. One day, it went too far. This was a month after my mom died. I grabbed whatever was nearby – a letter opener – and I hit him with it. I mean, it felt like hitting. But I stabbed him. I wanted him to get away from me. He died in the hospital the next day.'

Sal runs his hands through his hair and pulls so hard I worry he might pull some out. 'What did he do to you?'

I look my husband in the eye and try to speak and now, now I know what the hardest part of my story is. It's not the fact of the murder. It's the greater indignity of how I was singled out. The worst thing is having to recount everything he said and did to me.

I begin with the eraser incident. I keep my eyes on the place where the wall meets the tatami, just above Lily's sleeping face. When I tell him how proud and happy I was when Miss Danny humiliated Tomoya in front of everyone, I start to cry. Sal is unmoved. He puts a finger to his lips: don't wake Lily. I tell him about the Fatty Potato comic book, the grabbing and touching, the tacks.

'I'm sorry for killing him and everything that happened because of that. But when I remember it, when I put myself back there ... it's always scared me. When I put myself back there, I'm not sorry.' Saying this out loud gives me goose bumps. It's the truth, and it's a surprise to me.

Sal gasps. I feel like I'm lacking oxygen. 'And afterward?' he asks.

I describe Kawano, Dr K. Fighting with Hiro, waiting for visitors who never came. 'And when I was allowed to leave and start over, I was terrified. Relieved, yes. But terrified. I didn't know what life would be like. If I could even make it in the US.

In college. I was damaged. Less than human. I didn't know if I could ever be healthy enough. But I had nothing to fall back on. I couldn't risk messing it up. So when I met you, it was this burst of hope. Suddenly I could see my life turning out … happy. Like maybe I wasn't worthless, so fucked-up, after all.'

'And so you lied to me.' His voice is like a frayed rope about to break. His hands are shaking. He balls them into fists. 'That's the worst thing about all of this. Not that you killed someone. You were a kid. I feel *sorry* for you. But then you make up this whole life? Why not just say you had a rough childhood and you didn't want to talk about it?' He pounds his fist on the table and I jump as if I've been struck by lightning. He yells, 'Why *lie*?' Lily stirs.

Instead of blood in my veins, it's shame, and it rushes to the surface. My face feels hot and stretched out. 'It seemed like the only choice I had.'

'Why?'

I picture my mom in our apartment, painting canvases no one would see. Our secret shoebox. Her blossoming disenchantment with Japan. How she gave up so much to have the life she thought she wanted, far from her family, far from her first home. Her strength – or what had seemed like strength to me – and the abrupt loss of it. How could I reconcile all of this with what I had already been through at school, and with my father? There was no way I could explain it to anyone when I could hardly explain it to myself.

'I'd been lying for so long already, I half believed the things I told you about my high school years, my childhood. You have all these stories about your family. Staying up all night to make ravioli for Mayor Daley. Uncle Vito driving to Missouri to buy Coors Light. The party with the llama on the balcony. Hearing about that stuff made me feel so close to you. I wanted to share that same thing with you.'

'But you didn't. You *made them up*. Do you get how selfish that is?' I can't hold it back any more; I begin to weep. I am selfish. More selfish than my own mother, who couldn't or didn't want to figure out a way to keep going. At least she didn't hide her feelings. There was never a time when I felt like I didn't know who my mom was. She was never a mystery. But Lily – my daughter knows nothing about me. Lily's hair falls over her nose. I brush it off so she doesn't inhale it.

Sal continues, 'When you told me who you really were, it was like, *Aha!* Now I understand our marriage. I always knew there was a piece missing. You've been latching onto me to gain stability for yourself. Riding my coat-tails. But you weren't with me on things. You were riding until you fell off. Whenever I brought up something important, it was, "We'll talk about it later." Later, later, later. We'll talk about having another kid, talk about a bigger house, talk about going to Japan as a family – later. Sometimes I feel like I haven't married a person, I married a mask.'

He's right. I have been a mask. I look at Lily, who's so fragile, so trusting when she sleeps. I'm filled with a rush of love for her. She gets her trust in the world from Sal. 'No. My feelings for you, for Lily, for our life. They're real. You guys are everything.'

'It all makes sense. You can't watch violent movies – you flipped out during that scene in *True Romance*. And when that kid brought a pocketknife to Lily's school, you wanted to transfer her. And the envelope opener we got for our wedding from Frankie and Diane – you acted so weird about it. And it just disappeared.'

'I donated it.' The letter opener had been made of silver, not gold, but it had reminded me so much of Miss Danny's,

I couldn't bear it. Yet even as I tossed the fancy velvet box into the Goodwill bin containing wedding items we didn't want and couldn't return, part of me thought, Oops, Chizuru accidentally threw the wrong thing in there! You'll have to take it out later. All the while knowing I wouldn't. 'I shouldn't have hidden it from you. But can you at least understand why I did? Why I felt I had to?'

'Maybe. I don't know. I'm not you, I can't feel what you felt.' He looks at the ceiling. Looks at Lily. At me. 'Do you feel like a murderer?'

'I think about him. Tomoya. I wonder what he would look like now, a grown man. Who he would have married. He probably would have turned out to be a decent guy.' The room is so warm with the three of us in it. I'm sweating. 'His poor parents.'

'You didn't answer my question.'

'I don't know, Sal. That passion that used to build up in me – it's gone.' I remember Danny, the shed. 'But we all have breaking points.'

I tell Sal about my single nice memory of Tomoya. He was in the convenience store around the corner from my house. He carried a trumpet case, which he never had at school. I snorted when I saw it. Hiro despised the trumpet, called it the penis of the orchestra. He did an impression of brass musicians where he'd blow out his lips in an exaggerated fart sound that never failed to make me laugh.

With one hand Tomoya held the arm of an old man, what we called a 'ninety-degree man' for the angle of his bent back, and in the other was that boxy plastic case.

I followed them through the store. Tomoya didn't see me. I don't remember how long after he'd arrived at school this took place, how deeply he'd cultivated the art of picking on me, how much I hated him. I just remember the sense of wonder at watching someone betraying everything he was supposed to be. Everything he'd sold us at school contradicted this kid in the convenience store. I could even recall what they bought that day as I slunk around behind them: a three-pack of cotton underwear, a box of 'man' type chocolate Pocky, and a single pink carnation, wrapped in plastic and taken from the shelf in the refrigerated section above the egg salad sandwiches.

It was the rainy season and a downpour had started. I watched as Tomoya and the man stopped at the door, contemplating the rain. Removing his hand from the man's arm for just a second, Tomoya pulled an umbrella from his backpack, nudged the door open with his hip, and opened the umbrella so the man could pass outside without getting wet. Tomoya slipped out, holding the umbrella over the man's head while his hair got plastered to his own head. He managed to hold the trumpet case with two fingers while still guiding the man with the same hand.

'I could have helped them, but I didn't. I was too scared. I thought that if he knew I'd seen him weak like that, he'd punish me even worse.'

Sal picks up a puzzle piece and turns it in his hands. A boot piece. I can't tell if I'm getting through, if he's moved by what I've told him. He changes the subject. 'You said you wanted another kid. You were interested in Tuscany Terrace. Are either of those things true?'

'You were really into Tuscany Terrace, so I wanted to give it a chance. But, really – I like our house. It's *us*. That place felt uninviting – like a caricature of what upwardly mobile people are supposed to want. I didn't feel like I belonged there. We didn't belong there.'

Sal drops the boot piece onto the table and doesn't say anything.

'And we should think more about a baby. As a family. Like, can we afford it? The shop's barely breaking even, Lily will be in college in five years, and my salary's not enough to carry all that.' I begin to cry again; I have to tell him. 'Babe, I didn't stop taking my pills. I was too scared.'

He looks surprised, but not upset. 'Are you mad?' I ask.

'I found your pills weeks ago,' he says mildly. 'I'm just surprised you decided to tell me. Usually I have to confront you about these things.'

I am a child again, sitting in my room on the floor with my mom standing over me, asking me what these terrible, violent drawings are about. I am found out. My skin crawls; I want to cover my face and hide. But Sal continues coolly:

'The shop's doing fine. The economy's up. Yeah, that could change. Nothing's certain. It never is. What it all comes down to is, what do you *want*?'

Has Sal ever asked me this question so pointedly before? I wonder about the other lives I might have lived. What if there was a fork in the road a long time ago, and I took the wrong path? That other, phantom me is free. She is not being confronted with her own lies. Her life is not tangled in knots, because she made the hard decision to tell the truth when she first had the chance. Would it have been so hard to be that version of myself, the one I started to find on the trail? I wonder if there's still time. I want to take responsibility. I thought I had, but I haven't. Not really.

'I want to stay,' I say. I force myself to take a deep breath. 'I want to finish it.' I don't realise it's true until I say it. I need more time. Time alone to run, to be in this country, to be a pilgrim for the right reasons. I have often felt shame but I never truly felt humbled.

'Finish the pilgrimage?'

'I'll run it. I wanted to do that from the beginning.' Once I say it, I am certain. I'm at the top of a steep hill ready for a controlled descent.

'That'll take, what, a month? More? We need you at home. Lily needs you.'

At the sound of her name, Lily opens her eyes and mumbles, 'I'm hungry.' She pats around for my hand. I grasp her fingers. She is going to hate me for a while. My heart hurts imagining the look on her face when I tell her I'm not coming home with them right away. She is going to hate me, but it won't last. One day, she may even admire me. 'You asked what I want.'

'What about afterward?'

'I'll come home.' Who knows who I'll be after that month? What forks I'll have come to? What forks Sal may have come to? Lily's eyes flutter shut and I force the question out, whisper, 'Do you want to leave me?'

'That's a funny question, given that it's you who keeps doing the leaving.'

'You know what I mean.'

'I feel like I don't know anything any more. I need to process all this. We can talk about it when – if – you come back.'

Mrs Oeda sweeps into the house while the three of us are watching a video from Lily's camp that one of her counsellors uploaded to YouTube. Four girls on a film set, including Lily, who's yelling at someone to 'move the boom so it's not in the way of the spot beam'. She moves and sounds like an adult.

Mrs Oeda is all groceries, plastic bags looped around her arms, more bags clutched in each hand. Mr Oeda trails behind her, carrying a bag of golf clubs. 'There they are!' she cries in Japanese, dropping the bags unceremoniously on the table. A tube of mayonnaise rolls onto the floor. 'An American girl, right here in our home,' Mrs Oeda says when she spots Lily. 'Whoever would have thought?' I can't tell whether she's pleased by this turn of events or not.

I make introductions, doing my best to convey my gratitude to both Mr and Mrs Oeda without acknowledging there is anything to be grateful for. Now that they know who I am, does my past bother them? It doesn't seem to; at least, not on the surface. Mr Oeda shakes Sal's hand and bows at the same time. I can't read him; he seems, if anything, bored by our presence. But he touches Lily's shoulder and when he does he looks right at me. I look at my daughter and nod, and that is the extent of the communication between Mr Oeda and me about what happened.

Lily is not sure what to think of Mrs Oeda, who fusses over her as if she's a long-lost grandchild. Lily smiles politely as she touches her hair, her cheeks, exclaims over her neon-green fingernails. She buzzes around us, carrying on a one-way conversation with Sal and Lily in Japanese and arranging our itinerary for the rest of our time in Tokushima. I don't tell anyone else about running the trail.

'Can we at least help you prepare dinner?' Sal asks, gesturing toward the kitchen.

'You two can,' she says, pointing at Lily and Sal. 'We can get to know each other.' She turns to me. 'You go rest. I'm only whipping up a few basics.'

I sit on the mats and stretch my legs. My hamstrings are tight. Walking doesn't use the muscles in the same way. I look forward to being a runner again. To feeling like myself.

How am I going to tell Lily? Part of me wants to tell her immediately, now that I've made my decision. But if I tell her tonight, it might ruin the few days she has in Japan. I can't do that. Let her enjoy the Obon festival tomorrow night, at least. I'll tell her on Sunday, or Monday. I hope I can find the right words to explain myself.

Mrs Oeda calls everyone into the dining room. In the centre of the mahogany table, like two big eyes, sits a plate each of shrimp and vegetable dumplings. Arranged along their edges are six dipping broths – one topped with edible flowers – and beyond this a wooden vat of fresh noodles, pickled beets of vibrant yellow and violet in tiny ceramic dishes, seaweed salad, and deep-fried pork cutlets still sizzling in oil.

'You've gone to far too much trouble,' I say. 'This could be a wedding feast!'

'Doesn't hurt to practise,' she says, looking pointedly at Shinobu.

Mr Oeda, who has done little but sip a tall beer and grunt, grows eloquent as he pours sake from a pale blue bottle into the wooden boxes before each of us. Beside me, Lily gulps a strawberry Ramune soda. As Mr Oeda fills our sake cups to overflowing, he holds forth on the honour we've given his wife and him by allowing them to extend their hospitality. He is especially grateful to me for encouraging Shinobu to study hard for the bar exam, and for acting as a 'stand-in mother' on the trail. Shinobu shifts in his seat, his face as pink as Lily's soda.

Everything is delicious. It's like being back at Grandma and Ojīsan's house. The broths are luscious and greasy, the pork cutlet fried to perfection and tempting even though I don't like pork, the noodles fat and starchy.

Mrs Oeda notices I am avoiding the cutlet. 'I keep an eye on my figure, too,' she says, 'and personally prefer the leaner pork. But my husband insists on the fatty type.'

'The lean type makes terrible broth,' Mr Oeda says, draining his sake cup. Mrs Oeda reaches for the sake and immediately refills it.

'Eat lots and save your energy,' Shinobu tells us. 'Tomorrow, we will dance *bon odori*.'

Lily asks, 'What's Bono Dory?'

Shinobu lifts his arms gracefully and fans his fingers in front of his nose. 'Not "bonodory". *Bon. O-do-ri*.'

'*Bon. O. Do. Ri*,' Lily pronounces carefully. She puts down her chopsticks and mimics his movement.

'Excellent. After dinner, may I teach you this dance?'

'Mom, do you know it?'

'It's been a long time. We'll practise together.'

After dinner, Shinobu takes us into the small patch of sod out front. The neighbourhood smells like charred meat. He throws his arms over his head and bends his knees. Lily copies him. The two of them look like they're about to engage in a kung fu parody. Sal stands in the doorway, watching. 'Come out, and keep the air-conditioning inside,' I call to him.

Shinobu moves slowly, keeping his hand over his face, and slowly twisting it like a fan as he sinks into a crouch. He begins to whistle. I hum along.

On every beat, Shinobu lifts a foot, turns it, and sets it down across from the other while twisting his palm over his head in fluid movements. Lily's eyes are locked on him. She begins to clap in time to the melody.

Shinobu's tune picks up speed and though he moves quickly his bare feet make no sound on the sod. The rhythm comes from his clothes, the khaki weave zip-zi-zi-zipping as he shifts and spins. His legs bend while his hands flutter like leaves on an aspen. I clap as well, still humming the airy melody of the wooden flute I remembered hearing in courtyards across the city as a kid. It was the only sound loud enough to drown out the summertime cicadas.

'*Odoru ahou!*' Shinobu calls. Sweat beads at his temple.

'*Odoru ahou!*' I repeat.

'*Miru ahou!*'

'*Miru ahou!*'

'*Onaji ahou,*' I call, and together we finish the chant, '*nara odorana, son-son.*'

'What does it mean?' Lily asks.

'Dancing fools, watching fools, we're fools all the same, so you might as well dance.'

Lily insists I teach her the words in Japanese. After two rounds, she knows the chant by heart, jumping twice at the final '*son-son*'.

She's starting to seem like her old self. I turn to see if Sal approves, but he's no longer in the doorway.

After breakfast the next morning, Shinobu and Lily practise their dance moves to a video Shinobu has pulled up on his laptop. Mrs Oeda turns to Lily.

'This child needs a *yukata*,' she says.

I translate this and Lily agrees, then asks what a *yukata* is.

'It's like a wrap dress. The girls we saw from the taxi, on that bridge, were wearing them.'

Mrs Oeda looks at Lily and says carefully in English, 'Do you like shopping?'

Lily looks at me. I can see the indecision on her face. She loves shopping. But she doesn't want to leave me.

'I was going to go for a run, sweetie, but if you want me to come with you, I will.'

Lily knows how important running is to me. She's used to me going out most days, and understands that my runs are the same as the alone time she always has permission to ask for if she needs it. She says, 'I'll stay with Mrs Oeda. You should go running.'

They get a ride to the mall from Mr Oeda and Shinobu, who are on their way to Mr Oeda's law office. Now that Shinobu has passed the bar, he can make his official self-introduction to his father's firm. 'I think I prefer to work in a different office from my father,' Shinobu says as he puts on a slick navy suit jacket. 'But it is good to meet many people. Networking, yes?'

I take a run while Sal naps next to the near-complete sushi puzzle. I take off my T-shirt and run in my sports bra as soon as I'm in semi-privacy, climbing the steep path that spirals up Mount Bizan. From here, the city spreads out around me. It feels so good to demand things of my body and to feel my body respond. Thank god for the pituitary gland; endogenous opioid inhibitory neuropeptides are miraculous things. I feel both calm and exhilarated. I have no idea how far I'll have to go on the pilgrimage route before real peace sets in. I only know that out there, I can put something to rest for good. I can dissolve the black organ and emerge with an unbound heart.

I put my shirt back on and descend the back of the mountain, the side near Ame-Ame and the blue house. The streets and alleyways feel as familiar to me as they did when I was young.

After wandering the town a couple of times, I almost feel at home again. Like I belong.

I pass the narrow street where Tomoya used to live, then stop and walk back toward it. Might his parents still live there? I walk past the house. It's an old one that hasn't been updated like so many in this neighbourhood have. The nameplate on the mailbox contains only one character. It could be the uncommonly short surname 'Yu'.

I never had a chance to tell his family that I was sorry. All they received from my family was cash, and apology money is not the same as an apology. This is my opportunity: I can look at them and tell them that this has haunted me. That it's shaped my life. I can ask for mercy. If they want to scream at me, I'll listen. They can yell and slam the door in my face. At least then, I'll know what they think. But who knows? Maybe they've forgiven me. Maybe they had another child or children. Maybe they've managed to find a sliver of happiness.

This is absolutely the right thing to do. I am sweaty, but since I haven't used my T-shirt, I can appear relatively presentable.

Terrified but sure, I ring the bell. The sound of frantic, high-pitched barking penetrates the grey metal door.

The door opens a few inches and a woman peeks out, opens the door farther when she sees me. The barking worsens; it sounds like there's an entire kennel inside.

She shushes the dogs. 'Can I help you?' she asks. It's her. Tomoya Yu's mother. I didn't expect her to look so *old*. Her white hair is unstyled, and the regality is gone from her posture. This is the chic woman who clicked through the halls of our school in designer heels? It worries me that she's not wearing lipstick.

I bow. The formal verb endings stick in my throat but I force them out. 'I've come to give my greetings to your family. I knew your son, Tomoya.'

A short, thin man wearing bifocals appears in the doorway behind Mrs Yu. Three terriers with brown and black fur press in behind his legs. He opens the door wider. 'Who's this?' he murmurs to his wife.

But the woman doesn't speak. She just stares at me. Mr Yu stares, too.

'My name is – was – Chizuru Akitani,' I say. Something begins to happen to their expressions, a fast-forwarding of emotion: curiosity, shock, horror, and then the expressions are gone so quickly I can't be sure they were ever there. I wait for an explosion, but nothing comes. They both look at me with perfect courteousness, as if I'm of no more consequence to their lives than a fee collector for NHK broadcasts. One of the dogs sneezes.

'Please, come in,' says Mr Yu, and opens the door as wide as it will go. 'Don't worry, they won't run out.' The dogs sniff my shoes when I take them off. All three of them look at me warily. One of them has yellow goop at the corner of his eye. 'What cute little friends you've got,' I say. Behind Mrs Yu in the entryway is a photo of the dogs dressed as pieces of sushi.

'That's Chibi, Kibi, and Bibi,' Mrs Yu replies. 'They run this house.'

Mr and Mrs Yu lead me to the living room, which is traditional with a low table and tatami mats and seating cushions. The only light comes through a large curtainless window that needs washing. No plush carpeting or mahogany chairs here. The cushions are covered in dog hair.

'I'll bring some tea,' Mrs Yu says. 'Please sit and make yourself comfortable.' Her husband goes with her, as do the dogs. It's strange that he would go and leave me alone. He must want to discuss how to handle me.

In traditional houses, this room would be used for entertaining, and would contain things like family photos, scrolls, or the evidence of a hobby – vases for flower arrangement, paper and brush for calligraphy, a nice television. But there's nothing. It feels like a movie set. Just the table, cushions, and a doll encased in glass on a stand in the corner. The tokonoma alcove is empty. Empty! Though it's warm in the room, I feel a chill. An empty toko is like hanging a frame above your fireplace with no picture in it.

There are no photographs of Tomoya anywhere.

The room smells like wet fur. Part of me wants to get up and run out the front door. But I won't. I have to go through with this. I have to say my piece. My heart thumps as if I'm nearing the finish line of a long race.

Mrs Yu carries a tray into the room and sets it down. On it is a teapot and three mismatched cups. I kneel into a proper *seiza*, but Mr and Mrs Yu sit all the way onto the floor. A dog jumps into each of their laps, and the third dog, the one with the eye problem, blinks at me expectantly. Cuddling with a ball of old warm fur is the last thing I want, but, hoping to please Mrs Yu, I slide my legs out from under me. The dog shoves his cold wet nose into my palm, inhales deeply at my crotch, and curls into my lap.

Mrs Yu pours the tea and sets the first cup before me. 'Our condolences about your father. He was an excellent citizen and a true national treasure.'

Her formality catches me off guard. Of course she'd know about my father and feel compelled to say the appropriate set phrases. Still, it's strange to hear condolences directed at me in Japanese. She's the first one to do so.

'Oh – thanks! It's fine, though. I mean, please don't worry about that.' I feel terrifically awkward.

'I'm afraid we haven't prepared a mourning gift,' she says, ignoring my clumsiness. Her face is pained. 'Please excuse us. We didn't realise you would be coming by.'

'Well of course not! I didn't tell you.' Oh god. Do they really think I've come to talk about Hiro? My error in judgement settles over me like a shroud. I'm pretty sure the room is getting smaller as I speak, that empty tokonoma creeping up behind me. 'Forgive me. I've interrupted your day. But I felt compelled—'

'We weren't doing anything. Receiving visitors happens rarely for us and it's always an honour. Our home is so plain and uninteresting. Now, tell us about yourself. Where do you live these days?'

Mr Yu is holding his cup with two hands, gazing at the wall behind me. His eyes jump to mine when I don't respond right away. His pupils in the lampless room are empty black saucers.

I can't not answer her question. This is torture. All I want is to throw myself at their mercy. I mention Colorado, and Sal. They already know what came before that. I leave out Lily because it might remind them of Tomoya.

'No children yet?' Mrs Yu asks.

I hesitate. 'We do have one child, a daughter.'

'How delightful. It must be a joy, picking out dresses and getting her dolled up.'

Lily has never once let me dress her, but I agree with Mrs Yu that yes, it is indeed nice.

'As for us, we've both retired, of course. We're just two irrelevant old people now. I enjoy photographing the dogs – I can show you an album of outfits I've sewn for them, if you like. And my husband follows baseball.'

I have thrown myself into river rapids and there will be no climbing out. I must ride this conversation to its natural end. Each polite remark, each measured response, feels like a boulder I'm hitting in the water.

'Oh, how interesting,' I say. 'Who's your team?' Maybe I can break through Mr Yu's politeness and get him comfortable more easily than his wife.

Mr Yu sets down his teacup and sighs. 'The Hanshin Tigers have a few excellent players, but I draft from all around the country. The league doesn't let you draft more than three players from a single team, and each player has a ranking based on his past performance. ERA, slugging percentage, OBP, all the class-three sabremetrics. It's inefficient, the way they compile the statistics, and I've actually drafted a complaint letter to the head of the FSJ. I have ideas for reforming the league. For example—'

Mrs Yu interrupts. 'He runs a fantasy baseball team.'

'How wonderful!' I say with a little too much enthusiasm.

Mr Yu has not stopped talking. '... the way a player like Ren Sakamoto can just disappear from a roster when he gets picked up by a major-league American team is a disgrace. It leaves a hole in the fabric of the team. The balance is thrown off completely!' His voice gets louder. 'Honestly, I don't understand why these young players want to play in America anyway. For the money? Sure, but what about integrity? Everyone talks about the great Ichiro, how we can be so proud of him for representing Japan, but I call that bunk. If it weren't for Ichiro, I'd still have a scrappy second baseman with a three-hundred average on my roster.' He slams the table, rattling the teapot. The terrier on his lap yips and runs out of the room.

Mrs Yu touches Mr Yu's hand gently and smiles at me. 'My husband gets quite immersed in his hobby.'

'It sounds very interesting.'

Mrs Yu picks up the teapot. 'Oh, look, the tea's all gone.' The way she says it signals to everyone that the visit is over. Panic rises in my chest.

'Mrs Yu, Mr Yu, before I go, I'd like to say one more thing.'

Mrs Yu turns her cup in her spotted hands and maintains a placid half smile. Her eyes are slabs of concrete ten feet thick. I will never get behind them. I have slammed face-first into a wall of *tatemae*. I keep my mouth shut.

Mrs Yu rises, carrying a dog, and Mr Yu and I follow her toward the front door. The tension in the house is unbearable. Surely the walls are about to collapse any second. As we reach the entryway Mrs Yu says, 'It's awfully humid weather we're having today, don't you think?'

'Yes, quite sticky,' I mumble. I start to put my right shoe on, but feel wetness through my sock. A surreptitious whiff confirms it: a dog peed inside. I look up at Mrs Yu, who has not noticed the accident, and at the picture of the costumed dogs on the wall. I shove the shoe on and tie it. The urine seeps into my sock.

Mrs Yu's voice has gone dull. 'Thank you for your pleasant visit. We hope you'll come see us again sometime.' She opens the door and I step outside.

'I'm sorry to have bothered you,' I repeat. 'I only wanted—'

'It was no bother at all,' she responds, and shuts the door gently. As I walk down the short flight of steps to the sidewalk, I hear the lock *thunk* into place.

It's hard to walk straight. Shame is making my legs weak. It's as if I've cycled through and become worthless, disgraceful Chizuru again. My vision tunnels as I replay what just happened. What was I thinking, going to the parents of the boy I murdered and expecting them to open up to me? All for what – that dreaded lie, closure? This is a new low. This is the most selfish thing I've ever done. I don't deserve closure. I don't deserve their *honne*. I deserve to have to live with what happened for the rest of my life. Just like they must.

In the Oedas' living room, Lily sits on the couch between two large shopping bags. A collection of smaller plastic bags are at her feet.

'What's all that?'

'She looked so cute in the purple and the pink, we couldn't decide, so I just got both. And of course she needed slippers, and *kanzashi* for her hair and …'

Shinobu comes in. He gives me a look: I told you so. Sal follows behind him, looking groggy.

Mrs Oeda and Lily's lack of a common language doesn't matter. Mrs Oeda speaks in Japanese; Lily responds in English. They both look radiant. I can hardly look at Lily. I don't deserve her. I have devastated a couple's life.

'*Daijobu?*' Mrs Oeda asks if I'm okay.

'Too long of a run, maybe,' I manage. I try to put on a smile but it doesn't fit. My face wants to crumple. I clear my throat. 'Well? Let's see what you got.'

'Fashion show!' Lily cries, pulling open one of the bags. She stops herself and looks at Mrs Oeda, who motions her to go ahead.

The pink *yukata*'s print is youthful; bubbly flowers with rounded petals splash the fabric with shades of neon. When Mrs Oeda finishes tying the sash, it's as if the SpongeBob T-shirt

Lily wore seconds before was a silly illusion. She was born to wear these clothes. Tears well up, and I blink them back. Don't think. Don't think, Rio.

In her right hand, Lily holds a blue folding fan of Mrs Oeda's. The handle is lacquered black, made to slide open and shut with the delicate flick of a wrist. Lily waves it at her face.

'Wrong, wrong!' Mrs Oeda grabs the fan. 'It's not an air conditioner.' With one tiny motion, the fan closes. It opens before her face and begins to flutter. She keeps her eyes on Lily's. Quivering, the fan moves away from her body as she extends her arm beguilingly. Sal raises his eyebrows.

'Eleven is too young for this type of fan,' she says, dropping the pose.

Lily sighs. 'How old do I have to be?' she asks me.

'Usually a teen – hey. Did you understand what she just said?'

She shrugs. 'I know *juichi-sai* means eleven years old. The rest is obvious.'

Sal says to me, 'Pretty soon you two are going to be able to talk about me behind my back.' I can't tell if he's joking, or if the prospect actually troubles him.

Lily lifts her arms, flapping the long pink *yukata* sleeves. 'Now I'm definitely gonna learn Japanese!'

'Be right back.' I run to our room. In the side pocket of the green pack I find the plastic ring from the girl on the bus.

Mrs Oeda is wrapping Lily in the purple *yukata*. The material is darker, the floral design subtler, as if to imply the object of greatest appeal lies beneath the cotton. With her hair pulled up and held in place by the traditional beaded hairpin, Lily is a young woman. Mrs Oeda puts a hand to her chest and says a single English word. 'Beautiful.'

That's it. I start sobbing and I'm pretty sure I'll never stop. The room freezes and everyone watches me while I hiccup and gasp.

'What's wrong, Mom?'

'Nothing,' I say. 'It's fine. It's just—' I hug her. 'She *is* beautiful,' I say to Mrs Oeda, sniffling. She gives me a packet of tissues and I blow my nose.

I hand Lily the ring. 'I got this while I was hiking. It's from a girl who reminded me of you.'

'Thanks.' She puts it on and holds up her hand. 'Though it doesn't really go with this *yukata*. It's like more of a kid's thing, you know?'

I smile. 'Yeah. Maybe it is.'

'When do we get to go to the festival?'

'In a few hours. For now, you need a bath. And a nap.' Lily's eyes rest longingly at Sal's laptop. 'And no Internet.'

She grumbles but does not even try to make a coherent complaint, so I know she's exhausted. I am, too.

'I'll lie down with you,' I say. 'We can dream about being dancing fools.'

17

RED AND YELLOW LANTERNS line the downtown streets, which are jammed with people. Barricades have turned the area around Tokushima Station into a sea of brightly coloured *yukata* and *happi* waistcoats and fans and bobbing heads. Drums pound from every direction, shaking the air. Wooden flutes whine and hand-held bells clang as hundreds of *ren*, professional dance groups, perform wherever there's room. Lily holds my hand lightly, or not at all. She's no longer hanging on for dear life. Sal is on her left and the Oedas are ahead, leading us through the crowd toward the main stage. There is not a hint of self-consciousness on Lily's face as she takes in this new world.

Lily is beautiful like her grandmother. I have one picture of my mom when she was young, the only one she must have brought to Japan with her. In the photo she is a teenager, hair long and wild, a cigarette hanging off her lip. Her arm's around a mousy-looking girl with, my mom told me, 'the finest name I've ever heard'. Melody Lightfoot. Her best friend. Both have grinned their eyes into slits. My mom wears a tube top and low-slung jeans. She is so skinny, her belly button stretches vertically. She looks happier than I've ever seen her. Why did she choose Hiro? Impetuous, selfish, grandiose Hiro. But it's no use to blame her. I know about blame, now. It's only a place-holder for something much more difficult: acceptance.

Behind the main stage, food and trinket vendors have set up stalls. It's a little less crowded back here. Mr Oeda buys cans of beer from a teenager who fishes them from a kiddie pool filled with ice. He hands them to the adults. Lily picks out a Ramune soda – melon, this time. She delights in popping the metal buckle that releases the glass ball into the seltzer.

I have the photo of my mom and Melody in my wallet. I had to go out of my way to find a wallet that still included flaps for photographs – and in the slip next to it is a similar one of Lily with Dahlia, their arms draped across each other's backs, drinking straws replacing cigarettes. Sometimes I marvel at the resemblance between the two photos, the pose, the joy straining all four young faces, and other times I wonder if perhaps this image is universal, and I just happened to miss out. Of course, when Lily saw the photo of her and Dahlia, she cringed and asked, 'Is *that* what I look like when I laugh?' Sal has a collection of photos of the two of us standing together, posing at elevation signs or in front of a house, but they all have a plastic feel. No one has ever caught us in a moment of bliss. Maybe we can change that, starting with this trip.

A boy holding a plastic cage walks up to Lily. 'Wanna see my cricket?'

It's rare to see Lily shy. She looks away at first, then glances back at the cage, takes his meaning. The boy drops to the ground and Lily follows, my Lily who refuses to go into the bathroom if she sees a spider there, my Lily who insists on bleach in the wash so her white shorts glow, plops down next to this boy in the dirt. He cups his palms and brings them to Lily's. Her face screws into laughter as the insect dances into her hands. Lily's palms are ticklish but her feet are not. That's what new places can do for us – reveal facets that might remain in shadow, free us from ourselves.

Afterward, she sidles up to me. 'You like Japan,' I say.

'It's fun. And the girls are really pretty. Everyone's dressed up.' There's dirt on the hem of her *yukata*. After much deliberation, she chose the pink one. On her left hand she wears the plastic ring. She points to a group at the end of the row of stalls. 'What are those people carrying?'

'Lanterns. People float them down the river to remember people who've died.'

'Can we do one for Grandpa?'

'Sure,' I say, leading her to a stand selling the lanterns. The group follows us. 'You can pick one for your grandma, too. You look more like her every day.'

'I will buy for Danny,' Shinobu says. 'Choose one.'

I pick a green one with a kanji Shinobu tells me reads 'peace'.

Out of nowhere, Lily tells me, 'Megan T might die.'

'What?' Megan Teng has been in Lily's class since kindergarten. Her dad was a nurse at St Mary's when I first started working there.

'She has leukaemia. Her mom posted on Facebook that she's in the hospital and asked us to send her cards.'

'Did you make one?'

'I didn't have time. Dad said we had to come here, like, immediately.' She looks annoyed at the inconvenience. 'Megan's mom said there are kids in the hospital who don't get any mail so I want to send them something, too.'

'That's really nice. We'll go visit Megan when we get back.'

'Can we get her a lantern? Or are they only for people who died?'

'Sure. We can make a get-well wish on it for her.' Lily points to a green lantern, similar to the one I chose for Danny. I hand over the coins and we walk away.

'Mom?' Lily tugs at my hand. 'Are the lanterns very expensive?' When I tell her they aren't, she says, 'Can we get one for the other kids?'

She means the kids who might not get any cards at the hospital. It's hard to hold back my emotion. I lean down and hug her. Sal has been listening to this exchange, and I can see the emotion on his face, too.

'That is so thoughtful. Yes.' I think of Tomoya and his grandfather leaving the convenience store in the rain. Lily would have helped them.

Lily picks a white lantern with no markings, and as a group, we walk under the grandstand, where people are watching each *ren* perform their dance, and take a shortcut to the Riverwalk. The Yoshino River here is about fifty yards across, and there are bike and pedestrian paths along each side. The bridges that span the river are decorated with painted figures of Awa Odori dancers, the symbol of the city.

'Come, we can put in here,' says Shinobu. He kneels on a slab of blue slate at the river's edge and takes a lighter from his pocket. The slab has been cut from the earth, probably a riverbed twenty kilometres south, near the pilgrimage route. Shinobu drops the candle into Danny's lantern and in an instant, brilliant emerald light replaces the darkness. For a second the lantern does not simply represent her; it is not an object that exists to comfort the living with tradition and ceremony – its essence, the behaviour of light scattering across a barrier, *is* Danny.

Mr and Mrs Oeda each put a lantern in, though they don't say who they are for. He turns and lights a cigarette. I assume he's going to smoke it, but he hands it to his wife. She bows minutely and takes a drag while he lights one for himself.

Sal, Lily, and I kneel beside Shinobu. Inches below us, the river shines black and smooth. I place Hiro's lantern in front of Sal and give Lily her grandmother's. Lily insists on lighting the candle herself.

'I can't do it!' she says after failing twice to work the lighter.

'It's got a child lock,' Sal says. He shows her how to hold the switch with her left hand and flick the thumb of her right over the wheel. She's successful this time, light from the small flame dancing across her determined expression. She lights the final one, and I dedicate it to Tomoya in my mind.

The four lanterns drift away. Danny, Hiro, Elena, Tomoya. An unlikely family. I try to imagine them alive, at a festival like this: my father in a black T-shirt, Busano in hand, Elena gliding beside him in a long patterned dress. Danny's a half step ahead, red scarf swirled around her neck, excited to get wherever they're going, and beside her is Tomoya in his school uniform, munching something gooey and sweet from a stick, stopping to examine a pet cricket for sale. Where are they going? What if they are buying lanterns for us? What if *we* are the dead ones? The beer is going to my head, but it's not a bad feeling.

'Can you tell which one's yours?' Sal asks Lily.

'That one.' She points. 'I haven't taken my eyes off it.'

'Doesn't that one have a tall candle in it? Yours had a short one.'

'Or no, wait …'

Our lanterns have drifted downstream and joined the others. I catch Sal's eye. Neither of us looks away. A bubble of feeling rises in my chest. I have no secrets from this man any more. I have told the truth and my life has not fallen apart. The bubble pops and I can't help but smile at him. He gives a small smile back.

'I wanna dance,' Lily says.

We make our way back to the street. The feeling comes on slowly at first, a feeling of warmth, of welling up and spilling over. I can be *hafu*, if I want; I can always find someone to call me incomplete. But I can be whole, too; I can be unsplit and complete in the fragmented way that a life is a life. I don't know if we'll move or if I'll have another baby. Even Sal, I recognise now, offers no guarantees. Two things will have to be enough, the things I know for sure: I am a runner. And I will always be Lily's mom.

Suddenly we're surrounded by a *ren* that has just come off their main-stage performance. We dance among them. The men come first, fluttering their fans and crouching low. They get close, shout the nonsense syllable that's echoing everywhere tonight, *Yoi, yoi!* The women follow, subtle finger movements taking the place of fans. I watch these colourful block formations, these women in sync. What if one of them was in the detention centre with me? The point of one dancer's hat sits a bit higher than the others. Her face is pale and smooth, like a shell. As I watch, a lock of hair falls from under her hat and sticks to her cheek. I catch her eye and call, 'Yeehaw!'

A brown-skinned man in a ball cap forces a beer bottle into my hand, clunks it against his own, and drinks. I drink, too. Icy bubbles shoot up my nose.

Thousands of faces flicker under the glow of fireworks. One girl looks down at the river as the sky bursts with light while every adult looks up. What are you looking at, girl who sees what no one else sees? The girl in a thigh-length *yukata* and scrunch socks is at home as much as the man with his tie around his head like a bandana, drinking beer from a can and crushing it between his palms, a university trick he hasn't done in years; a drummer from one of the troupes steps out of formation to dance with a toddler and his mother. The mother holds the kid on her hip and the boy flails his arms in the air, laughing.

'This is part of you,' I say to Lily as she bounces amid a circle of strangers in the street. I step back and watch her. I have never seen Lily look like this. There is something in the blood, a quantum communiqué, a part that says *Hai*, a part that says, I am here.

Lily collapses against my side. 'I could live here when I'm older,' she says, out of breath. 'After film school. This festival would make a great subject for a short doc.' Anxiety flashes briefly through my chest. Hearing these words a month ago would have given me nightmares – what might Lily uncover in Japan about my past? – but tonight, the panic fades quickly, replaced by the reverberation of festival drums. Lily will be fine. She'll learn the truth when the time comes for her to learn it. Because my story is her story. I feel like a celebration, a whole stand of aspen.

She runs off, this time toward Sal, who is learning to dance from a group of drunk high school kids. I dance, too. With no one in particular and with everyone. If I have nothing else, I have this. I have my runner's body that carries me through spruce and aspen and violets and miner's lettuce and the damp smells of growth and I can name these things, name myself, in parts: the tarsals as they rotate, muscle fibres contracting and propelling me over the dirt, plantar fascia absorbing shock as my scarred feet carry all of this, whole, through the woods full of sweet blue air that soothes my lungs, a gift from the plants and an exhalation, my gift back.

ACKNOWLEDGEMENTS

My thanks:

To my agent, Katherine Fausset, a granter of wishes, an ear, and a champion of her writers. Thank you to her colleagues at Curtis Brown as well.

To Emily Bell, editor of indescribable talent and forthrightness, who took me to Balthazar, and who believed in Rio and made a place for her in the world.

To Doug Clark, for the introduction.

To Maya Binyam, Sarah Scire, Jeff Seroy, editing geniuses Lisa Silverman, Maureen Klier, Lyn Rosen, and Susan Goldfarb, and everyone at Farrar, Straus and Giroux who welcomed this novel and its author.

To Stephanie Koven, whose optimism and early support kept me working.

To Michael Adams, Stephen Harrigan, Elizabeth McCracken, Jim Crace, Rachel Kushner, and John Dufresne for your feedback, humour, grace, teaching, and well-set examples.

To Angela MacFarlane and Brian Beckey for a place to write and to call (tiny) home; the Shaperos, the Greene-Rosenblums, and the Bechtolsheims for the jobs and flexibility.

To the MacDowell Colony, Jentel Arts, Ragdale Foundation, Ucross Foundation, Kerouac Project, Sozopol Fiction Seminars, Sewanee Writers' Conference, and the Michener Centre for Writers for their gifts of community, encouragement, and financial support (and food), which were critical to the writing of this novel.

To Maya Perez and Rachel Kondo for their sustaining friendship and feedback on everything from new drafts to major life decisions. KLP, LLC.

To Kristin Kearns, my dear K, who's been there from page one.

To Justin Quarry, whose friendship and feedback have been invaluable.

To the literary community: book and lit mag editors, agents, conference organisers, librarians, publicists, designers, students, writers, readers, and Duchess Goldblatt.

To my ever-positive and loving grandparents, step-parents, aunts, uncles, and cousins, and to the Seymour clan, and to all my friends-who-are-family in Illinois, Texas, and California.

To my mom, who fed me books and knew this day would come, and to my dad for his sense of adventure, and to my 好きな人 Derek, who knows the secret.

To the real Shinobu and to my friends in Tokushima, especially Kimiko Kobayashi, for the welcome, the education, and your open hearts. やっとさ－！